A SIMPLE GAME

Hoping you have a simply wonderful holiday season, full of love and peace — Enjoy!

Kirk

A SIMPLE GAME

Kirk Wolcott

Copyright © 2015 by Kirk Wolcott

This is a work of fiction. Places, incidents, names, and characters with the exception of a few well-known public and historical figures are the products of the author's imagination or are used fictitiously. Any resemblance to actual persons, living or dead, is entirely coincidental. Where real-life public or historical figures do appear or are mentioned, the situations, incidents, and dialogues concerning these persons are entirely imaginary and are not intended to depict any actual events or change the entirely fictional nature of the work. All views expressed are those of the author and not necessarily those of the Department of State or the U.S. Government.

Victory Mansion Media, LLC

Cover design by Sladja Ivkovic

To Vonda

It may well be understood, once for all, that I shall not surrender this game leaving any available card unplayed.

Abraham Lincoln

Pregame

A Few Years Ago

Gentlemen Guerrillas Strike Seaside Resort

Hostages Unharmed in Bizarre Ordeal

Associated Media International

DUBROVNIK, Croatia (AMI) — A two-hour takeover of one of Europe's top luxury hotels ended peacefully today with the release of some 40 hostages and the mysterious escape of half a dozen gunmen who had earlier treated their victims to food, phones, and heartfelt apologies.

Beyond the surprising politeness of the hostage-takers, several peculiarities struck the shocked but unharmed guests at the five-star Elegancija Spa & Resort, overlooking the ancient city of Dubrovnik on the southern coast of Croatia.

The first oddity was the unusual nature of their demands.

"They said they wanted to bring an end to the fighting in the Sudan," said a Russian oil tycoon staying at the hotel. "They asked if we knew that over 2 million people had died there while the world hardly lifted a finger."

"The funny thing was none of the gunmen looked particularly African," said his female companion, both of whom preferred to remain anonymous.

Other guests confirmed that the hostage-takers appeared to be of European or North American origin based on their accents and the color of their skin, at least that which could be seen through effective disguises.

Some of the victims claimed the leader, who carried an assault rifle like the others, may have been Asian from the shape of his eyes peeking out through slits in a mask. One gunman went without face covering but wore a cap and sunglasses. Another was short and may have been a woman. All six were dressed in dark business suits with black leather gloves.

"They looked menacing at first," admitted an elderly patron at the Elegancija, which routinely tops travel industry lists of leading Mediterranean guesthouses. "In the end, they were downright friendly. They let us keep our wallets, our jewelry, even our mobile phones. They were real gentlemen guerrillas."

Another guest, Roberto Segna, said he was awakened around midnight by a loud knock on his door. "An anxious porter told me to proceed immediately to the lobby."

Segna thought the building was on fire until he found the gunmen rounding up other guests and telling them sternly but politely to sit on the floor and keep still. Some of the hostages ate snacks, while others smoked cigarettes, all courtesy of the rebels, who did not object when Segna, a 45-year-old wine merchant, asked permission to call his wife in Venice.

Soon the entire lobby, with the priceless stained glass windows fronting the sea, was abuzz with guests contacting families, friends, and the authorities to let them know what was happening.

"If I was a terrorist, the last thing I would do is let all these people make phone calls," said hostage Dietmar Rehmer, an automobile executive from Stuttgart. "But it seemed like this was exactly what the gunmen wanted, for the whole world to know what was going on. It was very bizarre."

Another detail people remembered as being bizarre were the shoes worn by the gunmen.

"They were all dressed in formalwear, except for their shoes," said Naoki Inamoto, a Tokyo computer salesman. "Each of them had these fancy lightweight athletic numbers, like Olympic sprinters wear, only without the spikes. I ran 200 meters at university, so I've seen shoes like those before."

The unusual footwear provided extra traction, Inamoto said, enabling the hostage-takers to move quickly across the lobby's slick marble floor.

Shortly after midnight, one of the hostages said, the leader of the group climbed on top of the concierge desk and announced: "We apologize for any inconvenience we have caused you. We simply needed the publicity. Please, tell your governments to act now. And enjoy the rest of your stay."

He and the others then dashed off toward the back of the hotel, from where they seem to have vanished. Police later found a hole carved in a wall opening to the water below, raising the possibility that the gunmen climbed down or jumped, although the fall would have been considerable.

The only additional clue left behind was a crumpled piece of paper one of the hostages discovered in the lobby, near the grand rococo fountain.

"It wasn't a ransom note," said the middle-aged American woman who found the slip of paper. "It looked more like a bill or a receipt, you know, for a list of products—rubber gloves, metal canisters, liquid chlorine—like someone was stocking their swimming pool."

"A pretty large pool," her husband quipped. "But who knows?"

None of the guests could claim the document nor explain exactly what these temperate terrorists hoped to achieve before stealing off into the night, leaving their victims behind safe but clearly unsettled.

"It was a strange experience," said the Russian oil tycoon's companion, while dropping her cell phone into a genuine Prada handbag. "Frightening, but at the same time not entirely unpleasant."

Now

1

Hong Kong: just before midnight

"*Bu shi-iii!*" sprang the cry, at once authoritatively, like a command, and dismissively, as if what was happening could never happen to him.

"*No-ooo!*" it was repeated a moment later in English, more plaintively if no less forcefully. It shuddered through the *wushu* training center, over the rows of neatly arranged bamboo mats, down a narrow hall adorned with photos of its owner – performing martial arts, accepting gold medals, mixing with celebrities, posing in movie stills – toward an open window, where it was consumed by the raucous city sounds below: night riders bleating horns, street merchants hawking goods, music from too many discotheques competing for attention.

The next cry came with even more force than the previous two, a wail really, a tortured plea. But it was lost to all, just like the others, save for the man in black, the man crouching down beside him, preparing to deliver the final, fatal slice. And this man held no sympathy for the owner of the scream.

"*Not my foot!*"

Amsterdam: the same night

With fame came precaution, Lazarius, the Golden Buddha, considered from the backseat of his private, armored limo, as it peeled away from the stadium. Yet even tucked behind heavily-tinted, bulletproof glass, he could still hear the cheers of the hometown faithful who would linger long into the night singing his praises.

"Bu-ddha!"

"Bu-ddha!"

"Bu-ddha!"

His nickname derived not from the shape of his stomach, rock-solid and muscle-taut like the rest of his body, but from the mane of flaxen hair that flowed like a river of gold off his forehead and the Zen-like composure he possessed around a soccer ball. While many in his native Brazil took exception to this blasphemy, who could argue with such God-given talent? His new team, Ares Amsterdam, recently flush with a welcome injection of Gulf Arab petrodollars, certainly could not, its governing board shelling out a Dutch record-smashing $100 million to lure Lazarius to The Netherlands. And, having just netted three sumptuous goals to single-handedly knock Real Madrid out of the Champions League quarter-finals, the investment already seemed justified.

"Bu-ddha!"

"Bu-ddha!"

"Bu-ddha!"

As the limo left the parking lot, the chanting finally faded from earshot, and only then did Lazarius' driver and bodyguard, Rafa, ask if he should proceed to the usual place.

"*Pois não*," Lazarius nodded in agreement, answering in Portuguese. Like his teammates, in their newly minted Porsches, Ferraris, and Lamborghinis, the Golden Buddha could have owned any automobile he desired, in an assortment of colors, but he preferred letting someone else navigate Amsterdam's congested roadways. Soon they were gliding past cheap hotels, porno shops, and the famed pleasure houses where young girls recently arrived from Russia and the Ukraine, Africa and the Orient paraded their wares. While his agent may have argued otherwise, Lazarius knew Amsterdam's red lights and liberal laws played no small part in his choosing Ares over one of the more celebrated teams in England, Germany, or Spain. Catching sight of his reflection in the window, he smiled appreciatively, for this place fit him like a goalkeeper's glove: the respectable Dutch capital of Rembrandt and van Gogh to bolster his public image; the Red Light District to cater to his every private whim.

But there would be time for that later. Right now Lazarius was on his way to meet an old friend, as he did after every home match. Marcelo was really more like a father, he thought, as the limo rounded a corner and left the red glow behind them. While his real father had been busy introducing him to the profit of petty crime at age 10 and the pleasure of prostitutes by 13, before disappearing from his life altogether, Marcelo did whatever it took to bust Lazarius free from one of Rio's roughest *favelas*. Countless letters written, phone calls made, strings pulled, and trips taken at personal expense eventually resulted in Palmeiras gambling on the young delinquent and probably saving the boy's life. So, when the life of Marcelo turned south, a victim of acute lung cancer, Lazarius knew it was scant return on a priceless debt owed to bring the old Brazilian talent scout to Holland to see out his final days under the best of European comfort and care.

"Here," he instructed Rafa, who guided the limo to the curb a couple blocks shy of the blue-lit Medisch Centrum Claes Pieterszoon. A handsome donation to the hospital afforded certain privileges, like keeping most mouths shut, but Lazarius could never be too careful, especially when stepping out of a limousine. While the paparazzi lacked many things – including beating hearts, as far as he could tell – patience and cunning were not on that list.

Climbing from the vehicle, Lazarius carefully avoided a puddle before crossing the street and starting down a steep incline toward a sign marked "Emergency Entrance." No other foot traffic here, but he tucked his trademark tresses under a woolen watch cap just to be safe. Reaching the bottom of the hill, he began angling toward the back of the hospital, when he spotted some-one approaching. *Maybe more cunning than I thought.*

Lazarius slowed and considered going back, when he saw it was only a woman walking alone. A nurse finish-ing her shift, he figured, until he noticed how she was dressed all in black, with a tight black sweater, a stylish black cape, and a hood of that same dark fabric shrouding her face. On her feet black leather boots ran halfway up bare legs, instantly turning him on.

But Marcelo will be waiting…

"*Ola*," he said, passing her by. The woman turned her head and held his gaze. In that moment, he caught something in her eyes that sent his heart racing faster than an incoming cross. There was an air of defiance in the way she looked at him, a challenge even, as if to say: *I am a lioness that won't be tamed.*

The soccer star chuckled. He didn't know this wom-an, but was certain he could have her. He was Lazarius, after all, the Golden Buddha, the savior of Dutch foot-ball, and the heir apparent to the reins of the Brazilian national team, one of the most cherished clubs in world sport, not to mention a man endowed with certain at-tributes found particularly pleasing to the opposite sex.

But Marcelo…

So he kept walking, putting her out of his mind, until he heard her speak behind him.

"Nice shoes."

Lazarius turned back to see the girl standing there, beneath a streetlight, smiling. She couldn't have been much older than 20. Her face was striking, with fair skin, elfin features, and those laser blue eyes. Her hair remained completely hidden under the hood.

"Berlutis," she said in accented English.

It wasn't a question, but Lazarius answered anyway. "Right," he said, taking a step toward her. "Care to go somewhere?"

"You're very bold," she replied, still smiling, as she halved the distance between them.

"Don't you recognize me?"

"Should I?"

He ignored the question, more surprised than hurt, for his face was everywhere these days. "My limo's around the corner. My driver, very discreet."

Now she laughed. "I don't think so."

Lazarius frowned, for he prided himself on reading women. "I'm sorry, I thought—"

She gave him another sly smile. "What about here?"

"*Here?*" he said, looking around. "What do you mean, here? There's nothing here."

"Not *here*," she answered, pointing across the street. "*There*."

Now it was his turn to smile. This was not exactly what he had in mind. He typically preferred savoring his meals in privacy, lingering over each tender morsel. Then, again, this was not a typical night – three goals scored, the Champions League semi-finals reached. Nor did she seem to be a typical girl, and he wondered for a second if she might be a pro, setting him up. But there was something in her demeanor, the way she looked at him, that suggested otherwise.

Marcelo will just have to wait.

Lazarius took the girl's hand and started in the direction she had pointed. They crossed the street, moving toward an alleyway flanked on either side by dark buildings bathed in inky green neon from a flickering Heineken sign. She entered first, tugging his hand. He took a few steps forward before pulling back.

"Far enough, baby," he said, drawing her into his arms. He kissed her on the neck, the chin, the lower lip, until she stiffened, defiantly, like a feisty lion cub. This only spurred him on, kissing her more roughly, burying his tongue deep inside the girl's mouth. She responded with a light moan, meeting the force of his tongue with her own.

Until, suddenly, *he* stopped.

She looked up and Lazarius placed his hands on either side of her head, sliding back the hood. A shaft of green light caught her skull and his reward was most unexpected.

She was completely bald.

"You like?"

"Very much," he breathed, attacking her mouth again, harder than before, until this time she halted proceedings. Reaching up, she withdrew the cap from his head, releasing a cascade of blond hair tumbling down around his thick shoulders.

"*You* like?"

She just smiled and then dropped to her knees, disappearing below him in the dark. Lazarius felt her go to work and wondered again if she was a professional. He had been around the world many times, sampling the finest creatures placed before him, but few if any had ever done what she was doing now, at least not with the same style, unique flare. *What did it matter?* If she wanted money, he was loaded. More than he knew what to do with, by far. Better to put that business aside for now, lean back against the wall, and enjoy the ride.

"Ouh," he said, wincing, opening his eyes. *What was that?*

Lazarius felt a sharp prick on his hamstring, just below the buttocks. Thank God his legs were insured for £10 million each by Lloyds of London, he thought, as she dug her nails deep into his flesh. *Easy now.*

Then he felt something else, something strange. It started high in his legs, working its way rapidly up his spine. It was difficult to define. Like a current of water, rushing waves racing through his veins, neutralizing his muscles, drowning his mind.

What was she doing? What had she done?

By the time these questions were formed, it was too late. The double dose of sodium pentothal housed in a glass vile connected to a syringe cupped in the palm of her hand had already reached his brain, begun performing its voodoo. At once he felt light-headed, confused. His breathing slowed, his heartbeat depressed. While Lazarius remained in a standing position, propped up by the wall, he could no longer move. His body was paralyzed, his senses warped.

In a trance, he heard the purr of an engine growing louder. Through a green veil, he saw a motorcycle approaching, its rider a lanky dude in black, sporting a Mohawk, like some freakish skunk in reverse: black stripe on a starched white skull. Ruby red pins stuck in one eye.

Lazarius let out a laugh, at least so he thought, as his body collapsed, began sliding down the wall. Sliding... falling...*crash*.

He came to a jarring stop, legs splayed out in front of him, head level with the bald girl still on her knees, so soft and pretty. He reached for her now, or was it the other way around, she reaching for him?

So confusing, so hard to tell...

"Nize verk," he heard the Skunk say.

Distant voices, funny accents...

"Shuddup," the Bald Eagle squawked in his face.

The words buzzed around him like insects, a hornet's nest inside his mind. He became aware of a hand on his forehead, pressing back on his neck. Careful now, he heard himself say. Or was that someone else?

So confusing, so hard to tell...

Lazarius sensed movement all around him, but was unable to focus any longer, his vision growing dim and dreamy. He suddenly felt like a character in a children's nursery rhyme, like the ones the nuns used to read. Only, this fairytale had gone horribly wrong.

> *See a brown leather satchel,*
> *There on the ground.*
> *Out pops a blade, dancing around.*
> *Hurry up, scolds the Skunk,*
> *With embers in his eye.*
> *Fawkoff, comes the Eagle's chirpy reply.*
> *(Humph, that's no way to talk! Chop-chop-chop!)*
> *Puncture the skin, slice through it like lace,*
> *A river of red rolling over a face.*
> *Hear the crowd cheering, calling your name,*
> *Singing so sweetly till the end of the game.*
> *Bu-ddah!*
> *Boo-da*
> *Boo*

Beverly Hills: shortly thereafter

With light traffic and a fast car the drive from Hawthorne to Beverly Hills takes under half an hour. Not bad for two places literally worlds apart.

This thought crossed Mo Mo's mind as he angled his race-registered Jeep Cherokee off the stretch of the 405 connecting these disparate LA suburbs and eyed the fine creature in the passenger seat next to him. "How'd you say your name again?"

"I told you, it's Zulu," she answered in a singsong voice, with an accent he had never heard before. "But you can call me Zu, if that's easier."

"Man, that's a funny name. You're not from around here, are you?"

The girl giggled. She couldn't have been much older than 20. "You call yourself Mo Mo. Now *that's* a funny name."

"The one they gave me," he said, returning his eyes to the road.

"Who did?"

"The sportswriters," he answered. "It stands for 'More Money.' "

"More money than *what*?"

"Than anyone else in the NBA ever made out of high school, that's what!"

This bit Mo Mo said with pride, watching the girl again as they approached his neighborhood. He enjoyed seeing her reaction to the towering trees, manicured lawns, and magazine-featured mansions all around them.

"That's Madonna's place over there," he said, pointing. "Cost more than $20 million. And that's where Brad and Angelina live, part of the year."

"You sure you're not a movie star?"

"*Basketball* star," he corrected her for the second time, still surprised she didn't recognize him, for his face was everywhere these days. The first time had been less than an hour ago, when he found her stranded by the smashed windows and harsh graffiti fronting Hawthorne's Ocean Gate Avenue, bent over the hood of an ailing Honda. Her long, dark legs and tight, short shorts were more than LA's most eligible bachelor – according to *People Magazine*, following his Rookie of the Year honors last season – could pass up, even if he was on his way to see Momma for dinner, as he did every Sunday night when he was in LA without a game.

Mo Mo had swaggered toward her then like some Indy mechanic, unwilling to reveal he knew absolutely nothing about cars. His family didn't own one when he was a kid. *Who had the money?* And now that he did, he also had a high-paid technician to care for his Ferrari and tend after his Jeep. Following the requisite few minutes poking around under the hood, careful not to soil his tailored silk shirt, Mo Mo shook his head, threw up his hands, and conceded defeat. He then offered the girl a ride to the nearest auto shop.

That never happened. For once he mentioned Beverly Hills, she said she'd never been, he joked he'd take her there one day, she agreed on the spot, and any further thought of dinner with Momma and his sisters faded into the LA sunset.

He only regretted now he hadn't brought the Ferrari. Until, that is, she placed a hand on his black upholstery and said: "I *love* Jeeps!"

Mo Mo had always wanted to be the one telling stories in the locker room. Wilt Chamberlain's 10,000 women were legendary, whether you believed it or not, and Magic and Kobe were well-known not only for their on-court antics. Yet despite all the talk of women and hoops stars, he had never really been one with the ladies. Sure, there were groupies in every city, and the older players looked after the younger ones, hooking them up when they asked. But aside from a couple parties at his mansion and that department store clerk who sold him his suits, he rarely had had a woman of his own in his own bed.

Now, he, Mo Mo, was in the middle of one of these stories, and this girl Zulu was all that. He still had no idea where she came from, or what she did for a living, or why she couldn't keep her car running, but at this point he really didn't care. Turning the Jeep onto a wide, palm-lined street, Mo Mo popped up a console on the dash and struck a sequence of colored keys. He then pointed straight ahead to where a security gate was swinging open, eliciting a gasp from the girl.

"If you like that," he said with smile, "just wait till you get inside."

Inside, Mo Mo showed her his world. He began by flipping a switch near the front door, which caused every room in his mansion to fill with mood lighting and R&B music. Standing together in his vast living room, she marveled at the designer furniture and expensive African art, easily able to identify more pieces than he could. She hung on his every word as he explained, like some cheesy floor salesman, each new appliance in his restaurant-sized kitchen. The girl seemed especially taken by the assortment of rare spices (in glass bottles never opened) and the set of tungsten steel carving knives (used only once, to pry the lid off a peanut butter jar).

"Now, baby, *la pièce de résistance*," he said, mimicking some French actor he saw in a movie. The girl giggled, before taking a long sip of Cristal from the champagne flute he handed her. Guiding her toward a shiny metal box by the doorway, Mo Mo opened a panel display-ing an array of buttons and lights. This contraption protected him daily from all those who wanted to pos-sess the treasures of an NBA star without possessing the talent.

"Is that the controls to your *spaceship*?"

"No, baby, this is your new best friend. It keeps the good guys in," he said, thumping his chest, "and the bad guys out. See, you push this button here, and it locks the front gate. This one turns on the electric current. And this one engages the lasers to—"

"Kill the intruders," she said, taking another sip of champagne.

"No," he laughed, "to alert the police, who will be here in exactly four minutes. I promise. Feel safe now?"

"Yes."

"Want to go upstairs?"

"Definitely."

Mo Mo tried to act cool as he ushered the girl up his twisting stairway, past the neatly framed pictures of himself with a slew of celebrities – LeBron, Denzel, the President of the United States. He stopped briefly before a glass case housing his most cherished prize, an autographed basketball from Michael Jordan, with an inscription that wished Mo Mo, "Good luck in the NBA!" She seemed genuinely impressed, and he couldn't help thinking about the tales he would tell his teammates. He had found this exotic creature all by himself, and she was no groupie, no call girl, not even a set-up date.

Mo Mo briefly considered taking a shower, feeling gritty from messing around with her car. But he dropped the idea just as fast, fearing the time it would take might spoil the mood. Likewise, he skipped the tour of his specially modified workout room, his library stacked with leather-bound books he one day planned to read, and the open-air planetarium with its kick-ass collection of telescopes. There would be time for that later. Right now, the only tour she would be getting was of the room they were entering, the master bedroom.

Reaching out, Mo Mo pulled the girl toward him, kissing her somewhat roughly.

"Hey, slow down, Movie Star," she said, placing her hands on his chest.

"*Basketball* star," he corrected again.

"Shh," she replied, slipping one of those hands inside of his and leading him toward the bed. Next to it, on the nightstand, stood a copy of the Holy Koran, the only personal item found in his father's cell. She picked it up and started thumbing through the pages. "Are you a Muslim?"

He took the book from her. "It was my father's. I got it after he died."

"Oh, I'm sorry," she said, placing a hand on his muscular forearm.

"Don't be," he replied, returning the book to its stand, before pulling her toward him again onto the bed.

This time she did not resist. They kissed for a while and then she playfully pushed him away. He pretended to fall back helplessly, arms spread out over the silk sheets on his oversized mattress. She climbed on top of his long body, straddling him with her legs, surprisingly strong for such a slender frame. He guessed she might be a dancer, or maybe a fitness instructor, and wanted to ask. But she was preoccupied and appeared to be enjoying her labor. First, she helped him take off his shirt, impressed by his athletic physique. Next, she kissed his skin, starting near his tight belly and working her way up his torso, toward his neck and face. Then, after brushing her lips against his, her tongue sweet with the taste of champagne, she suddenly stopped.

"What's wrong, baby?"

"Bedposts!" she squealed.

Mo Mo frowned, wondering how this discovery could make her so happy. Off the mattress she bounced, tight shorts wiggling magnificently as she rummaged through his bureau drawers. Failing to satisfy her needs, she disappeared into his walk-in closet, emerging moments later wearing bright red panties and nothing else. In each hand she held one of his silk neckties.

"What are those for?" he asked, trying to focus on the ties but failing miserably.

"Quiet please, Movie Star."

This time, Mo Mo chose not to correct her. He watched, instead, as she straddled him once more, reaching for his hand. He craned his neck to kiss one of her plump breasts and felt the necktie pull tightly around his wrist.

"Careful, baby, those are expensive."

"What, these ties?"

"No, my hands. They're insured for twenty million each by Lords of London."

"You mean *Lloyds*."

"What?"

"Never mind," she said, reaching for his other hand. "Just lay back, honey, and let Momma do the work."

Mo Mo cringed at the word "Momma," pushing aside any thought of his own. It wasn't hard to do, with this sweet freak climbing around on top of him. He felt the silk bind around his wrist and thought about $40 million. *That's four million per finger, and I hardly use the pinkies.*

This made him laugh.

"What's so funny?" She tied off the second tie.

"Nothing, baby, nothing at all," he said. "What happens now?"

"You'll see."

"You're not going to rob me, are you?"

"No, honey, I'm not going to rob you. Zulu's got different plans for you."

"What plans?" he asked, but the answer seemed evident, as firm hands clasped his hips, pulling down on his slacks and underwear.

"Is *that* insured by your Lords of London, too?"

"No," he said proudly, "that's all Mo Mo."

"It certainly is."

"Hey, where are you going now?"

"Quit worrying, Porno Star," she responded, stopping just inside the doorway. "I'll be back in a minute. I saw something in your kitchen that could be fun."

Mo Mo lay on his back trying to imagine what in his kitchen could be so much "fun." Honey? Whipped cream? Chocolate sauce? He had seen this once in a movie, but never thought it might happen to him. He only wished now he had set up his video camera, in case his teammates doubted what was about to take place. He could still ask her to film the two of them getting busy, but maybe she wasn't that kind of girl.

Mo Mo was pondering this dilemma when his R&B suddenly snapped off, replaced seconds later by the hard-driving rap and nasty-ass lyrics that could only be Two Hole Punch.

Maybe she was.

As he lay there listening to the music, he felt his arms going dead. What was taking her so long? Another part of his body was in a bit of pain, too. He couldn't be expected to keep this up all night, could he? What was she doing down there? More importantly, what did he know about this girl? She called herself Zulu, which sounded African. She had an accent, not from around here. She drove a cheap car, which she apparently couldn't afford to keep running. And she was downstairs, in his mansion, alone, doing God-only-knew what...

Mo Mo suddenly felt a pang of anxiety rising up through his belly. Just as quickly he drove it back down, not about to let anything interfere with this fantasy. *Trust your instincts.* That's what he always said, and look where those instincts had taken him so far. Out of the hood and into this dream world, with his expensive toys, celebrity friends, and dark little freaks, like the one in his house right now. Only, where the *hell* was she?

On the sound system, Two Hole Punch began belting out the same lyrics in militantly repetitious fashion.

"Lion in the bed! Gimme yo head!"

Mo Mo's arms ached and the music was too loud. He feared one of his neighbors might complain, even though the next mansion was quite far away. He was about to call out, when just like that, she reappeared in the doorway, completely naked. In one hand she held a plate of fat red strawberries; in the other, one of his tungsten carving knives.

"Pretty big fruit knife," he joked, trying to sound calm. *Trust your instincts.*

The girl didn't answer. She moved instead toward the bed, sitting down all lady-like, crossing one leg over the other. He could detect her scent as she placed the knife beside the plate of strawberries. She reached for a single piece of fruit, inserting it gently into his mouth.

"Good," he said, between bites. "Real sweet, just like you."

Zulu smiled, waiting for him to finish chewing.

"Now you gonna cut me loose? So we can get down to business?"

"Something like that," she answered over the music. *"Lion in the bed! Gimme yo head!"*

Still smiling, she reached for a second strawberry. A real winner, fattest of the bunch, it was country fair quality. Mo Mo had to open wide to fit this gem in his mouth. Only, this time, the girl shoved the berry in hard, forcing it deep down his throat.

"Lion in the bed!"

Mo Mo gagged, wild-eyed in surprise, as he tried shaking his hands free, but the more he pulled, the tighter the silk ties bit into his wrists. The girl knew what she was doing.

"Gimme yo head!"

Now she was lifting the knife, his surprise turning to fear. And now she was stepping away from the bed, his fear running to horror. For now she was reaching down there, as he flopped on the mattress, kicking out in all directions, trying to scream. Only, his scream came out more like a gurgle, a harmless little sound blocked by the berry wedged in his throat.

"*Lion in the bed!*"

"Sit still, Porno Star. I'd hate to turn you into *No* Mo."

Zulu laughed at her own joke, while grabbing hold of his manhood. Mo Mo's eyes bugged grotesquely as he fought to choke down the fruit.

"You *bitch!*" he shouted, the word sounding more like *butch*. Not that it really mattered, his curse drowned out beneath the misogynistic ranting of Two Hole Punch.

"*Gimme yo head!*"

"Not nice calling others names," the girl said, lifting the knife high in the air, "especially someone holding one of *these!*"

And with that, she swung the weapon in a violent arc, missing his favorite organ yet hitting her primary target. The razor-sharp blade, scientifically designed for butchering large game, had little trouble chopping off a human hand, even one valued at $20 million.

Blood spewed everywhere. Across his silk sheets. Down his oversized mattress. Onto the slats in his floor. Mo Mo howled out, thrashing like a wild animal caught in a trap. His arm was free now and he tried to club her with it, but the bloody stump did little good. Thick red spray shot like a geyser through the open hole in his wrist. His legs kept kicking, but she stepped back, out of range. His howls soon turned to whimpers, his whimpers to moans, and then he fell silent all together, as the last of his strength ebbed away and he eventually bled out.

Dressed again, with nylon gloves from her handbag, Zulu wiped off the knife and all other objects she had touched, before leaving the master bedroom, heading for the stairs. Filing past the photos – LeBron, Denzel, the President, and Mo Mo in much happier times – she carried with her two mementos: in one hand, his hand; in the other, his father's Koran.

Stopping at the trophy case, she used the book to smash the glass, setting off alarm bells.

Exactly four minutes, she remembered, before LA's finest would be pumping her full of questions, if not steel-tipped bullets.

Reaching through the jagged shards, she collected the Michael Jordan autographed basketball and continued on her way. At the foot of the stairs, in plain view of all those who would soon enter, she placed the hand, the Koran, and the ball. She attempted to arrange the hand on the ball to appear like it was taking a shot, but it kept rolling off, falling onto the floor.

Three minutes remaining. She opened the Koran and propped the hand on a random page, index finger pointing to a long passage in Arabic script. "That ought to keep them guessing," she said aloud.

Gathering her handbag, she took a look around Mo Mo's palace of pleasure. She paid no attention to his various riches, but the security system, with its blinking lights, caught her eye. She stared at the buttons, trying to recall what each one did. "Hell, what does it matter?"

Two minutes to go.

In the garage, she started for the Jeep.

"I *love* Jeeps," she said, laughing. "Yeah, right."

She climbed into the Ferrari.

From her handbag she extracted a set of keys with a prancing black stallion on a bright yellow shield, pilfered from Mo Mo's nightstand.

One minute left.

She revved the engine and popped open the console on the dash. This device, similar to the one in the Jeep, she had been careful to scrutinize.

Forty-five seconds.

She tapped a blue key and watched the door lift behind her.

Thirty.

A red one released the security gates out front.

Fifteen.

Foot to gas, the girl called Zulu winked at her reflection in the rearview mirror before blasting off into the nightlights of LA.

2

A few hours later, on the opposite coast, a man in black moved through dark streets with mischief on his mind.

He was the Jag, self-proclaimed for his cunning stealth and feline agility. His exploits were infamous, although few knew him by this second identity, his alter ego. He preferred to work alone, plying his trade in the dead of night. Under a cover of darkness he toiled, moving between shadows cast by landmark structures symbolizing the very seat of America's unrivaled power – the Capitol Building, the Supreme Court, the White House.

This night found the Jag in front of a different house, a posh Colonial in the trendy, gentrified neighborhood fronting Lincoln Park, a stone's throw from Capitol Hill. Only a few years ago, this area, like much of the District, had been teeming with drug dealers, gang-bangers, and other assorted degenerates. Quite unseemly, it seemed, for the nation's capital. So, with a clever twist of the legislative broomstick and a few well-directed handshakes over cocktails at the Hay-Adams, in swept the callous yet capable real estate developers, out went the peeved but powerless low-rent tenants, and soon the Park, like the

Hill, was home to Senators, judges, and other assorted celebrities.

The Jag knew this neighborhood. He appreciated the vast wealth held by its residents, so falsely secure in their showcase homes and multi-million dollar estates. But he wasn't after their money. That wasn't his game.

Crouching catlike and concealed behind a vintage BMW, he raised a lecherous eye toward the uppermost window of the townhouse in question. He knew the occupant was young. He knew she was beautiful. And, most importantly, he knew she was alone.

Nothing like the thrill of the hunt.

Crossing the street, the Jag scaled the front staircase with bold disregard. He could feel the juice rising, up through his spine, teasing his senses, firming his resolve. The trick now, he mused, while traversing the landing and pulling up just short of the front door, was getting in, getting what he wanted, and not getting caught.

From his trousers he extracted an object, which he slid through the slit in the door, wiggling it slightly before finding the spot.

"*Voilà*," he whispered, as the lock gave way like a virgin under his practiced hand.

Then he entered.

Inside, the Jag moved without hesitation, as if he had been here before. Across Spanish tiles he swept, past a grandfather's clock, toward a wall housing an elaborate security system. With the same deft touch employed breaking in, he dismantled the alarm before pausing to survey his surroundings. Fine Persian carpets enjoyed the company of genuine hardwood floors, while modern amenities commingled with original art. On a side table, he spotted a photograph, smartly framed and featuring a young woman in the arms of a man. From her radiant beauty and inviting figure she might have been a model, an actress, or most anything she wanted to be.

The Jag smiled, knowing what he knew. The man would not be in his bed this night, the woman would.

Nothing like the thrill of the hunt.

Now, up the stairs he went, ascending in a hurry. The Jag was a predator, a big cat on the prowl, and the juice kept rising. Reaching the second floor, he filed past rooms that would have posed a burglar's delight, stocked with laptop computers, high definition plasma TVs, gym quality workout equipment, and other assorted play toys of the modern American bourgeoisie.

None of this interested the Jag. He was on a different mission. His treasure waited for him at the end of the hall.

And then there she was, in the master bedroom, curled up all alone. Her firm body lay hidden under a down comforter that furnished relief against the night air yet scant protection from what he had in mind.

Seeing her there in the flesh, her innocent face openly exposed and primed for the taking, it was all he could do to prevent himself from attacking her on the spot. But that wasn't his style. There were rules to this game, a certain manner of doing business.

Standing in the doorway, mustering restraint, the Jag collected his thoughts while letting his eyes adjust. He noted with wry pleasure the his-and-hers bathrobes draped over a loveseat, the matching slippers tucked under a desk, the bookshelves offering Larsson, Lehane, Le Carré.

Slowly, he untied his laces and stepped out of his shoes. Carefully, he peeled off his blazer, never taking his eyes off the girl. Finally, without making a sound, he unlatched his belt and deposited it carefully on the carpet.

Only then did he advance on his prey.

Up close, she was a rare beauty, indeed, with soft skin, an upturned little nose, and chestnut hair spilling across the pillow. A debutante, no doubt, accustomed to champagne cocktails and summer cruises on the Cape.

Well, baby doll, your picnic is about to end.

Bending down, the Jag reached out until he was nearly touching her. The anticipation was killing him, and his fingers began to tremble. His mouth started to water. His breathing came harder and—

Her eyes popped opened.

"What?"

"Huh?"

"*No-oo!*"

The woman cried but the Jag was ready, slapping a clammy hand over her mouth, while using the other one to sweep away the comforter. Beneath it, she wore a silk negligee and nothing else. He couldn't be happier.

Pouncing on the girl, he pinned her arms down with his knees. She tried kicking out, but her legs were trapped under the comforter. Her thrashing proved useless, as he went to work. Rather than tearing off her clothes like some wild animal, he prolonged the moment, slowly un-hooking the top button of her negligee.

"No," she repeated, apparently too frightened to scream.

The next button fell away just as easily, exposing soft flesh underneath. The Jag smiled like a devil, relishing the elements of this twisted game. What he failed to consider was how the girl could play, too. Pretending to surrender, she relaxed her muscles and arched her back, giving him a better view.

The Jag took the bait. Leaning in to ogle her, he braced his weight with one hand on the mattress, as she craned her neck and bit into his wrist.

"*Ow!*"

Now she had a hand free and used it to shove against his torso, knocking him off balance. The Jag tottered sideways, rubbing his wounded appendage, as she wrenched her other arm loose. He still had her pinned to the bed, but now she had both hands out and went in search of a weapon. Nothing of use on the nightstand,

and the antique-style telephone stood just beyond reach. So, she grabbed hold of the only object she could find.

"*Ayye!*" he shouted, prying her hands away from his most private of parts. "Now you're going to pay!"

Casting aside his earlier composure, the Jag clawed savagely at the girl's chest, tearing a button off her negligee. The damage done seemed to anger her more than the assault, and she flew into a fury, slapping wildly at his face. He blocked her efforts, while clamping his hands around her wrists to avoid further attack. With his superior weight, he pressed in to kiss her, but she jerked her head away. This angered the Jag, who yanked the girl's hands apart before trying again. This time, she squirmed beneath him, foiling his advances.

On they struggled, pushing and pulling, fighting and panting, getting all caught up in bedclothes...he determined to conquer her...she determined to escape... neither making much progress...nothing diverting them from this peculiar contest until...

The phone rang.

They froze in place.

Stared at each other.

It rang a second time.

Now they lunged. He beat her to it, but in doing so she freed a leg at last. He held up the receiver. She leaned back. He put it to his ear. And she booted him beneath the stomach.

"*Ugh!*"

A direct hit, the impact sent him sailing, ass over ankles off the bed.

Now the girl retrieved the phone, while tracking the intruder writhing on the carpet, clutching at his wounded groin. The Jag was injured and angry, yet far from finished.

Pushing aside the pain, he started coming at her all over again. This time the girl was ready. Watching him crawl back onto the bed, she lifted up the receiver, poised to strike, just as he reached out, trying to grab her.

So she let him have it, dropping the phone harmlessly into his hand.

"It's for you, Rory," she said with a smile.

3

Rory Crandall peered out the first class window of the Boeing 787 Dreamliner as it soared 30,000 feet above the Atlantic. All around him overpaid passengers dozed in supersized seats, but he had too many thoughts on his mind to join them.

Much had happened since he received the call the previous night in the house he had "broken into." His house. Rory – aka, the Jag – smiled at his reflection and wondered if he and Melanie were taking things a little too fast, both in their relationship and in the bedroom, where she constantly amazed him with what she was willing to do. "Intruder-housewife" was the latest game she had conjured up for their mutual enjoyment. As appreciative as he was, it also meant she now had a key to his place, which signaled a certain level of commitment he usually worked hard to avoid. Upon his return, Rory decided, he would speak to Mel – at 24, over ten years his junior – and make sure she understood all the rules. He might even ask for his key back.

Following the call, the two of them had finished what they started, with a little more tenderness if no less enthusiasm, and she was out the door by dawn. Rory then showered, hand-squeezed a stack of Sicilian blood oranges – flown in weekly from the same orchard in Catania at considerable cost but worth every penny – and powered up his laptop. It didn't take long to find what he was looking for, as the grisly murder of Lazarius, the Brazilian soccer star, was splashed across his "Favorites": BBC, NYT, *Le Soir*, ESPN. This news he already knew, for it was the same information he received from Mrs. Markham when she called.

A few years ago, as Rory was first venturing out on his own, he managed to obtain information from an ex-Soviet soldier that proved critical to cracking the case around the mysterious disappearance of billionaire IT pioneer and philanthropist Robert "Mako" Markham, who vanished while delivering relief aid during the war in Chechnya. The widow Markham, forever grateful, repaid her unsolicited debt by steering work, whenever possible, in Rory's direction. Among her circle of acquaintances there seemed no end to the number who found themselves or their valued (and valuable) loved ones the latest victim of this or that kidnapping scheme. Equally impressive was the amount of money they were willing to pay Rory to act as consultant when ransom was demanded, confidant when the ordeal dragged on longer than expected, or, at especially profitable times, hostage negotiator when assistance from the authorities was, for one reason or another, not to be sought.

Yet this case was different. Against his better business judgment, Rory reminded Mrs. Markham that he was a conflict resolution specialist and occasionally a negotiator, but not a detective.

"You should contact the Amsterdam police or Ares team officials," he told her.

"Yes, Rory, dear, the police are involved, but we really need someone we can trust taking a look at this one. You do understand."

Rory thought he did, being aware that among the stable of lucrative investments Mrs. Markham inherited from her slain husband was controlling partnership in an international consortium that owned several flagship sports franchises in Europe and America. A Google search would reveal Ares Amsterdam to be one of them.

Nor did he make an effort to correct her, when Mrs. Markham added, "Please, Rory, dear, you are the best."

"Well, you know, Mrs. Markham, if I do take this job, I'll need to be put on retainer," he had said, while eyeing the original Ai Weiwei in vibrant red recently purchased at auction and presently hanging on his bedroom wall, although he thought it might catch the light better downstairs, next to his Gauguin.

"Of course, dear, the usual rate," Mrs. Markham replied, sweetening the pot with an open expense account. Rory accepted the offer and was later on his iPhone, booking a same-day flight to Amsterdam, while simultaneously scrolling through a members-only sports blog, when something caught his eye. An entry from a blogger, who called himself "Beijing Boy," read:

Any1 think laz & zc murders related?

Rory figured "laz" to be Lazarius but had no idea to whom "zc" referred. Following his only lead, he pulled up on his screen the English version of *Beijing Wanboa*, the Chinese mega-city's most popular newspaper. What the Western press failed to see as hugely significant their Eastern brethren held practically sacrosanct, at least according to the bold headline that screamed off the front page:

Zhou Chu Savagely Murdered!

Beneath it a grainy yet recognizable photo revealed the martial arts legend and chop-socky icon, more commonly known as Jin Dragon, dead in his *wushu* training center in Hong Kong. Returning to the blog, Rory learned that the police photo and the question of who leaked it to the press had already become a matter of intense social media speculation, topped only by the revelation that one of Zhou Chu's lethal feet had been severed at the ankle and discovered crammed up inside a most uncompromising location.

"My God," Rory said to the startled KLM operator, before apologizing to her and canceling his flight to Amsterdam.

Reading on, Rory learned how Zhou Chu had millions of fans not only in his homeland China but spread across Japan, both Koreas, most of Asia, and much of the world. The three-time Olympic gold medalist, who took his name from a Jin Dynasty warrior immortalized for slaying a local dragon, was widely admired and considered by many to be the promised second coming of Bruce Lee.

Rory placed his next call to a close contact at *The Washington Post*. A cub reporter when they first met several years earlier, she had impressed Rory with her compassionate handling of his controversial forfeiture of a coveted university track scholarship. Her choice of such phrases as "focusing on intellectual pursuits" rather than "being physically washed up" or "lost in a sea of late-night Euro partying" may have deprived readers in Northern Virginia of some juicy gossip on one of their favorite sons at the time, but it won Rory's eternal respect. Now a Pulitzer Prize-winning journalist on the *Post's* editorial board, she in turn had benefited over the years from "anonymous" tips provided by Rory from some of his more sensational cases.

"Yeah, we just heard about Zhou," the journalist said. "But that's small potatoes. Turn on your set, Roar. Hey, sorry, but I gotta run."

Rory did as instructed, putting down his iPhone and reaching for the remote. He found CNN and couldn't believe what he saw there. The screen was split, with a camera on the left panning over the heads of a roomful of journalists waiting for the start of a hastily assembled press conference. On the right, a second camera zoomed in on two stout men in starched white uniforms wheeling a gurney covered with a sheet as white as their shirts, save for a ragged red stain marring one side. A trio of policemen cleared space for the gurney, as shell-shocked neighbors looked on from a wide, tree-lined street.

At the bottom of the screen, the following line summed up the scene:

NBA Star "Mo Mo" Hicks Butchered in LA

Rory listened to the commentary while doing the math: three world famous athletes slaughtered on three different continents in a matter of hours. *Who could have done this?*

Muting the volume, he rebooked his flight for Brussels, Belgium. He then spent the next couple hours pulling together a stack of papers, which he placed in a sturdy folder, tucked inside a leather duffle bag, before boarding a limousine to take him to Dulles International Airport.

Now, as the morning sun sliced through his window, high above the clouds, Rory declined a cup of coffee, ordering instead a glass of chilled orange juice – not his preferred brand, far from it, but at least in first class it

didn't come from concentrate or, worse, a can. He retrieved the folder he had brought with him and opened it
across the dropdown table. This dossier contained page
after page of photos in varying quality and sizes, each
accompanied by biographical information detailing the
murderous activities of the world's most wanted villains.

There were the obvious ones, such as Ayman al-
Zawahiri, theological leader and heir to Usama bin
Laden's bloody al-Qaeda, followed by ISIL's self-
proclaimed "caliph" Abu Bakr al-Baghdadi and some
of his vicious, black-masked henchmen. Next came
several bearded members of the Taliban, followed by
the Mexican drug kingpin "El Mayo" Zambada, head
of the deadly Sinaloa cartel. They were all there: terrorists, warlords, Mafioso figures, weapons merchants,
narcotics dealers, human traffickers, mercenaries, hit
men, some leaders of rogue states, and even a few serial
killers still at large.

A real who's who of hatred, Rory thought, as he kept
thumbing through the pages awash in human misery. He
had been over these documents so many times during
the flight he could practically recite them verbatim, yet
knowing this information did little to help answer the
questions that had been filling his mind ever since leaving DC.

*Who was capable of killing three top athletes on three
separate continents? What was the purpose, the motive behind
the murders? Wouldn't kidnapping these multi-millionaires*

and demanding high ransom for them make more sense? Why these three: a Brazilian soccer star, an LA hoops phenom, a Chinese martial arts legend? Where was the connection? What did the killers want? Why hadn't they identified themselves? And, perhaps most importantly, when and where would they strike next?

Closing the folder at last, Rory massaged his neck before draining the juice in his glass. He glanced out the window again, watching the contours of Europe emerge, forming those familiar shapes from the map.

No use struggling further with all these questions, he thought, as the plane banked sharply and started its initial descent into Brussels. If anyone held the answers, it was the man he was on his way to see now.

4

Dr. Emile Amwaj, professor, peacemaker, Nobel laureate, septuagenarian, strode across the stage of the cavernous lecture hall tucked within the leafy grounds on the Brussels campus of Leopold University. His helmet of dusty gray hair bobbed with each deliberate step he took before coming to a stop just shy of the front ledge. Tilting his head to one side, he appeared more like a Shakespearean actor about to deliver a soliloquy then a lecturer in an introductory course on peace and conflict resolution.

Staring out at the scruffy assemblage of students, Dr. Amwaj knew all too well that other faculty members chided him behind his stooped back for continuing to teach this remedial course semester after semester, year after year. He also acknowledged that most of these students had little interest in peace studies. They only wanted an easy grade from a survey course. He further understood, better than most, that in the end it was all a numbers game.

For every 200 pupils each semester – the seating capacity of this vast, dimly lit auditorium, which other professors avoided like a tumor and most students referred to as the "Dungeon of Amwaj" – some 50 of them were intellectually stimulated by the course material. Perhaps five of those 50 grasped the deeper implications of his words, "the meaning behind the meaning," as he liked to say. Of those five students, on average one per year – through a combination of perception, perseverance, and intellectual panache – might actually formulate an original idea worthy of further consideration.

That student he made his teaching assistant.

Among his assistants, usually one a decade was able to develop a strategy for putting those ideas into practice, taking what he or she created in the laboratory of abstract knowledge and applying it to the concrete realm of human existence.

Those rare finds Dr. Amwaj called "gifted."

Gazing out across the student body, at the soft young faces forming a colorful palette of races and nationalities, waiting for him to fill their amorphous little minds, Dr. Amwaj realized that valuable gifts were hard to find. Yet he was a patient man who had been at this game for more years than he cared to remember. Whether addressing world leaders or combat soldiers or a group of restless freshman like the lot before him now, he approached each lecture like an archeologist setting out on a fresh dig. He expected little but remained ever hopeful his endeavors might unearth the next hidden treasure. In the end, though, putting gifts and treasures aside, he was simply happy to still be teaching. For him, there was no higher calling, no worthier ideal, and no better reason for getting up in the morning.

This morning found him midway through his favorite lecture, on a discourse titled, like his best-selling book, long considered a classic: "On the Theory of Evolutionary Peace."

"Now, where was I?" he asked rhetorically, raising his shaggy head to the congregation. "Ah, yes, I was about to tell you that never in the course of human history—"

A *clank* from the back of the room broke his concentration. A student, late to class, was attempting to sneak into the lecture hall only to interrupt Dr. Amwaj in his delivery.

"*Pardon,*" called a distant voice in apology, as the derelict ducked down in the dark confines of the back row. Other students pivoted in their seats, sniggering at the culprit, before turning back to see how the old man would respond.

Whereas other professors would have taken the slacker to task, making an example of him before his peers, Dr. Amwaj shook his head, cleared his throat, and carried on. It was a numbers game, after all, and that one in 6,000 might have just walked through his door.

Rory slipped into the lecture hall, his efforts to avoid detection ultimately dashed by a loud *clank* of the door. He was reasonably certain the elderly professor up on stage had failed to identify his former teaching assistant and protégé, nestled, as he was, in the dark confines of the vast, dimly lit auditorium.

From this hiding spot Rory studied the individual who changed his life. Dr. Amwaj. *Has it really been fifteen years?* Amazing, but there he was again, the great man, still teaching, still towering above his students in this wondrous space. A theater really, his theater, where he ruled supreme, striding so grandly, so majestically...so much *smaller* than Rory remembered. Could it be that Dr. Amwaj, still toiling in this same building more than a decade later, had become just a bit player on some forgotten stage? Then Rory stared more closely and scolded himself for even considering such betrayal. Despite the added wrinkles and aggravated stoop, it was clear the professor, even in his twilight years, retained that same ruddy strength and vitality, those ageless eyes that refused to take refuge behind a pair of glasses.

More remarkable still was his voice, a resounding baritone that emanated from deep within, carrying forth those prophetic words Rory had heard spoken so many times before. As Dr. Amwaj filled the lecture hall with his commanding voice, working his audience like a Bedouin chieftain recounting fables around a desert fire, Rory found himself being transported back to an earlier time.

*   *   *

"*Cran*-dall! Rory *Cran*-dall!"

Young, nervous, lost beneath a flop of greasy brown hair and an ill-fitting, hand-me-down suit given to him by his father before he died, Rory stood up clumsily from the back row, his note pages spilling out in all directions. He tried to impress the professor and his new foreign classmates with his best schoolroom French – "*Je suis ici!*" – causing laughter all around. His fellow students found great humor in his accent, which only seemed to irritate Dr. Amwaj.

"My office, after class, and for God's sake, English will suffice."

"Ooh," rang a chorus from other students as they gathered up their books and hurried out the door. Rory remained standing in place, fearful of what he had done.

"You're in big trouble now," said a cute girl passing him by.

Rory blushed, averting his eyes, and when he looked up again, she was gone.

It took directions from three different people to locate the office belonging to Dr. Amwaj, which occupied the upper story of an old cottage sequestered beyond a maze of gravel paths and overgrown shrubbery on the outskirts of campus. As Rory started up the weatherbeaten steps he couldn't help wondering if placing Amwaj in this backwoods repository was less a reward for his imaginative teaching style than a means of keeping this brilliant but clearly eccentric professor far away from the more conservative faculty.

Out of nowhere a clap of thunder shook the steel gray sky, followed by a burst of rain. Rory scrambled up rickety stairs in search of shelter, but the effort went in vain. By the time he reached the top he was completely drenched, his sad suit hanging off him like dead skin. The rain then stopped as abruptly as it started. Cursing his luck while catching his breath, he squinted through the only window he could find. The room inside looked dark and empty, and he contemplated a fourth set of directions, when the door suddenly swung open.

There stood Dr. Amwaj.

"You're wet," the professor announced, by way of greeting, his thick nose barely visible over the top of an open book. "Follow me."

Rory obeyed, shutting the door behind him. They walked down a hall smelling of onions and cooked cabbage. *Does the professor live here, too?* The next space they entered contained a single source of light, spilling from a lamp on a desk literally overflowing with student papers.

"Your competition," Dr. Amwaj informed, before settling into the only available seat, a tattered armchair that appeared to be even older than its owner.

Standing there, looking down at the man still buried in his book, Rory wondered if this was the customary mode of introduction in the professor's home country, wherever that might be. Or maybe it was some sort of test: let's see how the new kid responds to blatant discourtesy. Rory was uncertain. He was uncomfortable, too, hovering there in this dreary office-apartment, dripping cold water from his damp clothes, watching this odd character silently reading a book. *Look up, old man*, he wanted to shout but didn't. He just stood there, feeling large, needing air.

Rory considered excusing himself, heading back outdoors, and waiting for Dr. Amwaj to finish his reading. The rain had kicked up again and was really coming down now, bouncing off the roof like marbles on linoleum. He decided, instead, to take the only seating option left in this cluttered space, a lumpy couch covered with heaps of reading material. Carefully sliding one batch aside, he lowered himself onto the smallest patch of fabric capable of supporting his soggy trousers. At least this afforded him a chance to survey his surroundings.

Everywhere he looked, practically floor to ceiling, books were stacked like skyscrapers in a metropolis begging for better city planning. One tower tilted precariously in front of him, and he leaned forward to scan the titles. "Men and Conflict: From Caesar to Napoleon." "Getting to Yes: Negotiating Agreement without Giving In." "Sun Tzu: The Art of War." Further down, a slender volume in a sky blue jacket caught his eye: "On the Theory of Evolutionary Peace," by Dr. Emile Amwaj.

Rory looked up at the book's author, but the old professor kept reading, his lips moving noiselessly as he chased after words on the page. *What could be so damn captivating?* On either side of the man, Rory noticed, in the rare spaces of wall not fronted by jam-packed book-cases, hung a series of photographs depicting famous destinations. He recognized the Coliseum in Rome, the Egyptian Pyramids, and the Great Wall of China, while other pictures were equally impressive if less familiar. He was about to break the painful silence and ask Dr. Amwaj if he was responsible for taking all these photos, when something else grabbed his attention. There, festooned on the back wall and hidden upon entry by a slant of shadow, appeared a sight that would change the course of Rory's life.

Maps.

There must have been a dozen of them, maybe more. Richly colored, finely drawn, lovingly ensconced in ornate wooden frames. At first glance, from this distance, Rory assumed each map represented a different location – perhaps, like the photographs, places where Dr. Amwaj had visited. Without thinking, he stood up, left the couch, and crossed the room. Upon closer examination he realized these maps, while clearly different, were also remarkably the same. Each embodied a freeze-frame of the world at scattered points in history. First in the series was a long-dead cartographer's best estimate of ancient Earth, with a grossly oversized Europe dominating the center and frightening sea creatures patrolling rough waters or guarding shores of bizarrely named places. Subsequent maps became more precise and more familiar, with Europe shrinking in size as its best explorers converged on foreign lands, returning to paint increasingly accurate pictures of the planet. Vast empires gave way to nation-states, while the final map in the collection showed the world as Rory knew it then, with the United States prominently displayed and cautiously staring out in all directions at those who might wish to challenge her recently won lone superpower status.

Rory was staring, too, completely mesmerized. Through his mind hummed a hundred thoughts, embryonic in nature yet still momentous – the power of history, the thrill of discovery, the wonder of invention, of music and art, science and religion, war and peace and needful revolutions, an endless sea of change, all encapsulated here in these magnificent maps. It was far more than he could grasp at one time, and Rory knew in that instant that right here was exactly where he was meant to be. He sensed a purpose far greater than he had ever imagined possible. He realized without the usual self-doubt clouding most of his thoughts that he must find a way to spend as many hours as possible in this cramped and musty room getting to know this strange and reclusive man who was sitting there, calling his name.

"Mister Crandall…"

"Huh?" Rory wheeled around to find Dr. Amwaj eying him quizzically. *How long have I been standing here gaping at these maps?* "Sorry."

"Don't be," Dr. Amwaj said. "I didn't put them up there for lack of wallpaper." He shifted in his chair before addressing Rory again. "Do you know why I asked you here today?"

Rory couldn't imagine. That is, until he spotted a familiar object pinched between the professor's fig-like fingers. It was the paper he had submitted with his application to the university. Self-doubt came galloping back into the room.

"Did you read that?" he asked, realizing the absurdity of this question the moment it left his lips. So, he tried covering it up with another gem. "Did you *like* it?"

Dr. Amwaj frowned. "A bit fanatical, don't you think?"

Rory didn't know what to think, or say, so he just stood there, dumbly.

"We'll talk about it later," Dr. Amwaj said, dropping the paper onto his desk with all the others, like a fisherman tossing back a catch far too meager to bring home for supper.

Rory wondered what they would talk about *now*. His early dismissal from school? The procedures for returning his track scholarship?

But the professor had different plans. "Fancy a whisky?"

And so their friendship began.

Rory never knew why Dr. Amwaj chose him. Nor did he ever ask, content as he was with their new relationship and fearful of anything that might endanger it. The routine was always the same, Rory stopping by after his last class and afternoon training session ended to find the professor either reading a book or preparing the next day's lectures. Rory would light a fire in the hearth and then tend to his studies, settling into the lumpy couch, a full cushion cleared now for his personal use. A few hours later, Dr. Amwaj would put down his work, reach for a crystal decanter, and pour them each a long pull of single malt.

"Doctor's orders," he would say with a wink, handing Rory his tumbler of Scotch. "A devout man never drinks, and yet we never go thirsty."

Rory would laugh appreciatively, enamored more by the ritual than by the professor's favorite joke. He would then sit back and listen to Dr. Amwaj regale him with colorful accounts of historic battles fought and lessons learned from fallen warriors who vainly believed they could rule the world. One night it would be Julius Caesar storming across Europe, or Alexander the Great forging a Middle Eastern mega-empire. The next would find Genghis Kahn or Attila the Hun taking center stage, followed by Napoleon or Hitler or one of the modern-day dictators.

At first Rory only listened, trying to imagine what it would have been like filling the sandals or jackboots of these marauding behemoths of history, commanding armies, controlling men, taking land and life. But gradually he assumed a more active role, stopping the professor here and there, questioning what he heard, even offering up theories of his own – a brazen act he rarely had the confidence to make during class. It was at these moments that Dr. Amwaj would shift tactics, moving away from simple storytelling to presenting hypothetical suppositions. "What if there were no national boundaries, Rory? What if we had color blind civilizations? Or no more wars?" The professor loved playing this way, with words and ideas, every topic lending itself to new discoveries and novel ways of thinking about the world.

Dr. Amwaj soon made the young man his teaching assistant, an arrangement that suited both parties perfectly. Rory had since given up his track scholarship, a decision that did not sit well with all those who had supported the "Great Falls Golden Miler." While a strained patella tendon and a strong passion for Belgian beer and other sweet, after hour delights rendered obsolete his plan of taking the European 1,600-meter world by storm, Rory's main interest now lay elsewhere, and he actually counted himself lucky for his physical failings and weak constitution. For whatever reason, he had caught the eye of Dr. Amwaj, this learned scholar whose reputation was rapidly growing.

In truth, though, it was the professor who may have profited most. In Rory, he had discovered a mind, much like his own, unafraid to dance in the cerebral dark, to turn reason inside-out and back again in quest of deeper knowledge. He now had an eager apprentice. Not a disciple, like so many of his students, but a rare find, that one in 6,000. For not only was Rory an extraordinary listener, able to absorb a vast amount of information and apply it in a practical sense, he also had a unique talent, only then starting to blossom: the ability to place himself in another person's space.

Dr. Amwaj once tried explaining this enviable skill to a fellow faculty member. "It is as if this student of mine temporarily thinks like someone else. He sees through their eyes, hears with their ears, and approaches the world from an angle not entirely his own."

To which his colleague gave a sarcastic retort. "Maybe this student of yours should join the Drama Department…or see a psychiatrist."

Dr. Amwaj took it in stride, accustomed as he was to being misunderstood. He comforted himself in the knowledge that in Rory he had finally found someone with whom to match wits. He saw the young man as a kindred spirit, the son he never had. Their verbal jousts often progressed well into the night, a second round of single malt giving way to a third, as the fire crackled in its bed, competing with the latest jazz track to hit the streets of Brussels.

Some nights they would launch into heated debate, Rory gaining self-confidence and intellectual footing with each passing week under the professor's tutelage. Their discussions ranged far and wide, from such classical propositions as man's inherent good or evilness, to more topical discourses on the logic of nuclear deterrence or the moral justification for capital punishment. Eventually, the exchange would wind its way around to the subject matter favored most by both men – Dr. Amwaj's Theory of Evolutionary Peace.

"But why can't you force peace upon another country?" Rory asked late one night, punching the air sharply with his index finger.

The professor calmly answered the question, as he had done countless times before and would continue to do for years to come. "In the end, you will see, peace *must* evolve."

"Maybe," Rory said with youthful vigor, a splash of whisky spilling from his glass. "But what if it's too late? What if while we're waiting around for this evolution of yours to take place, another Hitler rises up and lays waste to us all? What then?"

"Then," the professor chose his words carefully, "it was never meant to be."

Rory glowered back dumbfounded.

"*What* was never meant to be? This planet? Mankind? Are you for real? Are you trying to tell me that we're just some cosmic experiment that eventually goes awry, that we annihilate ourselves so the cockroaches can rule the day?"

"Perhaps," said Dr. Amwaj, taking a measured sip from his glass.

Rory shook his head in disbelief, as the professor watched him.

"Only, my son, I believe it *was* meant to be. Any more questions?"

*   *   *

"Any more questions?" Dr. Amwaj was saying again now, as Rory sat hidden and much older in the back of the lecture hall. *How naïve was I then*, he asked himself, considering all that had happened since? Following graduation and his move to Washington to become a diplomat before setting up a much more lucrative shop on his own, Rory had been pleased to see, as were many others, the teachings of Dr. Amwaj put into practice, leading to peaceful negotiations between longtime combatants in Southeast Asia and a Nobel Prize for his mentor.

"Yes, Sir, I have a question." A tall boy in the second row stood to address the professor in English. "You say peace must evolve, but as far as I can see, in places like Iraq and Syria, Pakistan and Afghanistan, Libya, Yemen, Somalia, Israel and Palestine, much of Africa, Haiti, Mexico, and many of America's inner cities, the world is becoming *more* violent all the time. How much longer must we sit back and wait for this peace of yours to climb out of the water and start walking upright?"

Students burst out laughing. Clearly, it was their first time hearing this joke.

Not so, Dr. Amwaj.

As always, he feigned amusement before proceeding to lay down the foundations of his Theory of Evolutionary Peace, leading the classroom through a compelling history lesson. From club-wielding cavemen to the barbaric Middle Ages to blood-drenched empires and two World Wars, the professor demonstrated how in spite of the misery and terror that sadly remained today, humankind was steadily advancing and evolving as it went. Until one day, he promised, there would be world peace, maybe even within their lifetimes.

"Any more questions?" he asked.

This time no one took the bait, either unwilling to risk young egos or more likely eager to depart class early. So the professor began collecting his papers.

"*J'ai une question*," Rory shouted from the back, attempting his best schoolroom French. Laughter rang out all around him, just like in the old days.

Up on stage, Dr. Amwaj squinted but was unable to make out the questioner.

"Yes, what is it?"

"I just wanted to know," Rory said, rising from his seat, "will this be on the exam?"

Dr. Amwaj bristled before recognizing the owner of the shoddy French.

"My office, after class," he said in mock seriousness. "And for God's sake, English will suffice."

"Ooh," came a chorus from the students, as they gathered up their books to leave.

"You're in big trouble now," said a cute girl passing him by.

This time, Rory just smiled.

5

"**A**ny ideas?" Rory asked.

"Plenty of them," Dr. Amwaj responded.

"Too many, in fact," Dr. Gustafson added.

"It's the answers we're lacking," Franz Glick said, "obviously."

They were seated, the four of them, on the outer rim of a semi-circular stainless steel table bolted to an elevated platform in a stark white, windowless room. Replete with several bays full of the latest generation computers and specialized monitoring gear, the place held an ultra-modern feel, like a biotech laboratory or Mission Control for the space shuttle.

"Obviously," Rory repeated, staring at the last man to speak. He was positioned farthest from Rory at the table, a sprite young upstart with a pointy goatee and trendy rimless glasses, who had introduced himself as "Franz Glick, Junior Genius." *Why would Dr. Amwaj hire this punk?* Rory wondered, before pushing aside the question. He wasn't here to critique the professor's employment practices, but rather to obtain insights into the perpetrators behind the "Sporting Murders," as the world's press had already dubbed yesterday's trio of homicides.

"So where do we start?" Rory asked.

"With the usual suspects," said Dr. Gustafson, sitting next to Glick and laughing at his own joke. He was one of those roly-poly, middle-aged intellectuals, Rory thought, who liked to laugh – and *eat* – a lot.

"Right you are," Dr. Amwaj agreed, while tapping a sequence of keystrokes on a sleek computer console that had risen up through a hole in the metallic tabletop like a serpent poking its head above the surface of a silvery sea.

"Unless," Franz Glick said, "you want to wait for the killers to march in here and hand us a message."

Rory had a message for this twerp, but decided to let it go. He watched, instead, as a massive plasma screen descended from the ceiling two stories above them, reminding him of a theater curtain falling, while the lights began to dim. Dr. Amwaj struck another key, and the screen, fully extended now, came to a rest. The room went dark, followed by a cascade of colored lights dancing before their eyes. A hologram appeared in the familiar shape of the Earth, a three-dimensional globe spinning on an invisible axis. As the sphere rotated it began to unfurl, peeling apart like the skin off an orange, eventually engulfing the entire screen and turning into a tremendous map of the world, with countries cast in different splashes of color. Next came a hundred or more beams of red light, like fiery eyes or bursts of ammunition, the bulk of them burning in the Middle East, with a smattering in Africa, Asia, Europe, and Latin America.

"The usual suspects," Dr. Gustafson said.

"Right again," said Dr. Amwaj. "The information gathered here we share with friendly governments, researchers at leading think tanks and universities, and anyone else trying to peacefully resolve armed conflicts. At present, we have identified more than thirty major militant groups – the larger, brighter pegs you see on the map – plus many smaller ones, including state armies, terrorists organizations, violent cults, and other devious characters demanding attention."

"There must be over a hundred dots up there," Rory said.

"One hundred-and-fifty-four, to be exact," Franz Glick, Eager Einstein, chirped from the end of the table, theatrically crossing one leg over the other while pulling on the tip of his pointy beard. "Each terrorist cell you see up there represents a major network, and each network contains anywhere from five to five hundred operatives, and in some cases many more."

Who is this smug bastard? Rory realized he had been on edge ever since leaving the lecture hall but wasn't sure why. *Was I really expecting to spend the entire day alone with Dr. Amwaj in that weed-infested house of his on the outskirts of campus?* Instead, the professor, with the aid of a cane, had led Rory down a freshly paved, tulip-lined path toward a vast structure occupying much of the New Campus and christened the "Emile Amwaj International Peace & Conflict Research Institute."

"Amazing what a little thing like winning the Nobel Prize will do," Rory had said then, trying his best to sound impressed, while nostalgically wishing to have seen his former mentor in the old haunt where they had spent so much time together.

"Indeed," Dr. Amwaj had responded, while navigating Rory through the first layer of building security. "It may lack some of the charm of the old place, but just wait until you see the map room."

Seated now in the map room, Rory decided to drop whatever was eating at him. "Yes, now I see what you're talking about. This is all quite impressive."

"Ah, but you haven't seen anything yet," Dr. Amwaj replied, striking more keys. In front of them, on the screen, one of the fiery eyes began morphing into a life-sized portrait of a man, tall and thin in flowing white robes and skullcap, cradling a weapon.

"Usama Bin Laden," Rory said.

"And a pretty large gun," Dr. Gustafson added.

"A fifty caliber sniper rifle, to be exact," stated Franz Glick, while stroking his little beard again. "Capable of punching a hole through an armored vehicle, bringing down a fighter plane, or taking out just about anything it likes from a thousand meters away."

"Quite right," Dr. Amwaj said. "And what else do we know?"

Rory was about to say that al-Qaeda was not responsible. While the core of the terrorist organization had been decimated since the killing of Bin Laden, it still had the reach to commit three murders on three continents in a single day, plus the motive in Bin Laden's so-called *fatwa* of 1998, which demanded the destruction of America and the establishment of a strict Muslim state in perfect contrast to the lavish material pursuits embodied in the three slain athletes and their followers. But Rory knew al-Qaeda had not orchestrated these attacks because—

"These crimes don't fit al-Qaeda's *signature*," Franz Glick jumped in first, "for AQ typically engages in activities that cause mass casualties, with severe damage to the world economy and long-lasting dramatic shock. It's what we refer to as 'spectacular attacks,' like the World Trade Center or the American Embassy bombings in Kenya and Tanzania."

"*Obviously*," Rory said, mimicking the younger man, who was really starting to get under his skin. "The signature, as we all know, is the means by which an organization goes about its business, the method it employs to invoke terror. So we should take a close look at, but probably rule out, at least for now, the so-called Islamic State because—"

"—the IS or ISIS or ISIL favors gruesome attacks in its own backyard," Glick interrupted, "like the beheading of journalists, aid workers, and even other Muslims in Iraq and Syria. While the terror group does promote 'lone wolf' attacks by supporters in other countries, it would be a stretch to find these guys committing coordinated murders in LA, Amsterdam, and Hong Kong."

"Yes, it would be," Rory snapped. "Likewise, it's hard to imagine Lashkar e-Tayyiba, or the Army of the Righteous, being responsible for this case. While LeT does have global connections—"

"—it favors high-profile assaults in South Asia, such as the 2008 Mumbai attack that killed one hundred and seventy people, and it is not likely to take up individual slayings," Glick cut in on Rory again.

"Well done," Dr. Amwaj said.

He's encouraging this impudent elf? Rory was about to object, when he suddenly remembered. This was precisely how the professor liked to operate, pitting intellectual foes against each other for the betterment of the discussion. Dr. Amwaj always made sure his lessons were not just told but taught, which is what he used to say... *back when I was the student.*

Now Rory smiled to himself, recalling how Dr. Amwaj had encouraged similar behavior when Rory was a teaching assistant trying to establish credentials before some older gentlemen at the faculty club. *Now I'm one of the older gentlemen*, he realized, reminding himself why he admired Dr. Amwaj the way he did.

"Nor is Hezbollah," Rory said and then paused, holding open a hand to tee up Glick for the answer. "Because Hezbollah—"

"—tends to go for big, headline grabbing kills, like the two hundred and forty-one dead U.S. Marines in Beirut, or its more recent shelling of Tel Aviv," the younger man finished, with a nod to Rory.

"So, we must also reject the Haqqani Network," said Dr. Gustafson, showing he could play, too. "Since the HQN carries out—"

"—attacks typically around its base of operations in Afghanistan and along the Afghan-Pakistan border," said Rory.

"Right again," replied Dr. Amwaj, clearly pleased by the team effort. "All of the signatures are off. Nor should we consider the various Ansar al-Sharia in Africa, Jaish-E-Mohammed in Kashmir, the Kahane Chai in Israel, or any of the other groups whose terrorism is strictly religiously motivated, for our three victims were of different religions. Maurice Hicks, or Mo Mo, the basketball star, was secretly a Muslim like his father, while Zhou Chu, the martial arts champion, a Taoist, and Lazarius, the Golden Buddha, a seldom-practicing Catholic, despite his nickname."

With each terrorist organization mentioned, Dr. Amwaj tapped a key on the pad, causing the corresponding pegs of light to disappear from the screen.

"We can also cross off all those groups seeking purely territorial gains," he said, with additional keystrokes. "Such as ETA in Spain…the FARC in Columbia…the New Peoples Army in the Philippines…the Shining Path in Peru…"

He continued working his way through the names of organizations and individuals, including many of the ones Rory had studied on his plane ride over. Eventually, the four men sat staring at a blank screen.

"Which leaves us absolutely nowhere," Rory observed.

"I'm afraid, for the moment, you may be correct," Dr. Amwaj said, striking the keyboard again and sending the screen on its journey back into the heavens. A final keystroke brought up the house lights, and they all blinked against the intrusion.

"I wish we had answers," Dr. Amwaj continued. "There are many out there with reasons to create mayhem, but these three murders do not fit any of their profiles or unique signatures. There is really no precedent for a crime like this one, orchestrated in this manner, with no obvious connection between the victims beyond their celebrity status and—"

Dr. Amwaj suddenly broke into a harsh fit of coughing Rory had never heard from him before. On the opposite side of the table, Franz Glick and Dr. Gustafson acted as if this outburst was nothing out of the ordinary. Rory started to his feet to assist, but Dr. Amwaj waved him off. He eventually brought the cough under control and took a sip of water from the glass in front of him, resuming his explanation before Rory had an opportunity to inquire about his condition.

"Now, where was I?" Dr. Amwaj said, clearing his throat. "Ah, yes, there have been sports figures slain for ideology. The PLO's killing of Israeli athletes at the 1972 Olympic Games comes to mind, as does the murder of an Iraqi tennis coach and two of his players a few years ago for wearing short pants in public. Horrible attacks have taken place, as you know, at major sporting events, such as the Atlanta Olympics bombing and, more recently, the Boston Marathon. Although, in neither of those cases did the athletes themselves appear to be the targets. While several of those whom we monitor are capable of such actions, they would be swimming in uncharted waters here."

Dr. Amwaj paused to catch his breath, before counting off possibilities on his fingers. "In the end, this operation may turn out to be the work of a new terrorist group…a warlord seeking attention…a Mafia boss with scores to settle…or even a rogue state flexing its muscles. Until we discover what these killers hope to achieve, all of these options remain mere speculation. At this juncture, we simply lack too much information."

"Which, again, leaves us nowhere," Rory repeated, shaking his head.

"Well, not exactly," Dr. Amwaj corrected, addressing his former protégé. "We do have some leads to follow and one potential clue."

Rory raised an eyebrow and Dr. Amwaj continued. "I don't know if you are aware, but we learned today that at least in the case of the Lazarius murder in Amsterdam, the type of weapon used was rather unusual."

"How do you know that?" Rory asked.

"Because the killer left it behind at the scene."

"Why do that?"

"I don't know," Dr. Amwaj answered. "But I have a theory, based on the weapon."

"What is it?"

"A *sica*."

"Like those used by the Zealots?" Rory said, as surprised by the answer as Franz Glick and Dr. Gustafson seemed to be by how quickly Rory came up with his response.

Dr. Amwaj was smiling. "So you do remember my lessons?"

Rory smiled back. "Most of them."

"Excellent, then you should also recall how the original Zealots were a community of Jews living in the first century AD, who launched a ruthless assassination campaign against the Roman Empire and its occupation of what is present day Israel."

"In what many experts believe to have been the first acts of what we call 'terrorism' today," Rory said.

"Correct," Dr. Amwaj replied, with a nod. "And what may be most interesting about the Zealots was how they purposely attacked their victims in crowded places and in broad daylight, using a curved dagger, known as a *sica*, to cut their throats, while innocent bystanders watched the blood flow. These dramatic public displays were designed to cause great psychological trauma that carried well beyond the immediate assaults, sending a strong message to a much larger audience, including the Roman legionnaires and those who supported them."

"And you think our killers are trying to send a similar message to a much wider audience?" Rory asked.

"I do," Dr. Amwaj said. "The brutal murder of three international sports stars on three continents on the same night, not to mention the use of this unusual weapon, left behind for all of us to see, hardly seems a coincidence, does it?"

"No, it does not," Rory said, thinking. "But *what* message?"

"Again, I don't know, but at least we have a starting point to try to find out."

Dr. Amwaj now turned to the other two men at the table. "Franz, I need you to continue contacting museums of ancient history and warfare, plus any private collections you can think of that might be missing a *sica*. My hunch is there can only be a limited number of these artifacts still around."

Glick nodded, but to Rory's mind he seemed less than thrilled by this unglamorous assignment.

"Dr. Gustafson," Dr. Amwaj said next, "please reach out to your contacts, especially within the intelligence community, to learn what they have learned. And I, for my part, have a few wise old friends to catch up with – Jimmy in Atlanta, Desmond in South Africa, and Aung

San in Rangoon, now that she is free to come to the phone."

"And what about me?" Rory asked, starting to his feet.

"Well," Dr. Amwaj said, also rising, with some difficulty, "I should think you would proceed up the road to Amsterdam. Take a look at the site of the Lazarius murder. See what you can see. And, I imagine, as usual, you are well provided for, hmm?"

Rory registered the comment, keenly aware of how their respective motives no longer matched. *So, sue me for finding a way to make a little money in the field*, he thought, casting an eye on all the flashy toys in the room. "It doesn't look like you're exactly suffering here."

"Point taken," Dr. Amwaj replied with a wink. "Unfortunately, my friend, as you well know, all the technology in the world can only take us so far. In the end, it is human resources that matter most. That is why you should continue on your way, Rory, while we stay here and try to fill in some blanks. Unless, that is, you have a better idea?"

"No, I'm afraid not," Rory said, extending a hand to his former mentor. "Not unless, that is, the killers decide to march in here and hand us a message."

6

As Rory departed alone through the main entrance of the Emile Amwaj International Peace & Conflict Research Institute, the afternoon sun cast long shadows over Brussels, turning the tulips into rows of angry spears, while a flurry of questions flew across his mind.

Was this a wasted trip? Who benefits most from killing three celebrity athletes? Was I too hard on that kid Glick? Will the killers strike again? When, where, and why? So what if I make a little money off this venture? Is that Glick running at me now?

Rory had turned at the sound of pounding feet and now watched as a figure in full stride belonging to none other than Franz Glick came charging toward him. The graduate assistant was moving with considerable effort yet not much pace, leading Rory to conclude that he was more scholar than scholar-athlete. Rory also couldn't help wondering if he really had insulted this intense young man with his parting jibe about the killers marching in to hand over a message. While it seemed crazy to think the kid would chase him down to restore some sense of lost pride, Rory found himself dropping into a defensive posture all the same.

"Cran...dall..." Glick shouted as he drew near.

"What?" Rory said, bending his knees, hands at the ready.

"I've...got..." the kid panted, his chest heaving from the exertion.

"What?"

"A...message..."

"What message?" Rory relaxed as Glick kept struggling to catch his breath.

"A message...from..."

"Dr. Amwaj?"

Glick shook his head, no.

"Mrs. Markham?" He couldn't think of anyone else who knew his present location.

Another shake.

"Then *who*?"

Glick started once more, determined to finish this time. So Rory waited, detecting what might be the slightest hint of a grin cross the young man's lips before he finally spit it out.

"A message from the killers."

Game On

7

The Message, as it quickly came to be known in every major world language and scores of lesser-spoken ones, was beamed around the globe. It was contributed anonymously and distributed brilliantly to reach the maximum number of people in the minimum amount of time. Americans – North and South – first saw the Message on daybreak news programs or heard it on car radios while driving to work and were soon spreading it like a virus over the Internet before the steam had cooled in their morning coffee. The Message was simultaneously served up with luncheon chardonnays from London to Cape Town and all points in between, while Arabs, Indians, Asians, and Australians discussed the Message over evening cocktails or communal cups of tea. Brief and to the point, the Message was easy to remember and simple to pass along:

Niger Delta killings stop or another athlete
gets the chop!

But what was the Niger Delta? Where was it located? And why should anyone care? Fortunately, a slew of talking heads were primed and ready to explain all. With the aid of maps and charts and high-definition computer graphics, these self-appointed experts distilled this long-raging conflict down to its bare essentials: warring tribes in impoverished southern Nigeria were waging brutal battles against each other and an indifferent government in bed with multinational oil companies making a mint off the local population.

As soon as it was determined, however, by highly paid (mostly white) polling firms that highly agitated (entirely black) tribesmen killing each other and occasionally lowly regarded (white, yellow, and brown) oil workers were no longer pulling in big rating points, the world's news outlets shifted focus to the *sender* of the Message, who had been dubbed universally, as if through silent consent, as the Sporting Murderers. File footage of world-renowned killers – menacing stares from Ayman al-Zawahiri, Abu Bakr al-Baghdadi, Charles Taylor, and even Charles Manson – filled television screens, while somber newsmen and women asked each other: "Who could have committed such horrible crimes?"

Next, linguistic experts and cross-cultural specialists were tracked down and propped up before TV cameras and radio mikes to expound on the *meaning* of the Message and whether the words chosen provided clues to the nationality or religious affiliation of its sender. When no conclusions could be agreed upon, speculation turned from the originator of the Message to the most likely next *victim*. Athletes from every sport imaginable were considered. One London booking house even posted odds, offering a handsome return for anyone willing to wager on another trifecta.

Sports personalities pulled out of competitions. Skittish promoters rescheduled events. One pro golfer went so far as to declare early retirement from the game, just to be safe. In contrast, Formula 1 driver Jayden Ziegler refused to cancel his title defense at Monte Carlo, stating that while he treated the Message with some trepidation he was more likely to get killed doing his day job.

Everyone seemed to have something to say about the Message and the fate of professional sports. The UN convened a special session in New York. The OAU gathered African delegates in Addis Ababa to see what role it might play. A $10 million reward was offered for anyone providing information leading to the capture or killing of the Sporting Murderers, while TV producers and newspaper editors around the planet reserved top-of-the-hour broadcast slots and above-the-fold column inches for anything to do with the Message. From late night talk shows to social media platforms, from private clubs to local pubs, even school playgrounds were abuzz with predictions of who would be next to "get the chop." If a soccer star lost his head while a hoops sensation gave up a hand and a martial arts legend was found without a foot, one could only imagine what grisly fate awaited a bowling ace or a javelin thrower.

At first, the world watched and waited and wondered what would happen next. Then, when no more killings occurred and no legitimate suspects were apprehended, the public began to lose interest. There was always something else to worry about. The world economy was in bad shape, after all, with unemployment on the rise again, while fighting in Syria and Iraq kept lingering. And what about the Ebola virus? Within days, the Message found itself bumped from prime time television and dumped off the front pages of most metropolitan dailies. Relegated to the tabloids or the netherworld at the back end of the sports section, next to the black-and-white ads for rubber tires and discount Viagra, even here interest waned, as fickle sports reporters returned to covering the latest controversy over steroids use or the most recent scandal committed by overpaid superstars cheating or beating on their wives.

And through it all, armed conflict continued to rage in southern Nigeria, as it had done for years, while somewhere someone plotted the next Sporting Murder.

8

All heads turned as the one they were instructed to call Confucius entered the room, surprisingly fresh after a long day's journey from the Far East.

"How did it go?"

Easing his scorpion's frame into the seat reserved for him at the head of the conference table, Confucius waited for the others to abandon whatever pursuits had been occupying their time – iPads were powered down, Kindles bookmarked, flat screens darkened – and take their places around the table, before answering the question.

"Perfect."

The others – a dozen college-aged men and women of differing colors and nationalities – held his stare without being asked. Dissimilar to many in their demographic, these kids were no coddled slackers. They had been carefully selected, as had Confucius, who, at 26, was the oldest among them and their day-to-day leader.

"Were you scared?" one of the younger members couldn't help asking.

"Not really," said the woman seated to the immediate right of Confucius, stealing the question. Her elfish features and bald head were framed now in a wig of striking blond hair. The others called her Bettina, for she refused a codename, although many of them were hesitant to address this one at all, especially after her scalping of the soccer star Lazarius. "You just need to be brave."

"Ha-ha," said her partner in crime, the one they referred to as Tito, after the Yugoslavian revolutionary hero. Lanky and brooding in a black hoodie, his skull was closely shaven now but still retained a trace of that telltale Mohawk, like watermarking on a sheet of stationary. A wisp of peach fuzz needed wiping from his chin as he dismissed Bettina's dig with a blink of his eyes, the left one starched red at the bottom with a deformity from birth that gave it the appearance of a boiled egg dipped in tomato paste. Across from them sat the young woman they called Zulu, the tall, dark beauty who had left Mo Mo dead and disfigured in his Beverly Hills mansion.

"I don't know," Zulu said in her singsong voice, trying to find the right words for what she and those at her end of the table were feeling so soon after committing murder for the first time. "It was, what, I don't know, it was—"

"*Necessary*," said Confucius, before turning his oblong eyes on the others. "Don't worry. We'll coach you through it, when your turn comes. Right now, we need to get started. He's expecting our call."

They all watched as Confucius used his index finger to slice through cellophane holding together a stack of notepads positioned on the glossy tabletop in front of him. Some considered how these same hands had just executed the Jin Dragon, while others wondered if they would be able to fulfill their duty, their deadly rite of passage, should they be called upon next.

Above and behind Confucius, through a narrow slice of glass permitting the only natural light to seep into this subterranean chamber, snow had begun to fall, unusual for this time of year but not necessarily this locale, situated on a cliff high in the hills over Sarajevo. The window was frosted on the outside so any trespasser able to penetrate the fortified walls surrounding this structure – which its inhabitants had been instructed to refer to only when absolutely necessary and then just among themselves as the "Sanctuary" – would have had no reason to suspect the true nature of the proceedings within.

"All right then," said Confucius, as the last of the notepads were passed down the table. "Does everyone have paper? A pen? Sufficient caffeine?"

As if on cue, a young co-ed entered the room carrying a tray of steaming hot coffee mugs. She was short yet striking in her beauty, with skin the color of summer sand and a flush of dark hair trickling down her back. Confucius accepted his coffee first, smiling up at the girl until she shyly responded in kind, an act that did not go unnoticed by Bettina or Zulu.

"Let me remind you," Confucius said, as the others took their mugs and settled into their seats, "like before, this is a *brainstorming* exercise. There can be no wrong answers, only good suggestions. So, let's stay focused and be creative, you know, think outside the box. And this time, we only need to come up with one recommendation. Anyone care to start?"

Every hand around the table rose. Confucius purposefully skipped over Bettina and Zulu, much to their obvious chagrin, before choosing an intense, brown-skinned boy with a slash of black hair hiding most of the pimples on his forehead, who they were told to call Che, after the iconic guerrilla leader.

"I've got a good one," he said, lowering his hand.

"Then why don't you take the board."

Che did as instructed, leaving his seat and striding toward the foot of the table and the flipchart positioned there. Turning his back on the others, he wrote something at the top of the page, before stepping aside to let them admire his work.

l. Kang Coleman — boxing

"Kang 'Killer Whale' Coleman," he announced, watching the others nod in appreciation, although a few were seen to wince at the prospect. "Beat that!"

"Nice," said Confucius, blowing on his coffee, before taking a sip.

"*Ja*," said Bettina.

"*Da*," agreed Tito, which came as no surprise, since they all knew he had a crush on her.

"*Shit*," scoffed Zulu, refusing to join in their positive affirmation fest.

"What's wrong?" Bettina challenged. "He's rich and famous, he's global, and he's—"

"—*black*," she said. "Another African American male. All together now, can we say *racial profiling*?"

"He's half Asian, too," Confucius pointed out.

"Making him *three* of the categories we've already filled," Zulu said. "Black. Asian. Male."

But Bettina wasn't giving in so easily. "All right, Little Miss PC, do you have a better idea?"

"I might," she said, thinking. "How about Viviana Albescu?"

"The Romanian gymnast?" Bettina nearly spat, while a few of the others struggled to place the name. "That's ridiculous."

"No, it's not."

"Ladies, ladies," Confucius intervened. "Let me remind you, this is a *brainstorming* exercise. No wrong answers, only good suggestions."

"Yeah," Zulu said, mimicking Bettina. "She's rich and famous, she's global, and she's a *she*. One half of the world's population we haven't tapped into yet."

While the others thought about this, Tito said, "I'm with Bettina."

"Of course you are," Zulu replied, rolling her eyes.

"It's not that," he said. "It's just, well, I'm not about to kill a woman."

"Why not," Bettina said, "scared to try?"

Laughter erupted all around, which Tito attempted to contain by staring them down. He looked particularly hurt that this joke had come from her.

"Okay, that's enough," said Confucius, returning order to the room. "Write it down, Che. We haven't much time. He's waiting."

So Che added to the flipchart the name of the Olympic medalist who had stunned the gymnastics world when her nude photos went viral online. The others followed suit, placing this second entry under that of the juvenile delinquent-turned-prizefighter at the top of their notepads.

1. Kang Coleman — boxing
2. Viviana Albescu — gymnastics

"Any more ideas?" asked Confucius.

"How about Diego Colarusso," said a stocky teenager with broad shoulders and tight, curly hair they called Caesar, as he mimicked revving a superbike.

"Clever," said another, "but few women in that sport."

"What about figure skating?" offered a young Kashmiri woman with the codename Ramona, after the Zapatista freedom fighter. "There's Tami Mitsuya."

"Too Asian," reminded Bettina, smirking at Zulu.

"What about Jamie Meagher?" someone suggested. "She's rich and famous."

"Maybe a bit outdated."

"And hasn't she been through enough already?" Che asked, to more laughter.

"All right," said Confucius. "Let's stay focused. These are all good ideas, but I still think there's a better one out there."

The others nodded, as the room fell quiet. Some stared up at the flipchart, trying to figure out the best answer, while others looked down at their notepads. A few reached for coffee mugs, hoping to find inspiration there. Outside, the snowflakes were really fluttering down now, sticking to the tall trees guarding the Sanctuary.

"I know," a voice said, breaking the silence and startling the others. In the corner, by the door, the young coffee girl stood lingering.

"She's not part of our group yet," Bettina objected.

"This is highly irregular," Zulu concurred, turning toward Confucius.

But he decided to let her speak. "Go ahead."

"Well," she started, boldly staring at Bettina, "why not women's tennis?"

The others considered this suggestion before turning back to Confucius and the only opinion that ultimately mattered. They all knew their places in the hierarchy, and none among them sat higher than the man at the head of the table, the man contemplating what he had just heard, before uttering a single word.

"Perfect."

A collective sigh filled the room, followed by a clatter of applause, until Bettina shattered the reverie with a question. "Which one?"

"Which *what*?" Confucius demanded.

"Which *player*," Zulu said, looking conspiratorially at Bettina.

"Right, which player," she agreed.

The others watched this brewing drama with keen interest. After Confucius, Bettina, at 25, was the next oldest at the Sanctuary and always angling for a confrontation. Zulu, at 24, was undeniably brilliant and relished competition, whichever side of the fence she found herself on.

Again, Confucius took his time. As much as he valued their opinions, he wasn't about to be pushed around by these two, especially not in front of the others.

"Excellent question," he said at last, "and one we will answer soon enough, I promise. But first, I would like to address another matter."

"What's that?" asked Che, leaving the flipchart and returning to his seat with the others.

"Who wants to do the job?" Confucius said.

Now most eyes fell away, the youngest among them quickest to break contact. While they had spoken together about this very moment, in hushed voices in their sleeping chambers after dark, now that it was actually upon them the magnitude of the task seemed daunting.

Confucius waited, watching them all. He appreciated how they, like he, had given up so much to be here – further education, promising careers, families and friends. He knew he could order any one of them to step up and they would comply without hesitation, but he also understood how that wasn't what this was all about.

Next to him, Bettina gazed across the table, into the eyes of Zulu, who coolly returned her stare. Both women opened their mouths, ready to suggest a suitable candidate, or, more likely, to offer their own services again. Only, they were both beaten to the punch.

"I'll do it."

Every head at the table swung around to the far corner of the room and the forgotten coffee girl.

"You must be joking," said Bettina.

"That's precious, child," added Zulu with a snort.

But no one else was laughing. They were all too busy turning back to see how Confucius would respond.

Once more, he waited, ignoring the others while sizing up the girl. She was the youngest present and the most recently arrived at the Sanctuary. To either side of him, Confucius sensed Bettina and Zulu glaring defiantly, which only validated his decision.

"Perfect."

9

Rory glanced at his watch and couldn't believe he had been standing there for nearly an hour.

Even on a good day, Murtala Muhammed International Airport in Lagos, Nigeria, was not a very pleasant place to be. In the mid-90's, during the depth of Sani Abacha's depraved dictatorship, the airport topped most travel industry lists of the world's worst destinations. Passengers on continuing flights were strongly advised against deboarding for any reason, and those who chose to ignore this warning frequently failed to return for their onward voyages. Those who did remain onboard sometimes fared even worse, raided on the tarmac by armed thugs who relieved them of their wallets, watches, and jewelry. Despite the best intentions of the current government to offer visitors a more welcoming reception to Africa's most populous nation, Nigeria's principal airport continued to lack most basic amenities, let alone modern conveniences or anything remotely resembling hospitality or charm.

And today was not a good day.

This place stinks, Rory thought, wrinkling his nose while transferring his duffle bag from one hand to the other. He jostled for position with other travel-weary passengers inching their way through the cramped and unlit passport control area, which smelled as if farm animals had relieved themselves before dying.

The connecting flight from London had been a difficult one, with large black men in flowing *agbadas* and large black women in peacock-colored *kabas* cluttering the aisles, chattering in loud voices, and praying to God upon shaky takeoff and even bumpier landing. To pass the time during the flight, Rory placed a call over the first class onboard telephone system, billing inflated fees to his client, Mrs. Markham, to let her know of his new destination. He then skipped the rich menu of in-flight entertainment, opting instead for reading material provided to him by Dr. Amwaj, including the latest official travel advisory, which advised travelers not to visit Nigeria at this time. Full stop. "If you must go," the document read, "make certain you are met on the ground by someone known and reputable.'" Rory had not been worried then, smiling to himself as he thought about how he would soon be seeing his old friend Tunde, who was nothing if not well known, although few who knew him well would ever think to call him "reputable."

Now, standing here in these dismal quarters, packed in with a horde of sweaty passengers and no electricity – which meant no lights and no air conditioning, just like the bad old days – Rory was starting to have his doubts. Something wasn't right here. For one, they weren't moving. *Why not?* When he had earlier posed this question to one of the many policemen milling about, he had been rudely told to stand still and shut up. *And why are there so many cops here?* That was never a good sign, he knew, and the fact that most of their uniforms did not match was even more troubling. Yet that still wasn't it.

No, something else was bothering him, had been for some time now. Rory had that feeling – call it a sixth sense – that someone was watching him, following him. He felt it back in London, at the airport waiting for his connecting flight, and maybe even earlier than that. He felt it again now and—

There she was.

Fair-skinned and decent-looking, she was definitely out of place and strangely familiar. *An old girlfriend?* No, Rory answered his own question while craning his neck to get a better look. Medium height, well-fit, she looked to be in her 20s. *Daughter of a client?* Possibly, but Rory prided himself on putting names to faces and keeping them there. And this one didn't stick. He knew the face but not the name and wondered if he ever had. He also wondered how he had missed her on a plane full of Africans. But there was certainly no missing her now, for she was the reason for their delay.

"I told you, I don't have any money," the girl was protesting, her voice rising in frustration at the only passport control official who seemed to be working. He was a mountain of a man, with a big round head, who loomed over her from behind a raised platform surrounded by a few idle police officers.

So much for Nigeria's new anti-corruption laws, Rory thought. He had seen this scene unfold before during his first trip to Lagos several years ago as an exchange student conducting research on traditional conflict resolution practices. The more you complained, the worse it got, until eventually you were emptying your wallet at the counter or being strip searched at gunpoint in a back room. He had half a mind to leave this girl to her fate, not wishing to get involved or draw attention to himself. But the stench was oppressive, Tunde would be waiting, and he wanted to know who she was and what she was doing here. So, pushing through the mob, ignoring hot-tempered curses, Rory fought his way to the front, holding a $50 bill out in front of him like a magic wand lest any of the cops decided to hinder his progress.

"—come to my country with no money, when you know there are fees," the big-headed official was booming down from his perch. "I don't believe you."

"I don't care what you believe," the young woman said in a tone that drew interest from at least two of the policemen. "I have credit cards and friends who told me it would not be smart to—"

"Finish that sentence," Rory said, popping up between the two cops and slapping the fifty down on the counter, along with his passport. "She's with me, and what she meant to say was that *I'm* the one who handles the money."

Rory gave the official a hopeless smile, as if to suggest women the world over had no concept of financial dealings.

"Who are *you*?" the woman asked.

Rory played it off. "Cute dear, you're not getting rid of me that easily."

Still, the passport official wasn't convinced, nor the pair of policemen, who drew in closer to see what was happening. So Rory dug out a second fifty and added it to the first.

"Are you crazy?" she asked this time.

"You're welcome," Rory said, as the official scooped up the bills, pounded a stamp in each of their passports, and sent them on their way.

Beyond passport control the terminal was in chaos. Babies cried, a dog barked, and phones went ringing. Passengers dashed about in all directions, while more policemen in mismatched uniforms shouted out orders and waved large weapons. Rory grabbed hold of the girl's arm before she could escape into the crowd.

"Let go of me," she objected.

"Not until you tell me why you are following me."

"Following *you*? I was clearly ahead of you. Until, that is, you started throwing money around back there like Bill Gates. Who are you, anyway?"

"Somehow, I think you know the answer," said Rory, trying to place her accent as he steered her through the crowd. "My question is who are *you* and why are you here?"

"I don't give my name to strangers and none of your business."

Rory eyed the young woman before releasing his grip. "Okay, I'm sorry. Let's start over. My name is Rory Crandall, and I'm very pleased to meet you."

She stared back at him, rubbing her arm before responding. "Well, that's a little better," she said, as they kept walking. "I'm Veronica Bay, but you can call me Rani."

Rory doubted any of these were her real names but chose to let it go. Up close, he realized he had been mistaken. She wasn't just decent-looking, she was extremely attractive. Not model-like, where the beauty slaps you in the face, but in a more subtle sort of way, her disparate features – playful brown eyes flecked bright green, ski jump little nose, mouth small but mischievous – coming together to form a beguiling composite, like a well-crafted impressionist painting. Her body was compact but shapely, and she had this strangely aggressive manner about her that he didn't usually seek out in a woman, but for some reason in her case it turned him on. Rory decided to keep things professional between them.

"Okay, Rani, you can call me Mr. Crandall." He was about to ask again what she was doing in Nigeria, when they arrived at baggage claim.

Here, the crowd stood even thicker than before, with distraught passengers fighting over heaps of luggage, scruffy men wheeling dented metal carts, and more armed guards stalking around with menacing stares.

Rory kept close to Rani as he scanned their surroundings. Past the baggage carousels, a sea of bodies could be seen jamming a single exit, while further on, beyond the glass, hundreds of faces leered in at them like phantoms in the night, yet still no sign of Tunde.

"Who are you looking for?" she asked.

"A friend," Rory said. "By the way, who's meeting you? And where's your luggage?"

"This is all I've got," she said, holding up a worn backpack. "And what do you mean?"

"You can't just show up here, not now anyway. You must be met by someone."

"Who's meeting you?"

"Not your concern," Rory answered, staring again into the mob.

"Shouldn't we be moving?"

"Where do you want to go?"

"I don't know," she said. "Maybe get taxis or something?"

"Sure, why don't you go pick us out a nice limousine?"

Rani frowned. She wasn't pleased with Rory's sarcasm but remained by his side. It didn't take long for a couple of foreigners with scant luggage and anxious looks on their faces to draw attention.

"You need a ride."

They turned to see a squat man with a bent back standing next to them. His skin was such a light shade of brown it looked nearly gray, and the twist in his back made it appear as if he was permanently leaning to one side. It was difficult to imagine this guy being tall enough to see over a steering wheel.

"No thanks," Rory said. "We're fine."

"No, you're not," the stranger replied. "And it wasn't a question."

"Regardless, no thank you," Rory said more firmly, still searching for Tunde. "Please, go away now."

But the odd little fellow didn't budge. "I think you need a ride."

Rory followed his gaze toward three men in shabby uniforms heading their way.

"Shit," Rani said. "Who are they?"

"Don't worry," Rory replied. "I've done this before."

"Maybe so," said the little man, "but I really think you need a ride."

By now, even if they had wanted to reconsider his offer, it was too late.

"What are you doing here?" one of the uniformed men demanded, a gold tooth gleaming through rubbery lips. He was the shortest of the three but also the meanest looking and clearly the leader.

"We're waiting to be met," Rory said matter-of-factly, as if answering a consumer choice survey rather than being interrogated by a trio of gun-toting thugs.

"By whom?" asked Gold Tooth, stepping into Rory's personal space.

"Not *whom*," said Rory, holding his ground while thinking on his feet. "*Who*."

"What?" Gold Tooth shook his weapon, not pleased to receive a grammar lesson. The other two men moved forward, and Rory sensed Rani tensing up beside him. He also noticed a small group of onlookers, curious to see what was causing all the commotion.

"*Who*," Rory repeated. "W–H–O…we're being met by officials from the World Health Organization. My colleague and I are here for the international HIV-AIDS symposium."

The gunman lowered his weapon and looked from Rory to the young woman.

"These aren't doctors," one of his henchmen blurted out.

"And there isn't any symposium," the other said, as the crowd continued to grow.

"You know what I think?" Gold Tooth said, raising his pistol before answering his own question. "I think you're *spies*."

"And I think you're making a terrible mistake," said Rory, far from convincingly.

"American *spies*," he sneered, which seemed to excite the two beasts behind him.

"Working for the CIA," one of them chortled, shuffling his feet.

"We're not *spies*," Rory insisted. "We're *physicians*."

"Yeah, the CIA," the third guard sang out, which elicited chattering from the now rather sizeable throng watching on.

"And you know what we do with *spies*?" the lead guard said, thorough a twisted smile, as he touched the shaft of his gun to Rory's cheek.

Beside him, Rory could feel Rani starting to shake, which wasn't helping their cause. He considered offering these brutes some money, but worried doing so would be an open omission of guilt, plus he had already given most it away back at passport control. *Tunde, you've screwed me this time*, Rory silently cursed his friend, while contemplating a final gambit.

"Like I told you, we're with the WHO," he said as authoritatively as possible. "We're being met by Dr. Okocha from the Ibadan Institute for a three-day conference at the Sheraton on advances in AIDS remediation in Sub-Saharan Africa."

The lead guard considered this new information, before waving his handgun in front of Rory's face. "Okay, then, show me your papers."

"My *what*?"

"Show me your letter of invitation from this Dr. Okocha."

Rory paused, cursing Tunde again. *Really screwed me.*

"He doesn't have one," said one of his comrades.

"No letter," the third guard added, reaching for the girl, who let out a squeal.

Totally, comprehensively, screwed me, Rory thought, before hearing a fourth voice.

"I'm with the WHO."

Rory and the others turned to see the little man with the twisted back still standing there, holding up a hand-written sign with those three letters. "I'm here to give you a ride."

The cops eyed him suspiciously.

"Well, it's about time," Rory said, seizing the moment. "Where have you been?"

The little man shrugged. "Sorry, boss."

"You've kept us waiting here forever. And where is Dr. Okocha? He said he'd meet us personally. There is going to be hell to pay."

"Yes, boss," the little man said, as if born to play the part.

But the guards weren't buying it. "Not so fast, CIA man. I still need to see your credentials," Gold Tooth said, shoving the snout of his pistol up under Rory's chin.

The crowd gasped.

"Fine," Rory said, going for broke. "Tell Dr. Okocha there has been a terrible misunderstanding. Let him know that we arrived in country, but we have been detained under false pretenses. Ask him to alert the World Health Organization headquarters in Geneva to make them aware that I won't be able to deliver my presentation. Then contact the U.S. Embassy in Abuja to let them know we are being held. Oh, and tell Dr. Okocha I will try my best to ensure that next year's funding isn't affected by this incident. Hurry up now."

The little man started to leave.

"*Wait!*" shouted Gold Tooth, turning his weapon on him.

"He's lying," said one of the bigger goons.

"Yeah, shoot the bastard," the other said.

Hearing this, the crowd jumped back, stumbling to get out of the way. Gold Tooth took aim, then hesitated, not certain what to do next.

So Rory made it easy for him. "Go ahead, he's only a driver."

And now the crowd started hissing and swearing, shocked by what they had just heard. But not the lead guard.

"My apologies," he muttered, before turning back to Rory and lowering his gun. "I thought you were some-one else, Doctor."

10

Outside, the sky was slate black, the night air hot and heavy.

"How did you know to say *that*?" the woman, Rani, asked, as they exited the airport, following after the little man with the twisted back, who was limping along in a hurry.

"*Empathy*," Rory said, tapping his head.

"You felt sorry for him?"

"No, not really, and that would be *sympathy*," he explained, while dodging a slow-moving couple wheeling bulky luggage. "I tried to think like that cop, or whatever he was, and to feel what he was feeling. I put myself in his shoes, so to speak, and told him what he wanted to hear, what he thought a pompous white doctor from America might say."

"And nearly got me shot in the process," the pint-sized stranger said over his shoulder. "Let's keep moving. We're not out of this yet."

In front of them, the mob was large and restless, pushing and shoving and shouting, as a swarm of policemen strained to maintain order. The scene, Rory thought, resembled a sports crowd about to turn nasty or a street protest ready to ignite.

"Why are they trying so hard to get into the airport?" Rani shouted over the din.

"They're not," Rory yelled back, as they veered sharply to keep as far from the melee as possible. "They're trying to get *out*."

"Out of where?"

"Out of this damn country," their miniature driver snapped. "Now hurry up."

In spite of his small size and physical handicap, the man moved rapidly, putting distance between them and the crowd, while forcing Rory and Rani to jog after him to keep pace. They soon reached the end of the building, turned left, and started up a steeply rising trail framed on either side by waist-high shrub brush. The further they went the darker and more difficult it became, for the path was unpaved, Rory noticed, and all the street lamps had been busted up. Under his feet, he felt the ground crackle. *Glass? Animal bones? Something worse?* He couldn't tell and didn't care to find out. Instead, he kept an eye on the back of the little man, not wanting to fall too far behind him. He suddenly imagined himself racing down a dark alley in Washington, DC, chasing after a black man he had just met, and it was only then that he realized this might be up there on the list of stupidest things he had ever done.

"Okay, that's far enough," Rory said, jerking to a stop. "Your job is done. We appreciate how much you've helped us, but we'll take it from here. What do we owe you?"

The little man stopped, too. Turning around, he held a finger to his lips.

"I have money," Rory said, reaching into his jacket.

"I wouldn't tell *them* that."

"Who?"

"Them!"

Rory looked back to see the faint shape of several figures advancing through the dark, just visible in the hazy glow from the now distant airport lights.

"Shit!" Rani said. "Who the hell are *they*?"

"Hurry!" Rory shouted, as the pack of men started giving chase.

"This way," the little man yelled from somewhere up ahead, but it was too dark to see him. Rory clutched his duffle bag to his body like an NFL running back and started pushing through the brush again, hoping he didn't trip over a root or crash into a tree. As he scrambled up the steep embankment, a thought suddenly struck him. *Is all of this some big setup by the little man, a ruse to get us away from the airport so a bunch of hooligans can attack us?* Behind him, Rory heard feet pounding and the sound of something else, something whistling past him in the air. *Is Rani part of it, too?*

"Damn it!" she screamed.

"What?"

"I've been hit."

"Shot?" Rory asked, pulling up and fearing the worst, although he never heard gunfire.

"No, a rock, I think, but it really hurts."

Rory strained to see and decided if she was in on it, the rising welt on her calf was pretty convincing. "Can you keep going?"

"Do I have a choice?" she said, hobbling past him.

Rory rushed after her, wondering if in their present condition dropping to the ground and ducking for cover might be a better option. But it would only be a matter of time, he figured, before these crazy, rock-slinging Africans hunted them down like helpless gazelles and did God-only-knew-what.

"Over here!" the little man shouted from the top of the hill, as dim light seeped in from somewhere. Another rock sailed by, dangerously close, making a loud *ping* sound as it ricocheted off a metal surface. Rory ducked and when he looked up again the little man had vanished once more, but the sound of angry voices was growing louder. More rocks skipped past him in the dirt. Rory sprinted forward, looking around until he located a beat-up four-door sedan with its engine idling and Rani already in the back, the door wide open.

"Get in!" the little man yelled from the driver's seat, so Rory joined Rani behind him. Just then one of their assailants reached the vehicle and struck it with something hard.

"*Shit!*" Rani screamed, as a second attacker appeared out of nowhere, smashing his fist into her window, which shook but did not break.

"*Go!*" Rory shouted.

The sedan shot in reverse, spraying gravel in all directions, as a third man charged toward them. Inside, their driver shifted gears, and the sedan bolted forward, narrowly missing another pair of attackers, who leapt free of the speeding vehicle. One threw a stick, which glanced harmlessly off the fender. Another whipped a stone, which fell short of the escaping car. Rory swiveled in his seat to watch through the rear window as the gang of men ran after them for awhile before stopping in their tracks and eventually fading into the dark.

"Damn, that was close," Rani said, touching a finger to the wound on her calf.

By now, the sedan had left the parking lot and was racing along an unlit roadway. Rani looked over at Rory, but he was preoccupied.

"Where are we going?" he asked their driver, who remained separated from the two of them by a thick sheet of glass.

"I don't think he heard you," Rani said.

Rory repeated the question, louder, while rapping his knuckles against the partition. Up front, the twisted little man kept driving, paying no attention to his passengers in the back.

"Why won't he answer you?" Rani asked, giving Rory an anxious look.

"I don't know," he said, distracted, banging even harder on the glass. He grabbed at his door handle, yanking it this way and that, but it was locked. Rani's too. Now Rory started pounding on the partition, smacking it with his fist while hollering into the night.

"Where are you taking us?"

11

The *Rub' al-Khali*, or Empty Quarter of eastern Arabia, is the largest stretch of desert on Earth. A seabed of blinding sand, it is also one of the world's great graveyards. The rare scorpion, sand snake, or giant beetle residing here might see another of its kind scurrying for cover from an unmerciful sun, which punishes those foolish enough to venture out before nightfall or much after dawn, but little else survives. So inhospitable is this tract of land that several hundred miles separating the Kingdom of Saudi Arabia from its southern neighbors, Yemen and Oman, remain without demarcation, one of the few places on the planet where no international boundary need exist.

In contrast to this searing wasteland, the vast region to the north, known as the Eastern Province, with its elaborate network of *sabkhas*, or salt flats, and lush outcroppings of date palms, tends to be more forgiving. Here, near the town of Hofuf, ruled for centuries by Ottoman sultans, one begins the lonely journey eastward. A blacktop road snakes through rolling red dunes, tracing the contours of the Persian Gulf and linking the ever-pumping oil derricks, as herds of camel amble off in the distance. This twisting highway connects the Saudi capital of Riyadh to the seven-stoned jewel of the Middle East, the United Arab Emirates. The UAE, in direct opposition to its more pious neighbor, brims with all the trappings of the modern, Westernized metropolis it has become. Fueled not only by oil wealth but also a thriving market economy and an atmosphere of relatively free thought, the Emirates are home to most any vice imaginable – all strictly *haram*, or forbidden, in the cloistered Saudi Kingdom right next door. Needless to say, there exist several flights a day from most any major city to the UAE, with seats inordinately booked by men.

Still, some do have their reasons for venturing overland, and should one choose this route, be forewarned: navigation is a killer, literally. For Arab playboys in high-powered sports cars soar like daredevils across this largely barren land, either believing their reckless pace will help elude Allah's roaming eye, or their faith in Him will get them from point *alef* to point *ba* in a single piece.

On this day, at least one driver en route from Saudi to the Emirates appeared willing to take his time. His mission depended less on velocity than on ingenuity.

"How far to Dubai?" the man asked in Arabic, handing over a stack of colorful bills to a lone attendant at a roadside petrol stop. The heat outside was stifling.

"Two hours to the border at Sila," the attendant said through a cloud of sweet smelling smoke. He relinquished the coil on his *shisha* pipe long enough to collect the cash. "Another two until you reach Abu Dhabi, depending on your speed. After that, you should arrive in Dubai by nightfall, *insh'allah*."

God willing, indeed, the driver thought. He thanked the cashier and climbed back into his platinum Lexus LF-A, before re-entering the mad speedway.

The attendant watched him go, thinking there was something a little strange about this guy. Short and slight, the driver otherwise appeared like most travelers in this part of world – leather sandals, flowing white *dishdasha* with matching *ghutra* on his head, tanned skin, dark glasses, manicured moustache. *So what was it then?* He didn't know, nor did he bother himself too long trying to figure it out. He returned instead to his *hubbly bubbly*, enjoying the melodic pop and gurgle of the murky water percolating in the hookah's crystal bowl, filling the surrounding air with a green apple fragrance, as the Lexus disappeared over the horizon.

Inside the vehicle, the slight man settled in for the five-hour drive to Dubai. He increased the air conditioning and then ran the radio dial over the frequencies, searching for a connection. Toward one end came a crackle of static, under which could be heard the sound of a soulful dirge, with lyrics full of Koranic verse. The man listened briefly to the moody wail of the vocalist before sending the dial further to the right. With some fine-tuning, there came a masculine voice reading the news.

"—in Palestine a man wearing a belt of hand gre-nades climbed onto a public bus, setting off an explosion which killed eleven people from the Jewish Entity, as well as the suicide bomber, himself, while wounding twenty Zionists...In America, another high school shooting re-sulted in the death of two teachers and nine students, including the gunman, a freshman boy who took his own life...While in Africa, during a hastily called meet—"

The words were lost in a hail of static. The driver fiddled with the dial.

"—said Nigerian Defense Minister Shehu Akinbiyi. The official went on to declare that Nigeria was not will-ing at this point to accept UN peacekeeping forces on its territory to bring about an end to the violence in the Niger Delta, which had intensified in the days following the release of the Message...And finally, in related news, sprinting sensation Kimani Babb announced he was pull-ing out of this year's Indoor World Championships, both as a tribute to the three murdered athletes and as a mat-ter of personal safety, stating that—"

This time the signal went completely dead. The driver worked the dial back toward the other end, where even the Koranic singer was no longer raising his voice in praise of Allah.

The slight man shrugged before adjusting his *ghutra*, pulling the fine cloth away from his face. Through tint-ed glasses he watched the approach of several oil pumps, their long necks dipping gracefully toward the ground, like a flock of thirsty cranes. Further on he spotted a tent belonging to a family of Bedouin making the arduous journey to the next oasis. This was the last patch of scenery he would see for many miles. Here and there stood a cropping of date palms. Otherwise, he was left only with his thoughts.

An hour or so later, a black dot appeared on the horizon. The driver blinked his eyes and shook the knots from his neck. The dot disappeared and he wondered if it had been a mirage. The desert plays tricks.

When the Lexus crested a hill, the dot reappeared and began taking shape. A road sign read: "Sila – 3 kilometers." This was no mirage but rather the border crossing between Saudi Arabia and the Emirates, where a checkpoint was manned around the clock by uniformed guards with loaded weapons.

"*Marhaba*," said the customs official at the window, demanding the driver's passport.

"*Shlonak*," he answered in a standard greeting for his country, which carried the ironic double meaning of "What's your color?" He handed over a little blue book, property of Kuwait.

"Purpose of your trip?" the official asked, while opening the passport and eying the driver with suspicion. The photo matched its owner, while the family name coincided with the make and model of the car – new and expensive. Still, there was something odd about this man, something he couldn't put his finger on.

"Business," the driver responded.

"What sort of business?" the official started to ask, when his finger struck something unexpected – a short stack of hundred *riyal* notes tucked toward the back of the booklet.

"*Shukran*," said the customs official, thanking the slight man without waiting for an answer to his question.

"*Afwan*," said the driver, accepting his passport minus the "extra" sheaves of paper, before pulling away from the customs booth.

"Short interview," said another voice, tinged with sarcasm and belonging to a second customs official, older than the first, who watched the Lexus cross into the UAE.

"*Aiwa*," admitted his partner, while stashing the ill-gotten gains inside his logbook, without offering to share the profit. "Everything seemed to be in order."

"Hmm," responded the older official, suspecting what had just transpired but unwilling to register a complaint, lest his own next customer tender an even larger bribe. This was the unspoken pact between the two of them, an illicit ritual that helped pass long hours at the window.

"Although…"

"Although what?"

"Well, there was something a little unusual about that guy."

"How do you mean?"

"I don't know exactly. His hands were very small and, well, he didn't have a beard," the younger official said, still searching for the source of his consternation.

"Nor do you."

"I know. My wife hates the whiskers."

"What about your mistress?"

The two men laughed at the joke, their suspicions soon forgotten.

A kilometer or so down the road, the driver was laughing, too.

"*Mumtaz*," he said aloud, for his performance had been excellent. He watched in the rear-view mirror as the border crossing became a faint dot again and then disappeared from view altogether.

Night arrives early in the desert and already the skyline had faded from a comforting azure blue to an edgy slate of gray. Continuing along the Trucial Coast, the Lexus passed nondescript towns with forgettable names – Sila, Ruwais, Turit. Outside, gray turned toward black, and soon after that, magnificent lights burst into view, revealing the shiniest of the UAE's seven sparkling jewels, the diamond city of Dubai.

Without slowing down, the driver removed his *ghutra* and placed the headpiece on the passenger's seat beside him. He then reached back and unclasped a pin holding his hair in place, causing beautiful black tresses to spill down around his shoulders. Next, he removed his sunglasses, revealing a pair of startling brown eyes under long, thick lashes. Finally, with a stinging wince, he tore the moustache from his face and dropped the fake whiskers next to the other props.

"*Business*," he laughed in an uncommonly high pitch, for there was something strange about this man. He was a woman. And not *any* woman – it was the coffee girl from the Sanctuary.

Her name was Leila, but the others had been instructed to refer to her from now on only as the Arabian Princess. Had she been asked, she would have chosen Zenobia for a codename, after the 3rd century queen of Palmyra, or modern-day Syria, and a personal hero who had conquered Egypt and much of the Roman Empire. But no one had asked her, and she did not object. She understood her place in the system, and being sent on a mission of global importance at the age of 18 was far more than she ever could have expected.

Steering with one hand, she used the other to remove her cumbersome robe. Beneath it, a sleek evening dress rose and fell like the sand dunes outside.

From the glove compartment, she extracted a necklace and matching earrings. These she applied with impressive dexterity before smiling at herself in the mirror, realizing there would be no trace of her entering the country. No airplane manifest with her name on it. No history at all of a woman crossing the border from the Kingdom of Saudi Arabia into the United Arab Emirates – which, without a husband or male blood relative behind the wheel, was strictly forbidden, truly *haram*.

With a jolt, the radio suddenly sparked back to life. She immediately turned the dial, leaving the Arab singer to wail his plaintive cry to someone else. This was the UAE, after all, and seconds later she found a station playing nothing but European dance tunes.

Cranking up the volume, the Arabian Princess threw back her hair and let her luscious body sway to the pounding pulse of techno as the Lexus raced onward, toward the carnival lights of Dubai.

12

"*Stop this car!*" Rory shouted, pounding on the glass partition, but the twisted little man kept driving, speeding away from the airport. "You don't want to mess with me."

The driver finally looked up, into the rear view mirror, and let loose a hearty laugh. "No, I don't, Mr. Crandall."

Rory turned in surprise to Rani. "I never told him my name."

"You don't remember me, do you?"

"No," said Rory, shaking his head. "And if you're planning to rob us, it's not worth your trouble. I gave away most of my money back at the airport."

Again, the driver laughed, before flipping a switch that lowered the glass between them.

"I don't want your money, only your safety," he said. "I'm Femi, Tunde's brother."

"*Femi,*" Rory said, stunned. "My God, it is you. I haven't seen you in years, since you were a kid. And what happened? Tunde is so, well…huge."

"Yes, yes, I know, and please don't remind me. Tunde stole all the large genes in the family. As you may remember, Rory, we're only half brothers. I'm half and he's one-and-a-half."

Rory laughed, both relieved and astonished at the same time. "Why didn't you say something earlier? And where is Tunde? He was supposed to meet us at the airport."

Now Femi became serious. "I'm sorry about that, but I couldn't say anything back there. It's just too dangerous, especially for Tunde to be out at this time. Even saying his name in public these days can get you in trouble."

"Evidently," said Rory, "and no apologies necessary. You may have saved our lives, or at least saved us from a very uncomfortable interrogation. Oh, and now it's my turn to apologize. I want you to meet Veronica Bay. She's a—"

"Human rights worker and a student," Rani interjected. "And please, call me Rani."

"Nice to meet you, Rani," Femi said. "How do you two know each other?"

"That's what I'm trying to figure out."

"We don't," Rani said. "I mean, we just met. I'm from Denmark, from a little town outside of Copenhagen. I've come to Nigeria to do research for my doctorate. My dissertation is on African women's studies."

Rory studied her face as she spoke, weighing this new information. He liked what he saw but still wasn't certain what he should believe.

"Well, then, welcome to Nigeria," Femi said, steering the sedan onto a bridge that ran over the highway and provided them with a panoramic view of the dirty urban sprawl below. Across Lagos, lights were out in much of the city, leaving the unruly concrete patchwork cast in a dull glow from a smattering of manmade fires. "I'm only sorry you have to see it like this," he added with a sweep of his hand. "Is there someplace I can take you?"

"I'm staying at the university," Rani said, "the Nigeria Law School."

"Not anymore, you're not. The Law School is closed. Yaba College, Igbobi, too, even Lagos State. They're all shut down."

"What? When did this happen?"

"A day or so ago," Femi said, as the sedan reached the other side of the bridge and entered a two-lane road. "By the government after the student protests, the riots began. Several people have been killed already, including a few students. Just like the bad old days of Abacha all over again, eh Rory?"

"Yeah, what the hell happened? Guns at the airport, gangs in the street, riots on campus…"

Femi shook his head. "You know Nigeria. At the end of the day, it's like the great man said: 'Things fall apart.' Ethnic violence, religious wars, exploding pipelines. Step right up, we have it all. And nothing ever changes here. We had a few good years under Obasanjo. He put the military boys back in the barracks, cleared the vultures out of the Parliament Building. But they never went away. Once you get a taste for plunder, that taste sticks to your lips. As you know, Rory, our leaders not only have voracious appetites, they're good at biding their time."

"And now the vultures are circling again," Rory said.

"Right."

"Why now?" Rani asked.

"Because of the Message," Rory said.

"Right again," Femi agreed, while guiding their car off the roadway and onto an exit ramp. "This Message, as the press boys call it, gives the vultures some leverage. It gives them the excuse they need, the perfect reason to turn this country on its head again."

"So you think the Message comes from here?" Rani asked.

"Maybe, I don't know. This operation seems too sophisticated for our boys to pull off."

As if underlining his point, Femi turned onto a dark street flanked on either side by rows of run-down buildings. The smell of burning oil and the absence of light here added to the eeriness of their surroundings.

"Tunde will explain it all later," Femi added, as he slowed the vehicle. "Right now, I need you both to duck down and stay quiet."

"Why? What is it?" Rory asked.

"Too late," said Femi in a tight voice. "We've been spotted, trouble ahead."

From the backseat it was hard to see anything at first. Then, faint as a shadow, an object began taking shape, a solid beam running waist high across the street, blocking their path. On one side of this barrier stood an armed guard in uniform, like back at the airport. A second man could be seen on the opposite side of the road, also holding a weapon.

"Not a word," Femi whispered, before dimming the headlights and cutting the engine. As the car rolled forward, the only sounds that could be heard were the crunch of tires on the pavement and the cries of insects somewhere off in the dark.

"State your business," the guard ordered, as Femi lowered his window.

"Taxi," he said, handing over his papers.

"Past curfew," the guard informed, barely eyeing them.

"Airplane just arrived," said Femi, holding the other man's stare.

The guard didn't seem to like this answer and tossed the papers at Femi before pointing his gun toward the backseat. "Who are they?"

"Passengers."

"Tell them to get out of the car."

Femi turned around. "You better give him some *dash*."

"You're joking," Rory said, but Femi didn't look playful. So Rory dug into his jacket for his wallet. "Will a twenty do?"

"Not for both of you."

"That's all I have left. Rani?"

The girl shook her head. "Only credit cards, really."

"How about my watch?" Rory asked Femi.

"That should work, but you better hurry."

"Now I'm joking. Are you serious?"

Outside, the man with the gun began tapping the barrel against the car.

"Very."

"Damn," Rory said, unclasping the timepiece from his wrist.

"Quickly," Femi urged, reaching back as the tapping grew louder.

So Rory relinquished his watch, which Femi handed over to the gunman, who placed it to his ear. Smiling, he signaled to his partner to raise the bar and let them pass.

"I can't believe it," Rory said, shaking his head in disgust as they left the roadblock behind. "That was an expensive watch."

"Believe it," Femi replied, shifting gears and re-engaging the high beams. "I'm sorry, but as you can see, it has started all over again."

"But who were they?" Rory wanted to know. "Police? Secret Security?"

"Worse," Femi said. "Army."

"Why is that *worse*?" Rani asked.

"Better weapons."

"And they're not afraid to use them," Rory said, scratching at his empty wrist. "Remember Dele Udoh?"

"Who?" Rani asked.

"Our murdered track star," Femi said, as they passed by a thatch of tilting palm trees before turning onto a narrow side street, again bathed in black. "Look him up. Dele was one of our most promising athletes, a four hundred-meters man training for the Olympic Games. He was based in the States at the time, but came home to Nigeria to represent us at an international track and field event. He was on his way to the National Stadium in Surulere, not far from here, when he and some teammates were stopped at a roadblock, like the one we just passed."

Rani leaned forward in her seat. "What happened?"

"Dele apparently forgot the way of his country," Femi said. "Or maybe he just didn't give a damn anymore, figured his celebrity status would protect him."

"And that was that," Rory said.

"That was *what*?"

"When the men at the roadblock stopped him," Femi explained to Rani, "they either didn't recognize the boy or didn't care. Either way, they asked him for some *dash* – what we call a bribe here in Nigeria – and he refused to pay. Dele said he wouldn't give away a single *naira* to a bunch of hoodlums, so the story goes. So they killed him."

"No."

"Shot him right the face," Rory said. "He never had a chance."

By now the sedan had left the hard pavement and was bumping along a rough gravel road, making conversation difficult. As they drove on in silence, the sky became so dark there was no point looking outside either.

All of a sudden, Femi slowed the car, nearly to a stop.

"Not again," Rory said.

"What?" Rani tensed. "Another roadblock?"

"Yes, but don't worry," Femi said, lowing his window and then cutting the engine. "This boy is one of ours."

The barrier here, Rory noticed, was made of wood instead of steel. The man in front of it wore a T-shirt and jeans rather than a uniform. And his weapon of choice was not a rifle but a flashlight, which he aimed into the backseat of the sedan.

"Friends," Femi told him.

"Good," the other said. "We need all the friends we can get."

Dousing the torch, he opened the wooden gate. This time, Femi kept the engine off, and the other man used his hands to push them through.

"So, how do you like our neighborhood watch program?" Femi asked.

"Very impressive," Rory replied. "Fighting AK-47's with penlights. I like your odds."

Femi didn't comment. He strained to turn the vehicle now that the power steering had been disengaged.

The car left the gravel and rolled forward, through soft grass, until Femi applied the brakes, bringing them to a full stop.

"Quiet," he whispered. "And try to stay as close to me as possible."

"Why?" Rani asked.

"Because it's very dark here."

"And there might be snakes," Rory said.

"*Snakes?*"

"You have nothing to worry about," Femi reassured her, seeing how Rory was playing. "They only bite when you step on them."

"*What?*"

"Oh, and one more thing," Femi said, smiling at the girl before opening his door.

"There's *more?*"

"Welcome to Nigeria!"

13

Across a yard they went, through tall grass that smelled like soap and into a ravine that came out behind a row of flat houses. Femi stopped before one of these dwellings, which looked no different than any of the others, cupped his hands, and made a soft, birdlike sound.

"*Coo.*" Nothing happened.

"Coo-*coo.*" A few seconds passed and then a glass door slid open. From behind it a figure emerged faintly in the dark, as they were ushered into a room even blacker than the night. Rory heard whispers, sensed movement, and then felt soft hands pat down his arms, his legs, his stomach, and back. He reached out but grasped only air. He opened his mouth to ask what was happening when someone else spoke first.

"They're okay. Here, close the door. Light a candle."

A flame flickered and Rory caught a flash, like a snapshot, of people all around him. A black man with a white beard and thick glasses stood to one side, next to Rani. A black woman, tall and fleshy, stood to the other, beside Femi. And a much younger woman, soft and radiant, stood mere inches from Rory. The candle caught and he took in this lovely creature, who, only moments before, had been feeling him up, presumably for weapons, but what difference did that make? She saw him watching her and smiled before averting her eyes. Rory leaned in to say hello, only to find he was staring into the chest of the largest man he had ever met.

"Tunde!"

"Rory! Back from the jungles of the West," the giant said, before smothering his friend in a big bear hug. "So, you remember Smydge, my *daughter*."

"Ah, of course, your daughter," Rory stammered, before nodding more politely this time to the young woman. "My apologies, Smydge. It's been several years since I saw you last and you have, well...changed."

"And I see you haven't," Tunde said, laughing, as he looked from Rory to Rani. "So, who is your little friend?"

"Oh, yes, this is Veronica Bay," Rory said. "She's a—"

"Human rights activist, working on my PhD," Rani said, stepping forward and offering Tunde her hand. "And you can call me Rani."

Tunde gave Rory a sly smile.

"No, no, we just met."

"Right," Tunde said, still smiling. "Well, it's nice to meet you, Rani. You've already met my brother, Femi. This fine gentleman next to him, with the billy goat beard, we call him the Doctor. He's the one I was telling you about, Rory. And this is my wife Ola, who handles everything in the house."

"And let's keep it that way," she said, waiting for her husband to release Rani's hand.

Ola, like her daughter Smydge, wore a colorful gown, or *kaba*, with a matching head cover, or *gele*. The men were dressed in Western gear, jeans and loose-fitting shirts.

"Now," Tunde was saying, as he turned to Rory, sounding much like the armed sentry back at the first roadblock. "Do you have a gift for me?"

Rory pretended to look nervous while reaching into his jacket. "Will a twenty do?"

"I think not, boy," the big man said in mock seriousness. "To the gallows with this one!"

"Wait," Rory said, digging into his duffle bag and producing a bottle of Scotch, purchased at duty free in London before departing. He handed the whisky over to Tunde while announcing: "Let the games begin!"

The "games" were a tradition borne out of Rory's first visit to Nigeria over a decade earlier as an exchange student. Normally a men's-only affair, Rory suggested Rani stay with them rather than join the two women, who had disappeared into the kitchen. He still had his suspicions and wanted to keep her close. Tunde put up initial objections, complaining how Americans like Rory, with all their talk of women's rights and liberation, were ruining things for the African man. He then laughed before guiding them, Rani included, into the adjoining room, where they took up seats around a simple table in a space that contained a worn couch, some bookshelves, and little else. There was no TV or stereo, and the walls were bare, save for a sizeable map of Nigeria and an equally large, cheaply framed painting of Jesus Christ.

"Not exactly the Ritz," said Tunde, spotting Rani's gaze. "You'd never catch our fat cat Rory slumming it in a place like this, but it does have all the qualities of a good safe house."

"Who are you hiding from?"

"Excellent question," Tunde said, and he was about to answer Rani, when Ola and Smydge reappeared, carrying with them a pitcher of water and a tray of glasses. Tunde stopped talking long enough to splash whisky into each of their tumblers, before raising his own. "Here's to your health."

"And to your wealth," Rory said, clinking glasses first with his old friend and then with the others. They all took generous sips, straight up, and Rani couldn't help coughing when the firewater hit her stomach.

"I see our friend here has much to learn," Tunde said with a big grin, adding a little water to Rani's glass to lessen the sting. "So, tell me, Rory, who is this young woman? The last time you came to Africa, *you* were the student. Are you the teacher now?"

"Hardly," he said. "Rani tells me she's a scholar, an expert in women's studies and traditional cultures."

"Not an expert yet," she corrected. "But I hope to be one day. I've come here to do work on my dissertation, on African women and the practice of FGM."

"Female genital mutilation," Ola explained to her daughter, the two Nigerian women lingering to listen in on this conversation.

"Then you must know Effioanwan," Femi said.

"Who?" Rani asked, puzzled.

The others looked up from their drinks. Rory eyed Rani, his suspicions growing.

"Chienjini," Femi said helpfully. "She was one of Nigeria's top football players and a crusader for women's rights in Africa. You *must* have heard of her."

The room fell silent, the others waiting for Rani's response. Ola and Smydge exchanged glances, while Tunde shot Rory a tense look before starting from his seat.

"Anyone studying in this field," Femi continued, "would have to know that—"

"Effi scored seventy-six goals in ninety-four international matches for the Super Falcons," Rani said at last, "as they captured seven African championships in the nineties, losing only four matches on the continent, before turning her celebrity into a cause for good, becoming a UN Ambassador for women's health and safety in Africa and making the short list for the 2007 Nobel Peace prize. I'm sorry," Rani added, turning to Femi, "I didn't understand your accent."

"Impressive," Tunde said, lowering his giant frame back into his seat. "And no need to apologize. None of us can understand him most of the time either."

He gave Rani a wink, before topping off each of their glasses. "Well, Rory, we could sit here all night grilling this poor girl, but I think you've come for a different reason." Tunde then dismissed his wife and daughter, who left the room marveling at how the foreign woman had showed up all the men.

"Yes," Rory said, watching them go, still not sure what to think of Rani, although her bona fides did seem to check out. He turned back to Tunde. "Fun times at the airport tonight."

"These are dark days for Nigeria," his friend replied. "The evildoers have been lurking like big cats in the bush, waiting to strike, and now this Message gives them the perfect opportunity to stir up trouble again."

"I understand that," Rory said, "but why are *you* such a marked man?"

"Because he's a rebel, that's why."

The others turned their heads at the sound of this new voice, the first words spoken since they entered the room by the one introduced as the Doctor.

"He chooses, as always, to antagonize the system from without."

"Rather than cuddling up with the criminals from within," Tunde said, bitterly.

"Gentlemen," Femi interjected, from his seat between the other two, and Rory wondered if he had chosen this spot purposefully.

But the Doctor wasn't finished. "Once I am *within*, as you say, I plan to reform the system, to bring about changes."

"If you're not swallowed up by it first," said Tunde. "The good Doctor is leaving his practice tomorrow so he can take a position in the government."

"It's time someone took a stand," the other said, his voice rising. "I am sick of being enslaved in my own country. We should be lions, kings of the jungle. Instead, we are helpless insects, constantly mashed under the feet of oppression. We're known the world over as villains and scam artists. We possess countless wealth, more petrol than we know what to do with. Yet at the end of the day nothing here ever works. Last week, I was operating on a patient when the electricity went out. Again. The poor sod nearly bled to death on my table while I hunted around the office like a blind man in the dark for sutures to clamp him up. I have few supplies, less medicine, not a single workable computer to keep track of billings," he lamented, shaking his head. "Not that any of that really matters, since none my patients have any money to pay me."

"I agree, something must be done," Tunde said, putting down his glass. "I just want you to be careful, my friend. For when you get in bed at night with your master, don't be surprised if he treats you like a whore in the morning."

Rory didn't like the way this conversation was going and decided to change the subject.

"So," he said, turning to the Doctor, "Tunde tells me you have a theory about who's behind these so-called Sporting Murders?"

The other scowled.

"One of the Delta groups in the south?" Rory tried. "The Ogoni, maybe? Or the Itsekiri? The Ijaw Youth? MEND? Or possibly Boko Haram in the north?"

"No chance," Tunde said. "None of those boys could pull off a stunt like this."

The Doctor remained silent.

"Then one of the oil companies?" Rory suggested.

"Doesn't add up," Femi said. "Those corrupt bastards have as much to lose as anyone if this conflict ever becomes resolved. Plus, the murdered basketball player, Mo Mo, he endorsed a line of Shell products, so why would they want him dead?"

"What about your government?" Rory tried, thinking how this might spur the Doctor to join the debate, but the man kept his mouth shut.

"He's not talking," Tunde said.

"He does this sometimes," Femi added.

"Proud bastard shuts up like a clam," Tunde scoffed, returning to his whisky.

But Rory wasn't through trying. His main reason for coming down here was to learn what this man knew.

"You must have seen some terrible things," Rory said, still directing his questions at the Doctor, who sat tight-lipped in his chair. "Truly awful things, I would imagine."

Femi started to interject, but Tunde cut him off with a raised finger. At last the Doctor spoke. "I wouldn't say that."

"I just figured, you being a physician and all."

"Nothing out of the ordinary," said the Doctor, taking a small sip from his glass.

"I bet you saw some bloody battles," Rory continued, as the others watched on.

"No, I never was a soldier," the Doctor said, leaning back in his chair.

"But you have been on the front lines."

"No, no…well, not exactly."

"During a coup d'état, perhaps?"

"No, not a coup," the Doctor said slowly, seemingly torn over whether to say more.

"A protest, then? A demonstration?"

"Yes, a demonstration," he agreed at last.

"At the Presidential Palace?"

"No, that's not right." He stared past Rory, as if watching it play out all over again. "It was the Mayor's house. We were marching, waving signs, singing songs. It was a peaceful demonstration, only…"

He hesitated, and Rory picked up on his thought. "Others didn't see it that way."

"No, they did not," the Doctor continued in a soft voice. "They tried to stop us, you know, with a show of force. They had batons and rifles, even a few tanks. We kept marching, though. Yes, we kept marching right down the center of Chamberlain Street, past all those bloody bastards, until…"

Again, he paused, and again Rory supplied the words, lowering his voice to the level of the Doctor's. "They chased after you."

"Yes, they did. They beat us with sticks – men, women, even the children."

Next to the Doctor, Femi watched in fascination, while Tunde carefully put down his drink. Rani, too, stared on, caught up in this curious interaction.

"Everyone was getting beaten," Rory said, prodding the Doctor along.

"Yes, but not me. I was fast then. I kept moving. I kept…well, I kept—"

"—avoiding them, staying out of their way," Rory said, finishing the sentence.

"Yes, that's right, until they started shooting, everyone falling in all directions."

"But not you," Rory said in a voice that sounded much like the Doctor's, as if he was somehow sharing the other's experience.

Femi turned and whispered. "What is he doing?"

Rani answered. "I think he calls it *empathy*."

"*Shh*," Tunde admonished, while Rory carried on, filling in pieces as he went.

"So you were running," he said, as if he too had been there, "running quickly and—"

"—yes, running. Many of us were still running, running away from them—"

"—only one of them was fast too," Rory said. "Faster than the rest—"

"—yes, he was. He caught me from behind and struck me—"

"—with his rifle butt. He knocked you to the ground—"

"—yes, he did. Stood over me, pointing his rifle—"

"—right at you. Took aim, about to kill you—"

"—yes, he was, only, he never fired—"

"—no, he struck you instead—"

"—yes, with the butt—"

"—of his rifle—"

"—in the—"

"Head."

They both said the word together, as the others stared on mesmerized.

"Right here," Rory said, placing a hand on his skull, just behind his ear. The Doctor was stroking his own head in exactly the same spot. Tears welled in his eyes as he relived the horrible moment.

"They killed them all that day, every one of them dead," the Doctor said, practically in a whisper. "But he spared my life, he did. I wouldn't be here now if not for that man."

"Why did he do that?" Rory asked, also in a whisper.

"I don't know."

"Because he knew you from the past?"

"I don't know."

"Because he owed you something?"

"I don't know," the Doctor repeated.

"Because he wanted a witness," Rory said more firmly.

"I don't *know*," the Doctor replied, almost pleading now.

Rory kept on the offensive. "So, who was he?"

"I don't know." The Doctor's lips trembled.

"Yes, you do," Rory said.

"I can't say."

"Yes, you *can*," Rory insisted. "Who was he?"

But the Doctor held back, fighting to keep a long-buried secret.

"*Who?*"

Before finally letting it go. "It was Bola."

"Bola!" Tunde sputtered, shooting from his chair. "Not that kaffir bastard!"

The interruption jarred the rest of them.

"Who is Bola?" Rani asked.

"A right bastard," Tunde spat. "That's who."

"General Bola," Femi explained, "was part of Babangida's inner circle, a real cold-blooded killer. He put many innocent people to death and jailed even more on false charges, some of whom remain in prison today. Bola eventually had a falling out with Babangida and the other generals running the country then. He went underground and stayed there, reemerging a few years ago as a mercenary in the South-South. He would have been a corporal back then."

"Corporal Bastard," Tunde said.

"And this man, Bola," Rory asked, still addressing the Doctor, "he's the one? He's behind these Sporting Murders? Is that it?"

But the Doctor was through answering questions. He just sat there, staring straight ahead at nothing, one hand rubbing mechanically at the scar on the back of his skull – the scar Rory had noticed when they first met – while he repeated the same words over and over again.

"It was Bola…it was Bola…it was Bola…"

14

Leila, the Arabian Princess, stared into the eyes of a man-eating tiger shark.

At least that was what the plaque on the world's largest acrylic viewing panel told her it was, both in Arabic and English. She was only relieved to have this dense, two-story sheet of plastic separating her from the shark and the other 33,000 exotic marine animals the plaque informed her were housed within the Aquarium and Underwater Zoo at the Mall of Dubai.

"Don't worry, this plastic is so thick it can withstand ten million liters of pressure," she heard someone say and spotted a perky customer service rep educating a group of elderly tourists, who nodded and gawked appreciatively. "A few years ago, a leak in the aquarium did force us to evacuate a portion of the mall, but everyone is where he or she ought to be today."

The tourists laughed at the joke, while further on a grade school teacher struggled to keep a bunch of rowdy students under control. "Did you know," he said, hoping to grab their attention, "this aquarium holds over four hundred sharks and stingrays?" They did not, nor did they seem to care, the little boys more interested in being sharks themselves, opening and closing their arms like giant sets of jaws as they chased after squealing little girls.

"Okay, this way," the teacher said, giving up on the titanic fish tank. "Who wants to go skiing?"

"*Mumtaz!*" the schoolkids shouted, following after their teacher and leaving Leila behind, smiling to herself. The thought of Arab children falling over each other down a slope of fake snow – *inside a mall* – brought her a peculiar sense of joy.

Growing up in the Middle East, she had heard all about the extravagances of Dubai, which boasted the world's tallest skyscraper, costliest hotel, a fountain with over 6,000 lights, and the largest mall on the planet, where she was located now. This lavish one-upmanship, she remembered her father telling her, started in the 1960s, when word began to spread of a tax-free oasis on the Arabian Peninsula. Big-money investors soon came clamoring, with curious tourists hot on their heels. Everyone wanted to indulge in the unabated trade, whether in precious stone, Persian carpets, Indian gold, or most any vice the human libido could imagine. She also remembered her father saying how Sheikh Rashid had built the first golf course with real grass in the Gulf as part of a successful bid to promote Dubai internationally and lure even more money here. By the time she was born, the Dubai Desert Classic had become a regular stop on the PGA tour, prompting the government to host a lucrative desert rally, one of the largest air shows known to man, and, of course, a professional women's tennis tournament, where most of the world's top-rated players were at this very moment knocking practice balls in preparation for the start of tomorrow's first round.

Turning away from the aquarium, leaving colorful creatures gaping on both sides of the viewing panel, the Arabian Princess reentered the rush of traffic circulating through the mall's 1,200 stores. She passed by a group of girls roughly her own age wearing colorful *abayas* so form-fitting they would have made her grandmother blush, while other shoppers sported miniskirts and tank tops rarely seen in the rest of the Arab world. While she was no prude and even frowned on the practice of bundling up women in public like shameful cocoons, she couldn't help wondering what cost the faithful had sacrificed by cashing in on the ancient ways to pray at the altar of a consumer god clearly run amok.

Then, again, she thought, as she entered a brightly-lit shop and started up the first of its many well-stocked aisles, she had to hand it to her fellow Arabs. They finally got it right when they adopted one of the greatest gifts the West had to offer: the modern convenience store. What would have taken her half a day in the old *souk*, she now could mostly accomplish in a single stop.

"Cash or credit?" the foreign-looking clerk asked, as the Arabian Princess reached the front of the checkout line and handed over her shopping basket.

"Cash."

She watched the cashier ring up her items: a bottle of shampoo, a bar of deodorant, a tube of sun tan lotion, and three green sports drinks – all props – plus those purchases necessary to accomplish the job she had been sent here to do, including a roll of athletic tape, a pair of nylon gloves, a sturdy paint brush, and a cartridge of ladies razor blades.

"Did you find everything you need?"

"Yes, thank you," she said, accepting her change and a plastic bag full of her new acquisitions. She started to leave the store, only to turn back with a smile.

"I do have one question for you," the Arabian Princess said to the cashier.

"Yes, my dear, what is it?"

"Where can I buy a tennis racket?"

15

The journey began innocuously enough, Tunde and Femi driving Rory and Rani from Lagos southward to Port Harcourt. With Nigeria Law School still closed and riots breaking out all over the city, Rani said she had nowhere to go and asked if she could join them. Rory voiced reservations at first, given the trouble he expected to encounter searching for General Bola. But she claimed to speak a couple tribal languages that might be beneficial, said she could use the experience for her research, plus the way she filled out her safari gear didn't hurt her cause.

"Thanks for including me," Rani said, while settling into the backseat of the sedan for the lengthy car trip. "Why don't we just fly?"

The others laughed.

"Remember everyone praying on your plane?" Tunde asked from behind the wheel.

"Yeah, why were they doing that? Were they afraid to fly?"

"No," Tunde told her. "They were so damn happy *not* to be taking a domestic flight!"

"He's right," Femi said, from behind his half-brother, in the seat next to Rani. "With these riots, no one is getting in or out of that airport today, but even if you could, you wouldn't want to use an internal airline. A few years ago, the dictator Abacha's own son died in a plane crash between Lagos and Abuja, but most of us never suspected foul play."

"Only Nigerian engineering," said Rory, joining the conversation from the passenger seat up front, after pocketing his iPhone and unfolding a map of southern Nigeria on his lap. "That was an official at the American Consulate. He told me we were not to meet with General Bola or anyone else from the Wajé tribe. It has been declared *persona non grata* by the State Department. Nor should we go to Warri, he said. And, should we be stupid enough to go Warri, never, under any circumstance, should we go there after dark."

"Where *are* we going?" Rani asked.

"To Warri," said Tunde, pointing at the map, "near the diseased heart of the Niger Delta."

"To meet General Bola," Femi added.

"And the rest of the Wajé tribe," Rory said.

Rani shook her head. "Are you all crazy?"

"Probably," Rory laughed, "but don't worry."

"Why not?"

"I promise to have you back before dark."

On the outskirts of Port Harcourt, Tunde and Femi bid them farewell, the big man telling Rory it was just too dangerous for him to go any further. "My friend," he added, as he stepped out of the car to say good-bye, "may less time pass before we meet again."

"Deal," Rory replied, extending his hand, but Tunde gathered him up in another bear hug. He then handed Rory a knee-high Ghana bag, stuffed to the brim and tied off with plastic strands. The blue-and-white-checkered nylon sack, Rory recalled, was the type seen all over western Africa and extremely popular among those who couldn't afford a Samsonite. Rory thanked Tunde and Femi both before watching them climb back into the sedan and pull away, leaving him and Rani on an empty road outside a clean, if spartan, guesthouse.

"So, what do we do now?" she asked.

"I don't know," he responded with a sly smile, "unless you can think of a good way to kill an hour before dinner."

"I can," she answered, smiling back.

"Really?"

"Yeah, I'm going to take a nap."

"Oh," Rory said, disappointed.

Rani laughed. "And don't try any of your mind games, either. They won't work on me."

"You're no fun," Rory said, hoisting the Ghana bag in one hand and his personal luggage in the other.

"Hey, what's in that sack?"

"I'm not going to tell you."

"Come on," she said, playfully. "Why not?"

"Because, it's none of your business."

"Now who's not being any fun?"

"Okay, if you must know," Rory started.

"I must," Rani said, still smiling.

"It's full of cash."

"*Cash!*" she nearly shouted, her smile falling. "You can't be serious."

"I am."

"You're taking a sack full of cash into the jungle?"

Now it was Rory's turn to grin.

"No," he said, starting for the guesthouse. "*We're* taking a sack full of cash into the jungle."

The next morning, after a breakfast of fresh mangos and fried bread, Rani leaned against a fencepost near the jungle trailhead taking pictures of long-tailed lizards with her digital camera, while Rory negotiated the price of car hire with several hard-looking men. These characters were nothing compared to the trio of hoodlums who suddenly materialized like black ghosts from a gap in the trees. The leader of this gang, a dark scarecrow named Echs, like the 24th letter in the alphabet, introduced himself as a "guide" from the Wajé tribe. His sidekicks – a scrappy young woman in a colorful headscarf, who called herself Prissy and looked anything but, and a sawed-off bruiser named Yakuba, who the others called Yak – shook hands without smiling.

Formalities over, the three of them, plus Rory and Rani, piled into a beat-up Buick LeSabre, owned by a thin-headed man named Tafawa, who hailed from a neighboring tribe. His car was a tank, chosen by Rory for its bulk rather than any noticeable amenity. Entering the mangrove swamp, they started up a mangled road bordered on either side by lush vegetation and exotic-looking trees.

"That's black afara…and that's Nigerian walnut… and that's opepe…and that's camwood…" Prissy shouted over the rumble of the Buick. She sat to one side of Rani, who was wedged in the back seat, with Yakuba on the other flank.

While Yak never spoke, Prissy kept up a constant dia-tribe, alternating between offering amplified bits of mar-ginally useful information – "There goes a side striped jackal, very dangerous" – to literally screaming at their driver – "Keep straight, kaffir!" – every time their tires struck a pothole or large tree root on the unpaved road, which was often. Up front, Rory carried on a conversa-tion with the scarecrow Echs, despite these many dis-tractions, which included Tafawa, their driver, cursing at Prissy under his breath in a tribal language none of the rest of them could understand. At one point, the jungle receded and the road flattened out. The dirt became in-creasingly muddy, making it even more difficult to ma-neuver, although Tafawa kept the car moving at a steady clip. As they rounded a corner, passing by a large, rusty spigot – "That's the first oil pump in Nigeria" – Prissy's tone suddenly became shrill.

"Kaffir, *watch out!*"

Too late.

There, in the middle of the road, as big as truck, stood a forest buffalo enjoying a drink of water. Tafawa jerked the wheel to avoid the animal, and their tires hit a slick patch. The Buick spun sideways, out of control and heading straight for the buffalo, which refused to budge. At the last second, Tafawa yanked the wheel back in the opposite direction, and the LeSabre shot forward, narrowly missing the beast, which lifted a goateed chin to watch the peculiar metal creature flying by. They were now headed at breakneck speed toward a phalanx of tree trunks – black afara or Nigerian walnut, it was hard to tell – when their tires sunk down into something soft, and they came to a jarring stop. Rani was thrown forward from the back seat and might have flown through the windshield if not for Yak's powerful arm holding her back.

"Thanks," she managed, but he didn't hear, for Prissy was screaming louder than ever.

"*Keep driving you kaffir bastard!*" Then, turning to Rani, she said more kindly, "Don't you fret," in what was to become a signature refrain.

Behind the wheel, Tafawa cursed again in his tribal tongue. He then pressed down on the gas, but the tires just spun, the Buick sinking deeper in the mud.

"It's no use," said Rory, watching the buffalo lumber off on knobby knees, before climbing out of the car and doing his best to avoid the muck underfoot. Rani, shaken but unharmed, joined him by the side of the road in the only slice of shade to be found. They both donned dark glasses to protect their eyes from the midday glare and then watched in wonder at the level of teamwork displayed by the three Wajé tribesmen.

As Echs barked out orders, Yak and Prissy disappeared into the bush, reemerging a few minutes later with sizeable slats of wood under each arm. From Prissy, Echs took a short log and wedged it under one of the Buick's back tires to act as a fulcrum. He then accepted a heavy stick from Yakuba and guided it over the first piece of wood and under the tire, creating a lever. The remaining lumber he slid ahead of the front tires to serve as ramps.

All the while, their driver, Tafawa, stood off to one side, muttering under his breath and mopping his thin head with a rag. Only when Prissy started for the driver's seat did he spring into action, practically knocking her down.

"That's getting us nowhere," Rory said, stepping in between them.

A nasty exchange followed, before Prissy reluctantly joined her fellow tribesmen at the back of the Buick. Tafawa, with a triumphant sneer, slid in behind the wheel. On Echs' command, he revved the engine, while Echs yanked down on the lever, and Yak and Prissy pushed with all their might. The tires spun, kicking out fat clumps of mud, like black oatmeal, yet failed to climb up the ramps.

"We need more force," Echs said, so Rory slotted in beside Prissy, and they gave it another try. Still nothing. Now Rani joined the effort, surprising Rory, who until that point had thought of her only as an attractive passenger. This time the tires rolled several inches, the lever bowing madly, only to fall back into place again.

"What do we do now?" Rani asked.

"Fry in the sun," Rory said, wiping sweat off his forehead.

"Don't you fret," said Prissy, shielding her eyes with an arm.

"We still need more manpower," Echs said.

"One of us could walk back to town," Rory suggested.

"It's over twenty miles," Prissy said.

"What do you know, cow?" Tafawa said from inside the car.

"Take that back, kaffir," she hissed, rounding the Buick with clenched fists. This time Rory was in no position to intervene, when a new voice suddenly rang out.

"Quiet!"

It was Yakuba. Everyone stopped talking, startled to hear the man speak for the first time in nearly an hour. His hand was raised, one finger pointing skyward, in the "just wait" position. They all listened and then they heard it: a low rumble, growing louder. It sounded like a small engine, maybe two. A moment later, a pair of motorcycles rounded the corner, each carrying a young driver and a second boy as a passenger, all of them shirtless, with no shoes.

"Give us a hand," Echs called out, as the bikes rolled to a stop, several feet away.

The four boys eyed the strangers, distrustful gazes falling especially long on Rory and Rani, before noticing the car stuck in the mud.

"Two on each side," Echs said. Whether it was his expression or the tone of his voice – or perhaps a reputation in these parts that Rory was beginning to suspect – the boys decided it would be wise to help out.

So, climbing off the motorcycles, they found space among the others. All of them dug in and then waited for Echs.

"One-two-three-*go!*" he shouted, grabbing hold of the lever and ripping it downward. Tafawa stomped on the gas, the rest of them pushed, and the Buick sputtered in protest, like an old man wheezing, while the tires made a run up the ramps.

"Harder!" Echs roared into the blazing sun.

Rory felt his arms burning under the strain, as he shoved the car slowly forward with the others and watched the veins in Yak's neck swell like a river. He heard a tremendous cracking sound, like a ball slapping against a wooden bat, and felt something *whizz* past his face. He nearly toppled over as the object raced by, missing him by inches. When Rory regained his balance, he heard a familiar phrase.

"Don't you fret," Prissy was saying, crouched on her haunches in the mud.

Rory spotted Rani lying on her back and rushed over. "What happened?"

"She's fine," Prissy said, as Rani struggled to sit up, a red welt already forming on her forehead, near her right temple, but surprisingly no blood.

"She's lucky," Echs said, picking up Rani's backpack, while Rory helped the girl to her feet. "That piece of wood could have poked out an eye."

Rani just stood there dazed, not saying a word.

"Are you okay?" Rory asked, placing an arm around the girl's back, as the others looked on with concern.

"Yeah," Rani said at last, wincing from the pain. "I'm okay, but I don't feel very lucky."

For Rani, the next part of the journey was a blur, everything happening at once, fast and fuzzy. Tafawa's car was freed from the mud and leaving the scene. Arguments broke out. Voices were raised. A deal was struck. She then found herself squeezed onto the very back of one of the motorcycles, holding onto Rory, as their shirtless young driver sped through the jungle, chasing after the other bike, upon which Prissy sat tucked behind a second boy. Echs and Yakuba were soon left far behind.

"Watch out!" Rory shouted, his voice tossed into the wind and lost in a *whir* of the bike's noisy engine. The motorcycle suddenly plunged into a ravine, water spraying in all directions. It then vaulted up over a hill, forcing them to duck down beneath a low-hanging tree limb, narrowly avoiding decapitation, as they raced onward, the world zipping by in a million shades of yellow and green.

Rory had worried at first about putting Rani on a motorcycle, after the thump she sustained. *But what else can we do?* The jungle wasn't safe for either of them to be traipsing around in on foot. Plus, they still had one guide, Prissy, with them on the adjoining bike, and the driver of their own motorcycle seemed quite skilled, leaning into curves, anticipating dips in the road, steering around dangerous mud slicks.

With Rani grasping his waist, Rory even started to enjoy the wild ride through the mangrove swamp. His adrenaline was spiking, and a cool draft seized his face like a glove. At one especially hairy moment, as they flew inches off the ground, an uncontrollable laughter shook his entire body, making him want to shout: *This is freaking fun!*

Then, just like that, they rounded a corner and nearly crashed into Prissy, who was standing by herself in the middle of the trail, cursing. "That kaffir bastard rode off without me," she said, as they wheeled around to greet her. "He said he wanted all his money now. I told him to bugger off, and he did."

"So what do we do now?" Rory asked.

"I don't know," Prissy said, thinking. "I suppose we should leave Rani on the bike with this boy. You and I can walk. It's better to have two of us together out here, and it's only a few miles to the river. Don't you fret."

"No, you listen," Rory said. "I'm not about to send Rani off with some kidnapper to get sold into white slavery."

"Thanks," she said, climbing off the bike and gingerly feeling the wound on her forehead.

"What then," Prissy asked, "she and I walk while you ride? Gang rape is so much nicer than slavery. Not that you would ever know either."

Rory looked at Prissy. Her expression was deadly serious under her flowery head scarf, and he wondered if she might have suffered from one or both.

"Okay, point taken," he said at last. "Well, we can't just stand here. How about you and Rani take the bike to go look for help, and the boy and I will stay here."

"The bike stays with me," their driver said, giving Rory a cold stare before turning to Prissy. "I take you. We go for help. First, you pay."

"You heard the man," Prissy said. "He keeps the bike, I go with him, but first you pay. Otherwise, he's going to leave us all here."

Rory wasn't thrilled by this arrangement, but couldn't think of a better way to proceed. So, he untied the plastic strings on the Ghana bag, reached inside, and pulled out a couple bricks of colorful bills.

"Two now and two more when you return with help," he said, handing the driver a down payment. Prissy smiled and climbed onto the back of the bike.

"Don't you fret," she said, before disappearing around a corner, leaving Rory and Rani alone in the middle of the jungle.

16

"**F**antastic," Rani said, staring up at the crazy network of roots and vines and sinewy tree trunks that seemed to stretch on forever overhead. "What do we do now?"

"We walk," Rory said, picking up the Ghana bag and his leather duffle.

"And what if we run into someone?"

"What? Here in the jungle?"

"Yes, here in the jungle."

"Well, if that happens," Rory said, starting off in the direction the motorcycle had gone, "then I will protect you."

"Just fantastic."

Rani threw her backpack over her shoulder and stomped up the trail after him.

"What's wrong?"

"What's *wrong*?" she fired back. "What's right? First, you nearly get us killed at the airport, pretending to be some famous doctor. Then I get hit in the leg with a rock. Then I almost lose an eye. And now, the two of us are walking, alone, in the middle of an African jungle, carrying a ridiculously large bag of full of cash, trying to find some old general, because you believe you've got this rare ability to read other people's minds, or get inside their shoes, or whatever it is you think you do."

Rani caught up to Rory and passed him on the trail.

"What did you want me to do?" he asked, falling in behind her.

"I don't know. You've done enough already. Can we not talk anymore?"

"Good idea," Rory said, listening briefly to the symphony of unfamiliar sounds filling the surrounding air. "We probably should keep quiet. But first, you must admit one thing."

Rani didn't answer.

"This has been pretty exciting."

She kept walking, swinging her arms defiantly as she went. Rory kept pace, but couldn't keep quiet.

"Without *naira*, hard cash, how do you think we paid for those rooms last night?"

"I told you, I'm not talking to you anymore."

"And the car this morning? With a Visa card? In this place?"

Now Rani stopped.

"What is it?" Rory asked.

"You *paid* that car driver?"

"Of course I did. We made a deal."

Rani shook her head in disbelief and started walking again.

"Half now, half when he picks us up."

"*Picks us up?*" she wailed. "We'll never see that guy again. My God, now I'm really not talking to you."

On they walked in silence for several minutes, until they eventually left the jungle and entered a wide clearing. Here, a field of tall grass spanned out in all directions. The sky was nearly colorless, and the sun pounded down from high overhead. Rory watched Rani put on her sunglasses. She looked amazing, even when she was angry with him. He considered breaking her moratorium on conversation to tell her, when she suddenly turned and spoke to him.

"You know, it's not a superpower."

"What?"

"That thing you do, getting inside other people's heads. It's not like you can fly or become invisible or something."

"It's called *empathy*."

"No, it's not. Empathy involves *compassion*," she said, starting up the trail again, parting the tall grass with her hands, as Rory followed close behind. "What you do, it's just being observant. Like with the Doctor back in Lagos."

"Right, I felt his pain. That *is* compassion."

"No," Rani said, "that's deduction. You spotted a scar on the back of his head and made some assumptions. They turned out to be correct, I'll give you that. You were clever, but not empathetic. In the end, you tricked him, that's what you did. You forced him into revealing a secret against his will. A secret he had been keeping for some time, I bet, probably because he felt revealing it would put him or those he loves in danger. Just like you put me and Femi in danger back at the airport with your little stunt."

Rory thought a moment. "But I was able to get information from the Doctor, important information about General Bola which may end up saving lives, if he turns out to be behind the Sporting Murders. So, if that's not compassion, then—"

"It's not," Rani interrupted. "Not when you have ulterior motives, like I know you do."

"We all have to make a living."

"True, but there are many ways to make a living," she said, still walking. "Have you ever thought about fighting for a cause?"

"Sure, I do, all the time."

"Really?"

"Why else do you think I opened my own office? Started representing—"

"Rich clients," she finished his sentence. "So you can make a lot of money, that's what I think. So you can buy a lot of stuff and live in a nice house and travel all over the world on someone else's expense account and—"

"You know what?" Rory said, interrupting her now.

"No. What?"

"You're a very smart woman."

Rani sighed. "And you're a hopeless man."

She kept moving along the trail, which was difficult to trace through the tall grass.

"But an adorable one, right?" Rory laughed. "Come on, I'm just playing."

"You know what your problem is?"

"No, I don't, but I'm sure you're about to tell me."

"I am," Rani said, tapping her head. "You're up here all the time. You're always thinking, calculating. I never see you *feel* anything."

Now Rory turned serious. "I can feel."

"I'm sure you can."

"I can," he said. "And what makes you think you know so much about me? We only just met."

"I've been watching you."

"You have?" Rory said, interested. "So what do you see?"

Rani kept pushing her way through the grass. "I see someone lost, to be honest. I see someone who thinks he's on the top of the world, unstoppable, with all the answers. But in reality, he's only someone who has lost his way, someone who has given up on the one thing that matters most."

"And what would that be?" Rory asked.

Ronnie stopped and looked back at him. "Your heart, that's what."

"You're crazy," Rory said, shaking his head. He was not accustomed to women challenging him this way and found it frustrating yet at the same time curiously appealing. "So, what makes you such an expert on the heart, anyway? Have you ever been in love?"

"We're not talking about me," Rani said, starting up the trail again. "We're talking about you. And I know you haven't been, not really. But that's not what I'm talking about."

"You don't know what you're talking about," he decided.

"You said a minute ago I was a smart woman. Your words…"

"I'm reconsidering."

"Ha!"

"I don't think we should talk anymore," Rory said.

"Good, that's how I wanted it in the first—"

"*Shh.*"

"Don't be rude."

"No, I mean it," Rory said, grabbing her arm. "Stop. Listen."

"What is it?"

"I thought I heard something," he whispered, looking around.

"You're not playing with me again, because if you are—"

"No," Rory said, pointing. "Look."

"Where?"

"*There!*"

She followed his finger over the chest-high grass and saw a man coming straight at them.

"Shit!" Rani said.

"I know. How did we miss him?"

"You were talking."

"Right."

The man was moving quickly. In one hand he carried something that shimmered in the sunlight.

"What the hell is that?"

"A machete, I'm guessing," Rory said.

"What do we do now?"

"I don't know, run?"

"He looks fast."

"He does. Are you?"

"What?"

"Fast?"

"No," she shook her head. "Are you?"

"Not anymore."

By now the man had halved the distance between them. As he reached a gap in the trail, they could see he was tall and dark, with no shirt or shoes, and filthy trousers cut ragged beneath the knee. The muscles in his arms and chest bulged all over the place, while the machete in his hand looked perfectly suited for hacking into a palm tree or the side of some lost stranger's head.

"Let me handle this," Rory said, stashing his bags in the grass by his feet. He took a couple steps forward, toward the jungle man, who was now only a few yards away.

"Can we help you?" Rory asked.

The other stopped and glared back.

"I don't think he understands you," Rani said, standing next to Rory now.

"English is their national language."

"Maybe not down here."

The jungle man took another step forward, raising his machete.

"Do something," Rani said, her voice unsteady.

"I am," Rory responded, holding his hands up in front of him, but this action only seemed to anger the other, who started jabbing his long blade at Rani.

"Something else!"

She took a step back, as the man pointed the machete at her chest.

"Maybe we *should* run," Rory said. "On the count of three, you go left and I'll go—"

"No," she cut him off. "I have an idea."

Now Rory watched as Rani reached down with trembling hands to where the man was pointing and slowly lifted the digital camera hanging from a cord around her neck. She forced a smile, which the other returned, holding the machete out in front of him, as he posed for a picture.

"I don't believe this," Rory said.

"Can you hand me the Ghana bag?"

"What? Why?"

"I need to show you something," she said, snapping a second photo.

"Okay," Rory replied, confused, but doing as he was asked. He placed the fat nylon sack next to her feet. Rani bent down, undid the plastic strands, and fished out two bricks of *naira*, which she handed over to the other man.

"Thank you," he said in perfect English, accepting the cash. He then tipped his head in gratitude, before continuing past them down the trail.

Rory watched him go before turning back to Rani, who was visibly shaken by the experience. "Why did you do that?"

"What?" she asked. "Take his picture?"

"Yes, for starters."

"I don't know," she said. "I just had a feeling it was what he wanted me to do."

"Right, a *feeling*. And the money?"

"Ah, that…well, I could see he needed it more than we do."

"That's crazy," Rory said, shaking his head.

"No," she replied. "*Empathetic*. Think about it."

Rory watched her start up the trail again, before grabbing his belongings and following after her.

"Oh, and one more thing," Rani said over her shoulder.

"What?"

"Now *that* was exciting!"

17

At the water's edge, a twisting helix of tiny insects shimmied just above the surface, abuzz in a melodic code decipherable only to those of their own kind. But they were no match for the heated argument being waged by Echs and Prissy.

"No, *you* were wrong."

"What else could I do?"

"You could have used your head, woman."

It was Echs, reprimanding Prissy for leaving Rory and Rani behind in the jungle. The five of them were reunited now on a flat-bottomed boat, pushing off from shore, Yak at the rudder and Prissy, predictably, not taking well to public remonstration. The spat began practically the moment they arrived at the riverbank, Echs and Yak having managed to procure rides on two more motorcycles, and then transporting Rory and Rani the final few miles through the jungle to where they found Prissy waiting by the boat.

She was about to protest again, but the look on Echs' face suggested she save her breath. This she did, letting it out in an exaggerated manner before taking a seat on the far side of the motor-driven skiff, away from the others.

Rory watched as Yak fired up the outboard motor. The boat lurched forward and soon was scooting across the glassy surface, picking up speed as it went. Rani selected a seat not far from Prissy in what Rory imagined was a nod to sisterly solidarity, while he remained standing, grabbing onto a handrail. *I can feel things just fine*, he thought, still staring at Rani, trying to get her out of his head, while wondering if she could look any better than she did right now. *Oh, screw her.*

"Turn here," Echs shouted over the rumble of the engine. Yak shook his head and kept going straight. It was apparent he knew this river like the veins on his muscular arms, and Rory found himself gaining an appreciation for why this silent troll had been added to their traveling party. A moment later Yak powered down the motor, steering toward the entrance of a narrow tributary that looked pretty much like all the others they had just passed.

As the boat drifted on, tall reeds spiraled up on either side of them. Rory took his seat and looked over again at Rani, who was reaching out to touch the water.

"I wouldn't do that," warned Echs, still standing near the center of the boat.

"Why not?" Rani's hand hovered in the air, a couple inches from the surface.

"There's no telling what you'll find in there."

"Dangerous fish?"

"Or worse," said Echs. "Oil runoff, raw sewage, human remains..."

Rani yanked her hand back. "I thought you said this river was your lifeblood?"

"It *was*," Echs said, sitting down at last. "These swamps are part of the third largest wetland system in the world, after the Dutch canals and Rory's Mississippi River. They used to be stock full of more plants and fish than we knew what to do with, enough agricultural here to feed the entire Niger Delta, millions of people. Now, you would be lucky to find a few grunters or thread fins, and those you did catch would probably give you cancer."

"What happened?"

"And what does any of this have to do with General Bola?" Rory wanted to know.

Echs laughed. "I was wondering when you would ask about Bola. It has nothing to do with him...and everything. We will get to Bola, but first I want to talk to you about oil."

"Oil?"

"Yes, Rani, it is the reason we are here, the only reason any white person ever comes down to the Delta," Echs said, frowning. "Fifty years ago, we discovered the black junk and it should have been our greatest moment. In truth, it's been our worst nightmare."

"Why?" Rani asked, as Rory idly listened, having heard versions of this story told by Tunde and others several times before.

"Greed, plain and simple," Echs said. "Some people can never get enough. They say our last dictator, Sani Abacha, stole more than six billion dollars from the state.

He stashed it away in foreign bank accounts – Switzerland, Austria, the Cayman Islands. The day he died, his wife and children were caught stuffing handfuls of cash into suitcases. Now they spend their days on the Internet trying to get it back."

"Where did all the money come from?"

"Right here," Echs said, with a sweep of his long arm. "The Niger Delta accounts for more than ninety percent of Nigeria's wealth, yet we remain one of the poorest places on Earth. They pump the oil, our oil, and then send it up north to Lagos, Abuja, Kano, Kaduna. What do we get in return?"

"Not much, from what I can see," Rani said.

"That's right," Echs said, his voice growing louder. "Nothing. No schools for our children, no hospitals for our sick and elderly, no electricity, clean drinking water, or sanitation services. We shit in the same place we're supposed to get our food. We bathe in water greasy and putrid from so many oil spills. We breathe air choked off from half a century of open flaring. We die from diseases unheard of in the rest of the world. We live worse than animals down here so some fat cats in Port Harcourt can enjoy martinis in their mansions while they rape us until we bleed."

Echs was nearly shouting now, and Rani decided not to ask another question.

"So, you kidnap oil workers," Rory said, reentering the conversation. "Kill innocent people. The ends justify the means, eh?"

"That wasn't us," Echs replied, not at all convincingly. "Anyway, that was a mistake. We usually just hold them for ransom. Make them drink from the waters they pollute until they get sick. Eventually, the oil companies take notice. They build us a church or a community center to shut us up. The last thing they want is a bunch of journalists or aid workers running around down here talking to us. Things get better for awhile, but not for long. At the end of the day, they just don't care. So we make them care. We hit them where it hurts. We sabotage a few oil pipelines, take their filthy workers hostage."

"But if you're mad at the government," Rani asked cautiously, "why do you take it out on the oil workers?"

"They're available," Echs said. "The government boys aren't. They got smart. At first they sent their soldiers down here to keep us quiet, but those monkeys didn't know the Delta. They seemed to keep disappearing. Poof. Black magic. So they stopped sending soldiers. They came up with a better plan. Divide and conquer. Why send your own boys into the jungle, when there are plenty of us already down here, ready and willing to slaughter each other for a few *naira*? Throw the Itsekiri a bone and they'll gladly keep the Ijaw off your property. Toss the Ijaw an extra piece of meat and watch them butcher the Urhobo. Soon we had a tribal war on our hands, all of us drowning in our own blood as we groveled over a few dirty crumbs."

"That may be true," Rory said, "but there's still one thing I don't understand. If you're so destitute here, as you say you are, and so far you've shown us nothing to doubt that assertion, then how is it possible the Message comes from the Niger Delta? How do you have the capacity to pull off an operation like these Sporting Murders?"

"What makes you think *we* did it?"

"Well, I've been thinking a lot about that very question," Rory said, looking at Echs. "For me, it boils down to one word: *motive*. By most accepted counts, there are some forty major or minor armed conflicts raging around the globe right now, plus scores of smaller wars, the majority of them as bad, or worse, than this one. So you tell me, why would someone go to all this trouble – kill three star athletes on three different continents and then send a threatening message to the world – unless he had a pretty strong *motive*, a real vested interest in the outcome of this specific struggle? Why not send a message telling the world to stop the fighting in, say, Afghanistan, for instance?"

"Or Syria," Echs said, eying Rory closely.

"Right," he agreed, "or Iraq." Rory had altered the volume and tone of his voice to match that of Echs, just as he did with the Doctor back in Lagos. Rani sat watching this tense exchange unfold, wondering how far he was willing to push their host, here in the middle of nowhere.

"Or Yemen," Echs was saying now, sizing up Rory like a prizefighter before the opening bell.

"Or Niger or the Central African Republic or Somalia," Rory said, pressing harder.

"Because," Echs said, "maybe the killers didn't come from any of *those* places."

"Exactly," Rory stressed. "They came from *here*, from right here in the Niger Delta. You know that."

He held Echs in his gaze, waiting for a confession, or at least some information he could use. *Can it be this easy?*

"Or maybe," Echs started.

"Or maybe what?" *Am I really this good?*

"Or maybe it was finally just our turn. Ever think of that?"

Crap.

Echs continued staring at Rory, who eventually looked away. They both fell silent for a moment, until Echs spoke again.

"Turn."

"I heard you," Rory said, but Echs wasn't speaking to him any longer.

"Turn here."

Yak heard it, too, but shook his head again. He let their boat glide past the immediate opening in the waterway and eased it instead toward the following entrance.

"How does he know to do that?" Rani asked Echs, who seemed pleased to change the subject.

"His mother fished for a living," he answered. "Yak used to ride with her up and down these waters as a boy.

Only, they didn't have a motor then. He and his brothers paddled. They helped her with the business, catching moonfish and croakers, fat spades or whatever else the water gave them. She sold her catches at the markets along the riverbank, like the one we passed a few minutes ago. She made pretty good money back then."

"Until they killed her," said Prissy. It was the first words she had spoken since they pushed off from shore.

"Who did?" Rani asked. "The army?"

Prissy did not reply, while Echs looked away and Yak kept steering the boat.

So Rani tried again. "Was it the police?"

"No," Prissy answered at last. "It wasn't the army. It wasn't the police either."

"How do you know?" Rory asked.

"I know," she said, reaching up and slowly unfastening her headscarf, letting the red, yellow, and blue fabric fall away from her face, "because I was there."

The first thing Rory noticed was how beautiful this woman must have been, before her brown eyes turned cold and dark, before her full lips curled into a permanent sneer, before whatever device was used to disfigure her skull.

"I'm sorry," he said, averting his eyes, but not before catching a good glimpse of the horrible wound. A three-inch gash ran like a trough through her soft, kinky hair, but Prissy made no effort to cover it up. She let them stare. It seemed like she wanted Rory and the others to see what had been done to her, to witness the ugliness men could inflict on a pretty girl.

"Who did this to you then," Rory asked, returning his eyes to meet Prissy's, "if it wasn't the army or the police?"

"No, it wasn't either of them," she said, while putting her headscarf back in place. "It was members of another Delta tribe."

Silence ensued. Even if they had known what to say, it would have been difficult, for Yak had kicked up the motor again, sending a shudder through the mangrove swamps. The rumble startled a crane, which voiced its displeasure before relinquishing a good hiding spot among the reeds, pushing off on long legs and gliding like a feather across the emerald water.

Soon, they, too, were flying along the surface. Yak guided them out of one channel and into the next, then briefly toward open water, their boat going full throttle over small, choppy waves before delving back toward a tangle of twisting tributaries. Through a moss-covered tunnel they sped, a vista of blue and green leading onto a long, straight stretch where the boat picked up even more speed.

The wind felt crisp and cool against Rory's face, a thrilling spray of water in the air. At the same time, there was a strange sense of heat overhead, which seemed to be growing increasingly stronger. Rounding a corner, the mystery heat intensified even more, and Rory was about to ask what was happening, when Echs suddenly shouted.

"Turn back!"

This time Yak made no objection. He spun the rudder madly to the right. The skiff swung sideways, but the lane was too narrow here to bring it back around.

"Kill the motor!" Prissy screamed, while scrambling toward the stern.

"What's wrong?" Rani asked, standing to her feet. Rory did the same.

"Stay still," Prissy ordered, as the boat continued careening forward.

"What is it?" Rory demanded. The heat was overbearing.

"Look!" Echs pointed a bony finger, which Rory followed toward a platform with a rising tower and a tremendous open flame. That explained the heat, Rory thought. *But why is everyone so panicked?*

Then he saw something else. There, toward the front of the wide platform, a man stood with no shirt. His arms were pulled back and tied to a thick beam that rose from the floor of the wooden structure. His flabby white skin appeared to be painted black, but only up to the neck, and his feet were on fire, flames literally dancing from his shoes. The man should have been screaming but he couldn't, for someone had shoved a rag in his mouth.

"Not a word," Echs said, and they all obeyed, as Yak slowed the skiff, which continued coasting toward the platform, where Rory now noticed four more figures. They were young men, with dark skin, wearing matching headbands. Each carried a gun, and those guns were pointed at the boat.

"Shit," Rani said under her breath.

No one else spoke. They stood like statues, staring straight ahead, their muscles rigid as the platform approached, just meters away now. The young renegades hovered above them, peering down with hateful scowls, their guns trained on these unwanted guests. Rory suddenly felt dizzy. The heat was unbearable, the stench of burning flesh revolting. Against his better judgment, he stole a peek upwards, and within that glance he saw the fat white man tied to the post...flames moving up his legs, roasting him alive...a grinning black boy pointing a rifle...the barrel aimed right at him!

A trigger slip and Rory would take a bullet square in the chest. He tried not thinking of what that would feel like, metal ripping through his flesh, shattering bones, lodging in his heart, blood spattering everywhere. He had seen some nasty things in his life but this was right up there with the worst of them. He tried, instead, to think like those boys on the platform. *What had pushed them to this? Could they be reasoned with? Was there any point trying to escape?* And then he had another thought, which surprised him.

How is Rani handling it?

All of this crossed Rory's mind as he stood perfectly still doing nothing. Nothing but waiting with the others, listening to the crackle and hiss of the fireball overhead, certain any moment they would all be gunned down, those boys going crazy, wailing away with their guns.

But that moment never came. And soon they were drifting past the platform, beyond the searing heat, away from this living nightmare. No one spoke for some time after that. Not until they had floated a good distance up river, into safe water, toward a slowly sinking sun.

"That was bad," Rory said at last.

"Worse than you think," Echs said, shaking his head.

"Why?" Rani asked. "Was that another Delta tribe?"

"No," Prissy said, a look of raw disgust on her face. "That was our own."

18

Under a steadily setting sun, Yak navigated their boat into open water. Tall trees rose up on either side of the riverbank, creating a welcome shade that cooled the late afternoon air.

"I still don't understand," Rory said, taking a seat toward the front of the boat, not far from Rani.

"Nor do we," Echs said, dropping his long frame into the space between them. "At the end of the day, this was our worst fear. We've been riding these waterways since that Message was announced, meeting with tribal elders, trying to convince them the time has come for all of us to band together again, to reunite the Delta tribes."

"To carry on the work of Saro-Wiwa," Prissy said, joining them.

"Who?" Rani asked, making room for her to sit down.

"One of the greats," Rory said, surprised how she didn't know this already. He was about to say as much, when Echs started explaining.

"Ken Saro-Wiwa was from a different tribe, but we all paid him deep respect. He had an idea, a vision, a bold strategy to bring us all together, like in ancient times, before government oppression drove us apart and greed compelled us to take up arms against our own brothers and sisters. Ken spoke the truth. He told us to turn our anger and frustration into a single, unified force for peace and justice. He told us to rise above our oppressors. He gave us a reason to dream."

"Alone, we are but fingers on a hand," Prissy said, splaying her own open and then clasping it tight. "Together, we make a fist."

Rani watched her. "So, what happened to him?"

"Saro-Wiwa?" she asked, and Rani nodded. "They killed him, that's what."

"Government boys rounded him up with some others," Echs said. "Falsified charges, held a kangaroo court, found them all guilty, and put them to death."

"While the world sat by watching," Prissy said.

"That was a sad day for Nigeria, a sad day for all of us," Echs said. "We've been trying our best to carry on in Ken's spirit. That is why we agreed to meet you, why we brought you here. We hoped that perhaps this Message, whoever sent it, could provide a path toward salvation for the Delta, that it could help turn things around for us somehow. But after what we just saw back there on that platform, I fear our work is in jeopardy."

"Our own brothers pointing guns in our faces," Prissy spat. "Our work is *done*."

They all fell quiet, until Rory eventually spoke. "I don't think so."

"What do you know?" Prissy countered.

"This is what I do for a living," Rory said. "I look for ways out of difficult situations, and I get paid a lot to do it. In the end, no conflict is truly intractable. Nothing is ever static. Situations change, and you need to be ready for those changes. You need to consider all the options available to you and think about potential solutions you may never have thought of before."

But the Nigerians were not convinced. Prissy and Echs both shook their heads, while Yak kept silently steering.

"He's right," Rani suddenly said, throwing Rory a tiny smile, before addressing the two Nigerians between them. "I may not have read all the books Rory has, and, like always, he's cast it in purely cerebral terms. But he's right. You must keep fighting for what you believe. You can't give up now, not if you see something that needs changing. You must change it, no matter what the cost. You owe it to yourself and to all those you love."

This last piece seemed to resonate with Prissy. "But what if those you love are the very ones causing the problem?"

"Then you must love them even more," Rani said.

"What are you talking about?" Echs wanted to know. "That seems naïve."

"And dangerous," Prissy added.

"And logical," Rory said, returning Rani's smile. He was about to explain, when she took over from him.

"He's right again," Rani said to Prissy and Echs. "You have accomplished much already, but you are still not there yet. And that's okay. Sometimes you need to keep turning the other cheek and pointing out what you know to be true, while patiently painting pictures until everyone else sees exactly what you see. Look at Mandela or Gandhi or Martin Luther King."

"Or Rosa Parks," Prissy said.

"Or Ken Saro-Wiwa," Echs added.

"*Exactly*," Rani agreed, becoming more passionate as she went. "You must find the right approach and then you must make sure everyone else understands that you are determined to succeed, no matter what obstacles are put in your way. You must demonstrate how you are committed to making your enemy today become your brother or sister tomorrow. If you fight them, you will all lose in the end. But if you embrace them and convince them there is a better way of looking at the world, then you can all win together. You always have a choice."

Rory couldn't stop staring at her. *You always have a choice. Where have I heard that before?* He wasn't sure, but he did know that he had underestimated Rani. There was something about her, and it wasn't just sexual desire. There was more to it than that. He had been chasing women all his life, a series of admittedly beautiful girls, yet always ending up in the same place. And now, sitting here, right in front of him, for whatever reason, was this gorgeous, intelligent, challenging, vexing, mysteriously stimulating woman. Watching Rani explain how it requires both the head and the heart to resolve difficult conflicts, Rory could feel himself falling hard, being pulled ever closer toward her – the words she spoke, the way she spoke them, the way she looked at him, the way she looked, period: her lips, her cheeks, the curve of her chin, the sun in her hair, how it lit up her face, making the green in her eyes sparkle, Siamese-like, as she fed him another one of her private little smiles, enchanting, bewitching, spellbinding. He suddenly experienced a powerful sensation – like years ago, staring at those maps – and a desperate need to know if she somehow shared the same feelings for him, too.

Rory turned away just as Rani finished bucking up these war-weary Nigerians with her speech. "From what I've seen today, the world needs people like you, people unafraid to risk everything to right an obvious wrong."

"Well, I thank you for that," Echs replied, starting to his feet. "Those are encouraging words, Rani, and I pray you are right, I truly do. And soon, we shall see."

Prissy also had left her seat, while Yak brought the skiff around, angling it toward shore. Up ahead, a fishing village was coming into view, rows of small houses fronting a wooden pier.

"What shall we see?" Rory asked, standing up, as well.

"Not *what*," Echs told him, "*who*."

Rory waited.

"We're about to see the one man who may still be able to save us from ourselves," Echs said. "We're about to see General Bola."

To get to Bola required a long walk through a ragged town that reeked of dead fish and burning fuel. By now the sun was in full descent, dipping below the shaggy palm fronds on the water's edge and casting long, distorted shadows that made it seem as if their souls were pulling them back toward the dock.

"Something isn't right here," Echs said, taking the lead.

"What is it?" Rory asked, moving quickly to keep up with the other's lengthy strides.

"Are we in Warri yet?" Rani wanted to know.

"Not yet," Prissy said.

"But I thought we were supposed to get to Warri before dark."

"Don't you fret."

On they continued, past cheaply-built dwellings leaning in all directions. Some were made of rotting wood, others of rusted metal folded over to form meager tents, presumably to keep rainwater off personal belongings, Rory guessed. Not that these people had many. From the far side, Yak kept turning his head, looking back to make sure no one was following them. As far as Rory could tell, this village stood empty, save for a few stray goats and clucking chickens.

"I'm telling you, something isn't right here," Echs repeated, although he kept marching on, until they reached the end of a lonely street, the dock no longer visible. Now Echs stopped and pointed ahead, toward a steep rise and a thatch of tall trees. Tucked behind these natural sentinels stood a massive structure, far more formidable than the dilapidated homes they had just left behind. Without a word, Echs set off again, the others following after him, forging their way up, through knee-high weeds and grass. Occasionally, one of them slapped at his arms or neck to ward off the pesky mosquitoes that attacked like kamikazes in a Japanese war movie. Rory was glad he and Rani had followed Tunde's advice, swallowing the fat anti-malarial pills given them, which tasted salty and caused vivid yet not entirely unpleasant dreams. The "malaria nightmares," Rory had heard, were far worse.

They eventually reached the crest of the hill and were met by a tangled wall of ekki trees fronting the building, which turned out to be some sort of African fort. No moat or turrets, Rory noted, but well protected all the same, with heavy slabs of wood and concrete spiraling upward, several stories high. Emanating from within this fortress could be heard the slashing strains of searing music: thumping base and wailing guitars punctuated by crazy reggae lyrics. It sounded like Bob Marley on Quaaludes.

"I told you something wasn't right here."

"Not General Bola's sound?" Rory asked.

"Nor his taste in tobacco," Echs replied with a sniff.

They proceeded toward the front entrance, where they were stopped by two armed guards. In their late teens, wearing khaki shorts and shirtless, their dark muscle-laden arms and chests suggested far more time spent running through jungles than finding friends on Facebook. In their hands they gripped automatic weapons, taken off some unfortunate Nigerian soldier, Rory imagined. Their faces bore looks of hatred and mistrust, which softened only slightly upon recognizing Echs.

"We're here to see Bola," he announced, eyeing the taller of the two.

"Not a good time," the tough boy said.

But Echs was clever. "Okay, we'll bring our message back another time."

"What *message*?" The smaller thug eyed them suspiciously.

"I'm sure it's not important," Echs said, turning to leave. But the taller guard wasn't about to take any chances on his watch.

"All right," he said, raising his gun to let them pass, "but be quick, old man."

Inside, the place was pitch black and the music deafening, making conversation pointless. Rory stopped to catch his bearings and was shoved forward from behind. He stumbled upwards, his feet finding stairs in the dark, hands fumbling against walls that were cold and moist, mind reeling from the pungent odor of hashish and a stomach-wrenching drumbeat. For a second, he thought he might be having one of those malaria nightmares.

"Don't you fret," was whispered warm in his ear, providing little comfort. *Where's Rani?*

They reached the next floor, and a slit of light seeped out from under a closed door up ahead. Rory spotted Rani next to Yak. *Good.* Echs reached the door first and pushed it open, the others following. They next passed through a fog of smoke and a fragrance so strong it stormed the nostrils and stung the eyes. The odor was sweet and musky at the same time, a peculiar combination that both attracted and repelled. *"Nar-cot-ics,"* Rory mouthed, while moving close to Rani. She nodded and did her best to smile, although the tight look on her face told him nothing in her life so far had prepared her for any of this.

All around them music pounded from oversized speakers positioned in a room otherwise devoid of furnishings. The sound shook the walls and floor, further contributing to a sense of disorientation. Following after Echs, they stepped around the bodies of more young men and boys, some no older than 12 or 13, all clad in khaki shorts, shirtless and dark-skinned. There must have been at least two dozen of them, lounging on the ground or sitting on their haunches, engaged in a ritual that involved sucking on water pipes, coughing loudly, flexing muscles, and making scary faces. Through the haze their eyes burned red. Few of them paid much attention to the visiting party invading their space. Those who did look up merely opened their lips to let milky puffs of smoke drift toward the ceiling.

Across the room, the next door was locked. Echs pounded twice, waited, and then rapped a third time before it finally swung open. Guarding this room was a man dressed in camouflage trousers and a tank top, a string of bullets slung across his broad chest and shoulders. He nodded at Echs and ran his dark eyes over the others, before ushering them into an open room and closing the door behind them.

In here, the music vanished. *Soundproofed*, Rory realized, before his own eyes fell on a most amazing sight. Scattered around these quarters was a massacre's worth of weaponry: pump-action rifles, serrated knives, assorted pistols, rough-hewn machetes, an entire wall lined with submachine guns. There was even a rocket launcher propped in one corner, near a desk littered with hand grenades and what appeared to be a gardening tool, or, more likely, some crude torturing device. Further on, toward the back of the room, three black men sat huddled around a table.

"General Bola," Echs said, as two of them looked up, startled by the intrusion. The third man kept glancing downward, showing them his expansive back.

"I have someone important here – from America – who needs to see you."

At last he turned around, and Rory was struck by two details: first, the immense size of this man and, second, his unexpectedly youthful age.

"*Samuel*," Echs stammered, surprised as well. "Where is the General?"

"Brother Echs." The man named Samuel stood and nodded. "Always a pleasure to see you, although now is not a particularly good time."

"Why not? What's going on here? Where is General Bola?"

"Haven't you heard?"

"No. What?"

"He's dead."

"*What?*" Prissy lunged forward, causing the other two men to reach for their weapons.

"It's okay," Samuel said, raising his hand.

"*Dead?*" Prissy repeated. "That's impossible. We just saw him the other day."

Samuel did not answer her, speaking instead to the men at the table. "Go now and get the boys ready. Let them know I will be there soon. And tell them to lay off those water pipes. A little of that junk makes you fearless. Too much gets you killed."

His two lieutenants did as told, stepping away from the table and gathering up as many weapons as they could carry before filing out the door, trailed by the bullet-laden guard.

"What do you mean, 'get the boy's ready'?" Echs wanted to know.

"AK-47s," Samuel said, watching them leave. "Cost less than a live chicken here. They're like African credit cards. You don't leave home without one."

Echs ignored the old joke. "Ready for *what*?"

"Ready for war," Samuel said. "What else?"

"*War?*" Prissy cried. "Who are you fighting?"

"The boys across the river."

"What are you talking about?" Echs jumped back in. "The Igbo? We opened negotiations with them. You were there."

"Not the Igbo," Samuel said, moving toward the desk and opening a drawer.

"The Itsekiri? They're with us, too. You know that."

"Not the Itsekiri."

"Then *who*?"

Samuel found what he was looking for, a bone-shattering .44 Magnum, like Clint Eastwood's Dirty Harry might have owned, while Echs spotted the map on the table.

"What the hell is *that*?"

"I told you," Samuel said. "We're going to war with the boys across the river."

Echs froze in horror. "Not our own tribe?"

"You can't possibly," Prissy started.

"This is madness," Echs spoke over her. "Think of everything we've worked for."

"They're like *family*," Prissy persisted. "Our own flesh and blood!"

"Yes," Samuel said, anger rising in his voice. "And the General was *my* flesh and blood, my own father, until they killed him! It's time to trim the tualags."

"What did you say?"

At first no one took notice of this new voice, caught up as they were in the drama unfolding. Prissy had thrown herself at Samuel. Echs was imploring him to reconsider. Even Yak was doing his part, trying to block the big man's way.

"*What did you say?*" the voice repeated, louder.

Still, no one responded, so the voice became a shout. "*WHAT DID YOU SAY?*"

And now all heads turned toward Rory.

"I said, he was my father," Samuel answered. "General Bola was my father."

"This isn't your concern," said Prissy.

"No, not that," Rory said, ignoring her and staring straight at Samuel. He reached out and took hold of the rebel leader's arm. "Tell me *precisely* what you just said."

The other Nigerians were shocked by this gesture and the tone of Rory's voice, but Samuel hardly seemed bothered. "I said, 'It's time to trim the tualags.' It's an old saying that means the time has come to—"

"—go to war with those closest to you," Rory completed the sentence.

"Right," Samuel said, surprised. "When those closest to you begin to turn rotten, like the—"

"—branches on the tualag, they must be trimmed back to save the life of the entire tree," Rory finished the line. "But there are no tualags in Nigeria, or even on the

African continent. So where did you hear that phrase spoken? Who told you about the tualags?"

He increased the pressure on Samuel's arm, and for a second it looked like the other man might strike him. Instead, he calmly answered the question.

"I think we both know very well where I heard it spoken."

"Impossible," said Rory. "He's incarcerated for life in a South Asian prison."

Samuel shook his head. "Not when I saw him. He was very much a free man, shackled only by his inability to fully impart wisdom on an unworthy student such as myself."

"I don't believe you. I would have heard. When was this?"

"Not long ago."

"*Where?*" Rory demanded, his voice rising wildly.

Samuel held him in his gaze, the silence sitting heavy in the room.

"I think you already know the answer," he said at last, before yanking his arm away.

This time Rory did not respond.

"Now, if you will excuse me," Samuel continued, shoving a handful of bullets into the pocket of his khakis. "I'm in a bit of a hurry here, and I'm sorry, Brother Echs, if you feel I have failed you. Your quest to bring peace to the Delta is a noble one, and I hope one day you succeed.

God willing, I will still be alive to see that day. As for today, I must fight."

He then he pushed past them toward the door.

"Please keep me in your prayers," he added, turning back momentarily. "And, for your own safety, I beg you flee this village as quickly as you can."

19

Center Court.   Dubai National Tennis Pavilion. Excitement nearing fever pitch.

Earlier in the day, former world No. 1 Aya Coppens had opened eyes with a riveting performance, leaving retirement to stun a much younger and quicker yet ultimately outclassed newcomer from Australia. The crowd was beside itself then – truly something to tell the Country Club set back home. But now, as the sun dipped below the gently swaying palm trees lining the sold-out arena, history was in the making, courtesy of an unexpected heroine. Slight of build yet high of spirit, this irrepressible South African sixteen-year-old went by a single name – Tania – though there was nothing singular about her game. Just ask her opponent, a Wimbledon finalist previously ranked among the world's best, who had spent much of the past hour sprinting and chasing and diving after a dizzying array of laser-guided ground strokes launched with pinpoint accuracy from the oversized racket of this previously unheralded hard court ingénue.

Today was Tania's coming-out party.

The chore of grooming this budding flower, who hailed from one of Cape Town's more privileged postal districts, fell on the narrow but sturdy shoulders of two women. One was Tania's overprotective Coach, who saw in her star pupil bright flashes of brilliance reminiscent of her own meteoric rise to fame and fortune. The other was Tania's overprotective Mother, widowed at an early age, who saw in her daughter mainly just fortune. Alone together in a private courtside box reserved for players' families and friends, Mother and Coach alternated between smiling down encouragingly at their precocious protégé and confidently at each other. For, at this moment, no one present exuded more confidence than Tania, herself.

With bronzed skin and bobbed hair shimmering in the fading sunlight, she was rapidly racking up the score in a dazzling display. Her nubile young body, tucked inside a fashionably chic tennis ensemble, caught the eye of all the paying customers as she went about the business of dismantling her opponent, a veteran of numerous tournament championships before Tania was old enough to wear her first training bra.

The first set ended in just 34 minutes and was remarkable only for the surgical efficiency with which she dissected her more seasoned foe. Tania took the opener, 6-0, collecting five aces out of 12 service opportunities and making only one unforced error. That lone blemish came in the second game of the set, a scorching cross-court forehand that many in the stands thought they saw clip the line for a winner, but the chair umpire and instant replay system judged differently.

And that was the last point Tania had lost.

The crowd, initially ambivalent to yet another coltish teenage wonder girl on the circuit these days, finally began to sit up in their hardback seats and take notice. As the match progressed, point after blistering point falling in Tania's favor, the reticent crowd moved further forward, toward the edge of those seats, to get a better view of the magic show being performed for them. It must be sleight of hand, for how else could one explain the exacting precision of those down-the-line winners, which seemed to vanish on the other side of her opponent's racket as if there were holes in the strings?

The second set began as an even more one-sided affair than the first. It wasn't until Tania captured the third game, without losing a point, just like the first two – *15, 30, 40, game!* – that the crowd began to realize something truly special was happening. Enlightenment may have flowed first from the pen of a young boy keeping score, who informed his father that the South African lady had now won 30 points in a row. The older man checked his son's arithmetic and then confirmed it with a glance toward the stadium press box, where the typically reserved scribes were chattering away gleefully. A murmur soon began moving through the stands.

"Thirty straight!" one fan gushed.

"Three games from a perfect shut out!" said another, while all around them urgent questions were being asked.

"Has this ever happened before?"

"Against an opponent of such high quality?"

"In a tournament that actually mattered?"

By now the audience had become part of the show. As game number four raced by in similar fashion to the preceding three – *15, 30, 40, game!* – people rose to their feet and began cheering, encouraging an impossible Tania forehand to land just inside the baseline...and it did.

Urging an improbable Tania backhand to bounce just out of reach...and it did.

Willing a feather soft drop shot to fall just over the net...and it did.

15-30-40-game!

The crowd – *her* crowd – responded to each mounting point with enthusiasm bordering on delirium. Her charming smile, her curvaceous body, and her blitzkrieg approach to the game had won over even the staunchest skeptics among them. The entire throng was behind Tania now, abandoning polite courtside decorum. This one, they seemed to be saying with their rowdy applause – prompting the umpire to quiet them from his elevated chair – might truly be a notch above. She might be the real deal, the next Hingis, Graff – dare we dream? – Chrissie Evert, still the undisputed girl queen of women's tennis.

Game number six began with a patented Tania ace, her opponent caught flat-footed by the sizzling serve.

15-love. Thirty-nine points in a row!

Some started to wonder if Tania's opponent had given up. Could it be she was conceding the match? Saving face? Yet those who knew tennis well knew better. This was one entry in the record books to which no one wanted to sign her name. In fact, the sapient spectators among them agreed, she was fighting harder than ever to steal at least one of the remaining three points in the match, and the ensuing play put all doubts to rest.

Faced with another smash down the line, Tania's adversary did all she could to get there. Lunging to her left, scraping her knee in the process, she managed to nick the ball with the top of her racket, producing a crazy spin, which sent it fluttering like a wounded bird shot from the sky. Barely clearing the net cord, the ball plunged back down to earth, as the spectators moaned, certain this return meant an end to the perfect run.

They were wrong. Tania arrived in time.

30-love. Forty points in a row!

The crowd went mental, totally out of control.

"Quiet on the court, please," the chair umpire admonished, first in English and then in Arabic. *"Oskoot, min fudlik."*

They finally settled down, taking their seats again, yet refusing to be muzzled.

"Two points to go!" one shouted.

"A perfect set!" another yelled.

"Who is this kid?" several asked.

None of them knew the answer to this last question better than the two women sitting courtside. Sharing a smile, Mother and Coach reached down below the railing of their private box, away from the roving cameras beaming the fresh face of their valuable property into television sets around the globe, and squeezed each other's hand.

At the baseline, Tania was bouncing the ball – once, twice, as was her custom – while preparing to serve. Before tossing it skyward, she repeated another superstitious ritual, glancing down at the inside of her left wrist. There, just below the rise in her palm, a tiny object glistened. It was a butterfly, with translucent wings shimmering in the six colors of South Africa. A teardrop of a tattoo, it had caused major ripples when Tania snuck off with a girlfriend to have it done. Mother had been furious, threatening to pull her daughter from the Junior Regional for such an irresponsible stunt, but Coach saw it differently. Ever the diplomat, she came to Tania's defense, contending that while this action was childlike and foolish, it did reveal a degree of rebelliousness vital to all great champions. In the end, Mother relented, Tania won the Regional, Coach congratulated herself as a master armchair psychologist, and the little good luck charm stayed on the girl's arm.

Quiet as the wings on that butterfly, a hush fell over Center Court as all eyes locked in on the ball. Up it went, Tania's racket retracting like a quiver. High overhead the ball sailed, hanging there on an invisible thread, waiting for Tania's titanium frame to race around and greet it.

Across the net, her opponent dug in. Legs spread, arms loose, mind clear; she would have roughly one second to react.

Whack!

The ball shot from Tania's high-tension strings like a bazooka, the laws of physics dictating its trajectory. Soaring and then dipping with a wicked twist, it skipped just inside the service line for another ace.

40-love. Forty-one points in a row!

Unreal, the crowd screamed in appreciation.

"Tania! Tania!"

Down on the court, she pumped her fist and let out a girlish squeal that made her undeniably irresistible. A star was rising and all her fading opponent could do was shake her head, bite her lip, and trudge to the other side of the court to await her fate, one point shy of a destiny no one desired.

"Tania! Tania!"

The crowd had to be silenced again.

"Quiet on the court...*min fudlik*."

And then it was quiet, deadly so. For a moment, it seemed as if time had somehow compressed.

Tick.

The crowd held its breath.

Tock.

Tania bounced the ball.

Tick.

Bounced it a second time.

Tock.

Her eyes fell again on the colorful butterfly carved into her flesh, an innocent creature trapped beneath a bead of sweat. The insect then disappeared, as up went the ball and with it the hopes of practically all present, save one.

Around came Tania's racket, driving ahead with commanding force. A loud gasp escaped from the crowd, a collective sound that seemed to carry the ball in Tania's favor.

Another ace?

Not this time. Her beleaguered rival scampered to her right, determined to avoid the ignominy this point represented, committed to scoring at least once in this demoralizing affair. Her racket found the ball, sending a surprisingly solid shot skirting back over the net. Tania's positioning off the serve appeared to prevent her from reaching the return. The ball was moving too quickly, slicing away at an odd angle and hurtling toward the corner, an inch or so within fair territory.

The crowd's sigh became a groan. How could this be? So close to perfection but now just another tennis match, for clearly it would take everything the teenager had merely to reach the ball, let alone to manufacture a meaningful response.

In the opposite court, Tania's challenger stood her ground, watching what surely must be a winner at last. Her mind fast-forwarded, as those belonging to the great ones do. It flashed through a fantasy scenario in which she not only took this point but actually climbed back into the match, winning the game, the set, and eventually teaching this impudent toddler a well-deserved lesson.

But it was only fantasy.

With catlike agility, Tania sprang forward, throwing herself at the advancing ball and spearing it with an open-faced racket. As she tumbled to the ground, the ball shrieked over the net, kissing the baseline one more time.

Game-love!

The unreal was real.

Tania had won the set without losing a point.

Match over in under an hour, crowd ecstatic, begging for more. Tania's handlers swooped in before a single autograph could be signed. Mother draped a protective arm over her daughter's shoulder, while Coach marched ahead, deflecting questions from the press. "Not now!" she barked, parting the way with powerful arms. "Tania will talk once the job is done."

On they went, away from Center Court, a quintet of burly policemen encircling the three ladies, lest any well-wishers get the wrong idea. If the Monica Seles stabbing was too far removed for some memories, the Message surely occupied everyone's attention these days. None more so than the tournament promoters, fully apprised to the damage a resort city like Dubai would suffer should the next star athlete happen to die here.

Among the first major events to take place following the Sporting Murders, the tournament organizers had pulled out all the stops. They doubled the police force, tripled the security cameras, and installed state-of-the-art metal detectors at every possible choke point. They even engaged military helicopters to patrol the skies over Dubai, politely yet firmly overruling protests from the Player's Union that the noise would be too distracting for their temperamental clients.

"Safety over everything" became a mantra instilled on the swarm of security forces manning this event, including the five who now ushered Team Tania toward a tunnel that led to the ladies' dressing room.

"That was good Mother," beamed a radiant Tania, waiting for the approval that mattered more to her than all the gold in the Emirates.

"Yes, darling, that was good," Mother smiled back. "Now let's keep moving."

As Tania's entourage entered a shaded corridor, Coach instinctively fell back, taking up a rear position, ever watchful for intruders who might slip past their safety net. She remembered all too well, for she had been there that fateful day in Berlin, when a knife-wielding lunatic brazenly attacked Seles in broad daylight in front of a stadium packed full of fans. Monica was never the same again.

Such thoughts ran through the minds of Mother and Coach as they corralled their nest egg toward the outer entrance of the ladies' dressing room. Here, they were met by a pair of brawny policewomen in crisp uniforms with loaded pistols strapped to leather hip holsters. Rarely seen in this part of the world, the lady cops were a special touch tendered by the tournament hosts, hired for the week and flown in at exorbitant expense from the Chicago Metropolitan Police Force.

Mother and Coach nodded at the officers, who scanned their surroundings before opening the door to let Tania enter. The two older women would remain outside, joining forces with the security gauntlet. Nine adults to guard a single teenager might seem excessive, but these days you could never be too careful.

Tania giggled at all the attention.

"I feel like Charlize Theron," she said, batting her eyes. And then she was gone.

*　　*　　*

Inside, Tania passes through a second door, patrolled by two more female officers, as tough as their male counterparts and equipped with the same standard-issue weaponry.

Next, she approaches the main dressing area, a place of peace and solitude, where players gather their thoughts before engaging in athletic combat.

Further still, protectively sequestered behind thick concrete walls and a final door, she enters the showering facility, a white-tiled haven where fragrant smells, wafting steam, and the gentle thrum of warm water conjure up images of a womb.

And here, sitting alone on an empty bench, innocently wrapped in a terrycloth robe, with a sports bag full of recent acquisitions, Tania meets the Arabian Princess.

20

It was dusk by the time they found the landing, untied the boat, and pushed off from shore. Yakuba kept the motor running high until they had put considerable distance between themselves and the spooky river town, where young boys emboldened by hatred and hashish were rushing into battle. Even so, the unmistakable *pop-pop* of gunfire reached them down on the water, and Rory watched Prissy and Echs cringe with every outburst.

For a long time no one spoke. The only sounds heard were the rumble of the motor and the mournful calls of insects settling in for the night.

As they continued on their journey, the moonless sky eventually became so dark Rory had trouble seeing his hand in front of his face. He moved toward the middle of the boat, listening to the wetland noises and wondering why exactly it was so important to reach Warri before nightfall, when they struck something in the water.

"Sorry," Yak grunted from the stern, giving Rory his first answer.

"I think we're here," Prissy said.

"Where's *here?*" Rani asked.

"The outskirts of Warri," Echs replied.

"The one place we were told not to go with you, especially after the sun went down," Rani said. "So what horrible fate awaits us now?"

"None," Echs said, "as long we stick together and be careful."

Moving in the dark, they stashed their gear and climbed out of the boat.

"Let's link hands," Rory heard Prissy say, as they huddled on the shore.

"Good idea," Echs agreed, grabbing Rory's left one with his coarse mitt. He felt much softer flesh press against his right.

"Prissy?"

"No, Rani."

Rory squeezed her hand and felt her squeeze his back. He smiled, but it was too dark to tell if she responded in kind.

Connected this way, they climbed up a short hill, their feet sinking in the sand. Rory's eyes began to adjust, and he realized they were on the fringe of a grubby beach town.

"Where are the lights?" Rani asked.

"Nothing that fancy here," Prissy said from the far end of their human chain.

"Even if this beach had lights, they'd be turned off now," Echs said in a hushed voice. "Dusk-to-dawn curfew. Soldiers everywhere. Let's keep quiet and try not to draw attention."

This they did as best they could by keeping toward the tree line, not far from shore. Every so often Rory thought he saw figures on the opposite side of the road. *Nigerian soldiers?* He couldn't be sure. Occasionally, he heard voices spilling out of the rough shacks they passed, speaking in a strange language that only added to his general anxiety about this place.

"Hold up," Echs suddenly said, while tightening his grip on Rory's hand.

"What is it?"

"I don't know, but it's coming our way."

Indeed, something was headed straight at them. Human or not, it was too dark to tell.

"Who's there?" Echs said, yanking his hand free, and Rory had the uneasy sensation of floating away.

"I have a gun," he heard Echs lie.

Rory held tightly to Rani's hand as the figure kept advancing. Tall and thin, it turned out to be human after all.

"Mr. Crandall?" a man's voice said in the dark.

Rory was stunned and looked to the others before answering. "Yes, I'm Crandall. Who wants to know?"

"A friend," the voice said. "Please, come this way."

They followed after the stranger, a local fisherman, who said he had been instructed to look out for them but would say no more. They passed along a narrow side street, even darker than the main road. The smell was sour here and their feet sloshed through something wet.

They soon arrived at the man's shabby quarters and were treated to a most surprising sight. There sat

Tafawa – their driver from earlier in the day, the one who got stuck in the mud – smiling up at them from a wooden table. The features on his long face were caught in flickering candlelight. "I told you I would finish the job."

"Unbelievable," said Prissy, shaking her head.

But Tafawa was in no mood to fight. He pointed at a cheap windup radio in the center of the table, near a dying stub of candle wax. At first all they could hear was static, until Tafawa fiddled with the radio's plastic knob. Then, through the interference, came the voice of a news announcer, speaking in English.

"—to repeat, earlier today, at the International Tennis Pavilion in Dubai, promising South African starlet Tania van NieKerk was brutally murdered minutes after winning her first major professional match in stunning—"

"My God," Prissy interrupted.

"*Shh*," shot Rory, straining to hear the rest.

"—teenager's face was so badly mutilated she could only be identified by a small tattoo on her left arm," the reporter went on. "At present there are no known suspects, but authorities have reason to believe this heinous crime was the work of the so-called Sporting Murderers. For on the wall in the ladies' dressing room—"

The radio crackled again and Rory lunged for the table, grabbing at the plastic knob, just as reception was restored.

"—a second message painted in the dead girl's blood."

Stakes Raised

21

"Yes, Mrs. Markham, of course I've seen it. I have it on now."

Rory had muted the sound when his iPhone rang, but it wasn't difficult to follow the news. It had been the same all morning, each of the alphabet soup channels – ABC, BBC, CNN, all the locals – carrying the haunting image of that darkly stained sheet draped over the butchered remains of the young tennis player, Tania, dumped in the corner of a changing room in Dubai. The $10 million reward for information leading to the capture or killing of the Sporting Murderers had been raised to $15 million, but what really grabbed the viewer's attention was the dramatic phrase scrawled on the wall above the corpse in the victim's own blood:

Stop a war any war or soon will die many more!

"No, I'm not sure what to make of it either," Rory said, turning from the television back to the breakfast table in his hotel room, where he had just poured himself a glass of juice when the widowed billionaire sports tycoon phoned. "I think it's fair to say, though, that someone has just raised the stakes."

Rory tried a sip – fresh papaya instead of orange but still delicious. "Yes, Mrs. Markham, a little extra cash in the account is always appreciated, thank you."

He took a seat at the table while scanning his hotel room, quite lavish by Nigerian standards: a big comfortable bed, new if gaudy furniture, and hot running water in a shower that actually ran. Given yesterday's ordeal, it was no less than he deserved.

"No, Mrs. Markham, I'm not sure where I'm headed next, but you will be the first to know," he said, as a knock came at the door. "Sorry, Mrs. Markham, but I need to go now. I'll ring you later, I promise."

A second knock followed.

"Come in," Rory called, putting down his iPhone. "It should be open."

He picked up his glass just as Rani entered, and the juice never reached his lips. *My God, she's gorgeous*, he thought, running his eyes over her body. She had exchanged yesterday's gritty safari gear for a simple sundress and matching sandals, her long hair freed and falling over tanned shoulders, her chest—

"Good morning to you too," Rani smiled, bringing his eyes up to meet her own.

"Sorry," he managed. "May I offer you some breakfast? The fresh fruit is fantastic."

"Thank you, no," Rani said, moving toward the table. "But I'd kill for some coffee."

Rory frowned.

"Sorry, wrong choice of words." She spotted the TV in the corner, as she reached for a cup and saucer next to the French press. "Any new news today?"

"No, not really," said Rory, deciding not to mention the $15 million reward and how it might be changing his thinking about this case. He glanced, instead, at a pad of paper on the table, next to his breakfast. Toward the top, he had written the text of the two Messages.

1. Niger Delta killings stop or another athlete gets the chop!

2. Stop a war any war or soon will die many more!

"What are you doing?" Rani asked, taking a seat at the table opposite him.

"Trying to figure out what this all means and where to go next," he said, watching her and wondering how best to ask her to join him. He returned to the notepad, opting for a casual approach. "What about you?"

"Me? I'm drinking coffee with a handsome man."

Rory looked up to see Rani smiling at him.

"Teasing," she said. "You're old enough to be—"

"Don't finish that sentence, unless it ends with 'a good friend of my older brother.' "

"Don't have one," Rani laughed, before sipping from her coffee.

"What makes you think I'm that much older than you?" he asked.

"Aren't you?"

Now Rory smiled. "How old are you, anyway, if you don't mind me asking?"

"I do mind and I'm not going to tell you."

"Fair enough, twenty-four."

"Thanks," Rani smiled back, licking a dab of coffee off her upper lip. "That's sweet but really rude, you know, guessing a woman's age."

"You're right, and I'm sorry, twenty-six. That's my final offer."

Rani laughed again. "It's not negotiable, not even for *you*. I'm twenty-nine."

"Get out of here."

"What's wrong? Can't handle someone close to your own age?"

"No, it's not that, it's just—"

"Got a pretty young thing waiting for you at home?"

Rory thought briefly of Melanie back in DC and dodged the question. "You seem to think you know a lot about me."

"That's because you're an open book," she replied, not missing a beat. "I read you the first time we met. You're smart, you're driven, you're wildly successful, and—"

"Thank you."

"—cocky, self-centered, always thinking, trying to find an angle, afraid to let yourself go. You know, be passionate, in the moment, live for a cause larger than yourself."

"Wow, is that what you see?"

"Yep," she replied, placing her cup back on the saucer. "That's what I see."

"Okay, then, Ms. Twenty-nine," Rory said, shaking his head. He didn't want to fight. He wanted to figure out a way to keep her here with him, and a way to get his hands on that $15 million. "Have it your way."

"My way, your way, it doesn't really matter, anyway."

"Why not?" Rory asked.

"Because," she said, "I'm going back to Copenhagen. This trip has been educational and, of course, *exciting*, but another day with you and I'll get sent home in a body bag."

"Sorry," Rory said.

"No need to apologize. I made you do enough of that yesterday."

"I wasn't apologizing. I'm sorry because I thought we were becoming partners."

"*Partners?*" Rani asked, raising an eyebrow.

Now it was his turn to laugh.

"Okay, *colleagues*…colleagues in solving these crimes, these Sporting Murders."

"Are we?"

"Are we what?"

"Solving these crimes?"

"Oh," Rory said, looking again at what he had written on the pad of paper. "Honestly, I don't know. It would seem these two messages come from the same source and that someone is trying to hold the world hostage, if such a thing is possible, by systematically killing our best athletes. But who that someone is and what they ultimately want to achieve I still have no idea." He looked up again. "I had hoped by coming down here to the Niger Delta and meeting General Bola that I – that *we* – would be able to shed some light on this mystery. But now Bola's dead, we've got no useful leads, and I'm starting to wonder if this entire trip was a mistake."

Rani thought a second, while reaching for her cup again. "Maybe it wasn't *General* Bola you were meant to see."

"What do you mean?"

"Well," she said, taking another sip of coffee, "maybe you were meant to see his son, Samuel. What was all that talk about the trees?"

"They're called *tualags*," Rory responded. "They grow wild on some of the islands in the Indian Ocean, off the coasts of Australia and Indonesia. I've been wondering about that myself, but it doesn't add up. Samuel was referring to a man called Daemon, a man who has been locked up in a high security prison there for most of the last decade."

"But Samuel said he's out now."

"I know he said that, but it can't be true. I would have heard."

"So, who is this Daemon?"

Rory hesitated, wondering how much he should tell her. *Hell, she's leaving today, back to Copenhagen. What does it matter?*

"Well, Daemon," Rory began, "before he was captured, was a rebel, a freedom fighter, and a merciless killer. Though, he didn't start out that way. In fact, his real name is Vieges Jekriél, and he began his career as a scholar and well-respected if relatively inconsequential professor of ancient history at Romitsae University. That is, until one of his papers questioning the legitimacy of authoritarian governments landed him in jail on trumped up charges of treason and inciting public disorder – even though, at that time, order was still firmly in place on the island nation of Romitsae, a repressive police state if ever there was one. While incarcerated, the humble professor suffered repeated beatings and other tortures for refusing to recant his research. When this regimen of pain and abuse failed to achieve its desired result, the government went after the man's family. They raped and murdered his wife and young daughter—"

"No," said Rani.

"—and beheaded his sons. They took pictures of the remains and posted them online as a warning to anyone else on the island with thoughts of challenging the regime. It was at this point that Dr. Jekriél shaved his head and adopted the traditional namesake Daemon, which loosely translates in the local vernacular to 'ophidian' or 'serpent.' It was also at this time that Jekriél-cum-Daemon approached another inmate to serve as his master in the age-old custom of *hortia*, a forbidden practice that fuses deep religious meditation with vicious martial arts. Soon the pair was training other inmates who held personal grudges against the governing junta, and there were many. In the government's zeal to crush dissenting voices, it had not only produced a growing cadre of freedom fighters across the island but had unwittingly created in Daemon a vengeful, ruthless, and natural born leader for these rebels to follow."

"But he still remained in prison, right?"

"Not for long. Daemon engineered a daring escape, resulting in the massacre of an entire guard force. The government moved quickly to quash the news, fearful of the impact it would have at home and abroad, while ramping up its campaign of murder, rape, and torture. Daemon, meanwhile, began traversing the island on a recruiting spree, uniting minority groups against the far better equipped government troops and state-run militia. He also reached out to mercenaries in neighboring countries – Cambodia, Sri Lanka, Viet Nam – to help his cause, hiring these trained guns with the promise of future payment once he staged his rebellion."

"Maybe this is when Samuel met him," Rani said, reaching for the French press again.

"Maybe," Rory said, "but the window would have been small, for Daemon soon made a critical mistake. Trusting one of his lieutenants, who had secretly been bought off by the government, he showed up one night with a band of men near the base of the island to purchase weapons to launch his attack. He was ambushed at the docks, most of his men were killed by waiting government troops, and Daemon was forced to surrender to save the rest. Only, the government reneged. Forcing Daemon to watch, they lined up his remaining fighters and shot them one by one in the head, before tossing their bodies in the sea and then throwing their leader back into prison, this time under solitary confinement."

"My God."

"Nice guys, right? But the ploy worked. With Daemon caged again, the opposition soon splintered. The rest of his rebels went underground, or, in this case, high into the hills above the island, where they've been hiding in the dense forests ever since." Rory paused for a moment, before concluding. "Meaning the civil war that Daemon had planned never materialized, which is why none of this makes sense."

"What doesn't?"

"This," he said, pushing the notepad across the table. "See, this Second Message says, 'Stop a war, any war,' yet there's no war in Romitsae to stop, since it never got started. So, if your theory is correct, that we came all the way down here to listen to Samuel, then his telling us about Daemon and the tualag trees clearly wasn't the point."

Rani took the pad and turned it in her direction, reading the two lines written there.

"Unless," she said.

"Unless what?"

"Unless it means stop a war *before* it gets started. This Second Message really isn't clear on that point."

Rory reached for the notepad.

" 'Stop a war, any war,' " he read aloud, thinking. "You're right. That's amazing. You're amazing. Why didn't I see that before?"

"I don't know," she said. "Why didn't you?"

Now Rory looked up. "Where are you going?"

"I told you, I'm leaving."

"Right, back to Copenhagen." He couldn't hide his disappointment.

"No," she corrected, stepping away from her seat, "to Romitsae, wherever that is."

She started around the table toward him.

"To stop a war," she said, stopping in front of him, "before it gets started."

Rory opened his mouth, but she placed a finger on his lips, whispering in his ear.

"*Partner.*"

22

High in the hills over Sarajevo the snow had all but melted, a few clumps clinging here and there like gauze to the spidery branches of the looming trees. Inside the fortress known to its occupants as the Sanctuary, an edgy buzz filled the conference room as they found their places around the table.

"I don't know," said Bettina, still in that striking blond wig, slotting in near the top and ignoring Tito, who grinned up hopefully with a blink of his blood-stained eye. "He only told me to drop what I was doing, round up the others, and for all of us to come here with our thinking caps on."

"Personally, I was planning on wearing a beret," Zulu smiled back from across the table. "But I'm ready for anything."

Further down, Che was telling Ramona about the social media churn generated by Tania's murder in Dubai, while the one they called Caesar and some of the other younger members spoke in animated voices about the same subject. The only two missing were the main architects of this topic, the coffee-girl-turned-assassin, now called the Arabian Princess, and the man entering the room.

"Greetings," said Confucius, taking his seat at the head of the table, between Bettina and Zulu. In his right hand he held a short stack of envelopes, which he placed on the tabletop in front of him. "Our marching orders. I received them from him and—"

"You've seen him?" Bettina cut in. The others were surprised by this blatant interruption, yet eager to hear the response.

Confucius weighed his answer. "Yes, I've been to see him, and he told me our mission is proceeding exactly as planned, although the steepest road still lies ahead. Once we make our next recommendation, I will pass out the new assignments," he said with a tap on the stack of envelopes. "And, for her outstanding work in Dubai, the Arabian Princess will be exem—"

The door at the back of the room suddenly swung open, but it was not the Arabian Princess. It was her replacement, a playful young thing of barely driving age.

"*Seriously?*" said Bettina, watching the predatory look on the face of Confucius as the new girl started up the table with a tray of coffee mugs.

"I hear *boys* can serve, too," Zulu sniped.

Tito also looked disturbed. Not by the jailbait doing her job, but by the fact that Bettina seemed to care so much about how another man reacted.

"I don't pick them," said Confucius, accepting his mug while smiling up at the new girl until she blushed and turned her face away. "Now, where were we? Ah, right, as before, let me remind you, this is a *brainstorming* exercise. No wrong answers, only good suggestions. So, let's try to be creative and think outside the box. Unless there are any more questions, I would like to get—"

Confucius stopped again, this time catching sight of Che, who had one arm raised. He waited for Confucius to acknowledge him before lowering his arm.

"Well," Che began, clearing his throat. "I was just wondering, aren't there any other ways to proceed?"

A murmur sped around the table and then the room fell silent. All heads turned toward Confucius, whose face betrayed no emotion as he considered this question. He would have expected it coming from Bettina or Zulu, both of whom sat watching him, but not from this intense young man, who until now had always seemed so eager to please. Confucius wondered briefly whether Che was attempting to challenge his authority, which might signal a larger break in the ranks. But the sincere look on the kid's face convinced him otherwise; this was merely a fair question.

"Yes," Confucius said at last, choosing his next words carefully. "You are right. There certainly are other ways to proceed. But I am following orders, just like the rest of you, and this is the way *he* instructed us to proceed. I do hope you understand."

Che nodded that he did.

"Good," said Confucius, turning back to the others. "Then, if there are no further questions, I have one of my own. Who would like to go first?"

This time Bettina did not wait to be chosen. Standing, she marched the length of the table, carrying with her a red, felt-tip pen, which she applied to the top of the flip chart.

"Always hated those bastards," she said, stepping back to let them see what she had written.

"*Da*," Tito agreed, as did several others, although some could be seen struggling to mask their true feelings, while a couple of them openly cringed at the notion.

Zulu went next.

"Excellent," said Confucius, watching Bettina jot down the second entry under the first. "Once we have finished the list, we will make our selection. Now, who else has an idea?"

All around the table hands lifted high in the air and young voices filled the conference room as one after the other provided the name of a professional sports team for slaughter.

23

The day was achingly hot, the room too small, like the brother who shares it.

Out of bed, the smell of fresh bread beckons from the kitchen. Not now, you must wait, says the sister, older, playing mother, the other mother.

Yes, wait my hobgoblin, says the real mother, covered in powder from baking, always with a name to give.

Down the hall, skipping past the cave with the dragon tap-tapping on his tap-writer. Never disturb the dragon.

Through a window comes a voice. Hurry, the game will start.

I must watch my brother.

We need you for our team.

Just a minute then.

Back to the kitchen, past the tapping dragon, begging for a piece of bread, warm and soft with oil dripping, a second for the window friend.

Outside, outrunning the wind, flying by houses and yards and women selling fruit and fresh bread, oil running down young hands.

Faster, the game will start.

Stop!

A checkpoint full of soldiers, stinking black uniforms and dirty loud laughing, rough in thick beards and accents, fingers on triggers.

Where do you go little men? You must pay a tax.

Holding up bread as loud laughter swings the gate open.

Running again, past sharp whiskers up the hill, where other boys chase a ball like a planet, cool above the village, the father and mother, sister and brother all forgotten.

Then, that sound, never forgotten: loud as a bear and shaking down the hill, over the lip and into the mouth, full of smoke that chokes the sad houses.

Running faster, falling down and up again, through the gate, littered with cigarette husks but no whiskers. Angry voices shout from trucks, women scream and wail. Running now past fruit on the ground, toward the smoke-filled houses.

Hot wind, joyless sounds, black smoke with orange feet, running into the sister, red liquid leaking, like juice from bad fruit.

In her hands a doll, like a brother, lifeless and limp.

He's DEAD.

The word hangs in the air with the smoke and orange feet. A mother, the real mother, lies covered in powder and dark ashes, the dragon beside her, no longer tap-tapping.

All DEAD, cries the sister. You were supposed to be here, cries the other mother. You were supposed to do something, sobs the only mother now.

But the hobgoblin just stands there staring. He is eleven years old.

*   *   *

Rory woke with a start. He had been dreaming, something awful, but he couldn't remember the details. On his lap lay a copy of yesterday's *New York Times*, a photo of that murdered young tennis star, Tania, smiling back at him from her obituary. The newspaper had been bought at an airport stall before leaving.

But leaving from where? To where? And where was Rani?

Rory felt pressure on his shoulder and looked over to see her shifting her position in the first class seat beside him, all the while keeping her sleepy head resting there. He remembered now. They were on an overnighter to Bangkok, from where they would catch a charter flight for the final leg of the journey and their ultimate destination, the turbulent island nation of Romitsae.

Rory smiled to himself. *Partners.* Hours earlier, he and Rani had sat side-by-side sipping mimosas in the luxury lounge at Nairobi International Airport, waiting for their connecting flight while working together on a plan. Rani had seemed so genuinely excited about the lives they would save by stopping a war that Rory had refrained from denting her enthusiasm, deciding not to reveal how slim their chances were or to admit to the 15 million other reasons he had for giving it a shot anyway.

During the conversation then, and again watching Rani asleep on his shoulder now, Rory couldn't help thinking of Melanie back in DC, and the sticky mess he was about to create. *Poor Mel, but we're not committed, not even defined, and Rani and I haven't done anything, yet...*

With this thought in mind, he closed his eyes and drifted back to sleep.

*   *   *

Tito's eyes snapped open. He glanced at the illuminated clock on the bedside table in his cramped quarters at the Sanctuary. He had been asleep for less than two hours. Next to the clock there stood a photograph. In it, he and Bettina, slightly younger, were alone together, smiling, happy.

Tito rolled over and looked at the other side of the bed. Empty.

He fell onto his back and stared at the ceiling. Something had changed between them. Definitely. But he wasn't sure what or why.

Ever since she killed Lazarius, while I sat there watching her do it, she hasn't been the same. We used to have a connection, the two of us against the world. Now she's distracted, erratic, even cruel at times, and she doesn't give a shit about me.

Rubbing at the peach fuzz on his chin, Tito wondered where Bettina was now. Rolling over again, he closed his eyes, and tried not to dwell too long on the answer.

*   *   *

In a noticeably larger room at the Sanctuary, Confucius followed the numbers on his wristwatch as a smile creased his wet and rigid face. It took all the will power he could muster to maintain the rhythmic pace of concentrated motion necessary to accomplish the task at hand.

He had been at it now for nearly 40 minutes, pounding away on the innocent creature trapped and thrashing beneath his legs, the newly arrived coffee girl.

Tightening his grip on the nape of her neck, he focused his attention on the contracting back muscles pushing through her baby-soft skin, while considering whether the muffled squeals emanating from inside the pillow represented joy or pain, and realizing he really didn't care.

*   *   *

In another room at the Sanctuary, a woman climbed out of a bed and began dressing in the dark. Completely naked, she slid on silk panties and bra, followed by a tight black skirt and matching top. The final accessory she fit over her bare head, which shone momentarily in a slash of moonlight.

Finished, she moved back toward the bed, careful not to wake the body lying there. Face down and partly exposed beneath the covers, its sturdy shoulders and muscular back stirred slightly upon her approach. Ignoring the body, she reached instead for an item on the bedside table, a still-sealed envelope, which she dropped into her handbag, removing a similar-looking packet, opened but resealed, which she left as a replacement for the one she had just taken away.

Satisfied, she turned and started for the door, when a voice, strong yet feminine, called out to her in the dark. "Where are you going, Bettina?"

"It's okay, Zulu, go back to sleep."

* * *

Half a world away, another woman lay alone on a bed. In one hand she held a frameless photograph of an eminently happy family – father, mother, and two little girls, one of whose features mirrored exactly those of the woman on the bed, only several years older now.

In her other hand she held a newspaper in Arabic script, a bold headline hanging over the innocent face of the tennis star, Tania, also from much happier times.

Looking from one photo to the next, Leila, the Arabian Princess, couldn't stop sobbing.

24

A t the United Nations headquarters in New York, an emergency session of the newly created Special Committee on Global Security and International Terrorism through Sport was moving into its third hour. Convened at the behest of the Secretary-General and consisting of representatives from the most powerful nations on Earth, the meeting was designed to draw up contingency plans for where, when, and how "to stop a war, any war," even though a decision had yet to be reached by the members of this assemblage on whether the UN would be willing to bow to terrorist demands.

On a separate floor, several flights down and below ground level, in an area of the complex rarely used, the decision-making process was far less constrained. Here, eight men with extremely high security clearances were bringing to close a secret meeting of SECTOR – the Strategic Engagement for Counterterrorism Operations with Results – as the outfit was referred to in the unclassified world. Conceived in the aftermath of the September 11 attacks on New York and Washington, SECTOR consisted of a small pool of agents from "friendly" countries who shared a wealth of experience in the fields of intel gathering, black ops, and other matters of national security.

"All agreed?" asked the leader of this elite group, staring at the single notepad on a metal table supporting eight plastic coffee cups and a map of the world. Scribbled on the paper was a list of names that included a few well-known terrorists, some lesser-known hit men for hire, and a handful of warlords, drug barons, and other charming individuals.

Hunkered around the table, the seven agents nodded in turn. By creating a streamlined unit that traded secrets, up to a point, through a centralized command system, it was hoped that the SECTOR operatives could strike far more quickly than the bureaucratic structures from which they were drawn. So far, this brainchild of a Cold War spymaster had proven effective, helping snare three Yemeni terrorists en route to demolish Big Ben before they ever left the London Underground, after earlier following a trail of dirty money to the hutch of a Central American narcotics ring funding al-Qaeda cells in North Africa. News of these two operations never hit the airways, while the money recovered from the drug raid failed to reach accredited banking establishments, both of which suited SECTOR fine. Unlike their more celebrated bosses several floors up, these eight reveled in anonymity, considering deep cover one of their most powerful assets. Plus, tracking global terrorists was never a low-budget affair.

"Spare no expense" was the motto of their enigmatic leader, a legendary figure in espionage circles who went by a variety of names, spoke even more languages fluently, and regularly employed methods, which, had they become widely known, would have been deemed by most in civil society as unconventional if not outright inhumane.

"It's decided then," he announced to his colleagues, before ripping the top sheet off the notepad and stuffing it deep inside the pocket of his cargo pants. Rolling up the map, he couldn't help thinking about the circus going on several floors above them. *What chance do those diplomatic yahoos have of ever catching the Sporting Murderers when they can't even agree on boundaries in the desert?* Fortunately for him and the other seven men filing out the door, their job was far more straightforward – search, capture, destroy.

*   *   *

"We're about to change the world," said Mills Greenblatt to one of his overpaid aides, as he was helped down from his private helicopter. One look at the man's shriveled physique and pinched weasel face and it was hard imagining him changing much of anything.

"Put me down," Mills shouted over the blades' metallic flutter, receiving his leg braces from a second supplicant, who had given up a promising modeling career to tend after her billionaire boss. His power resided not in his body, but in his mind and in his uncanny ability to keep one step ahead of the masses. Even now, as the world shuddered with the death of that South African girl, Mills was thinking. Thinking of how this Second Message was exactly what the media lived for these days: a dramatic story with a beautiful young victim and the intrigue of terrorist activity. Thinking of how this story cut across race, gender, nationality, and most every marketing demographic imaginable. It was O.J. Simpson, Nancy Kerrigan, and 9/11 all wrapped into one. But mainly he was just thinking of dollar signs. He didn't kill any of these athletes, but he planned to make a *killing* off their deaths.

"Crutches," Mills ordered another subordinate, before shuffling across a makeshift stage to address the journalists who had gone to great lengths to reach this secluded location. Squinting out at the sea of faces, Mills had no love for any of them. These hacks were simply an antiquated tool required to get his message out to that portion of the world which still believed it necessary to receive consumer information from messy newsprint or flickering picture tubes. The bulk of his audience was watching him through unseen eyes, logged onto PCs or mobile devices around the globe in fervent anticipation of whatever new creation this eccentric cyber guru and computer software legend had in store – and soon to be in stores – for them.

Give the people what they want.

"Welcome," Mills said, lowering the microphone and lifting his misshapen head, which appeared absurdly large tethered to such a meager frame. "I stand before you as a citizen of the world – the *new* world – and the future of possibility that lies within every one of us."

Mills paused to catch his breath, while staring straight into the lone TV camera permitted to record this event. Property of his personally owned cable network, he would make all others pay dearly for the feed.

"The recent attacks against these athletes – *our* athletes – are ugly, unjust, and morally repugnant reminders of how truly horrible people can be. I know, some of you are thinking these athletes got what they deserved. They're rich and spoiled and couldn't care less about you."

Here, Mills stopped again, looking like the poster boy for all the wimps of the world. "Well, get over it, because you're missing the point. These athletes are the stuff from which *dreams* are made."

As a child, his own dreams, like those of most boys his age, were shaped by bats and balls, rocket ships and comic books, where men leapt over tall buildings and outran locomotives. Mills had trouble getting out of bed each morning, and the rest of his day didn't get much better. Few playground teams were in the market for asthmatic oddballs.

"But let's face it," he went on, facing the reporters. "Their dreams are our dreams. We watch them. We talk about them. We want to *be* them. And they, in turn, teach us something about ourselves. They teach us that in life all things are possible. Look at me, I'm certainly no he-man, no sporting star," he said, pausing to wait for all to have their private chuckles, as they always did, before raising a scrawny index finger. "Heck, I can barely lift a finger. But with this finger, all things become, yes, *possible*."

And all things had for Mills, with the aid of a secondhand McIntosh and a basic programming course at a local community college. It wasn't long before he was marrying an innate ability to organize code with a wild longing for high adventure to produce some of the most authentic and profitable computer games ever conceived in an industry that now topped $100 billion in annual worldwide revenue.

"So now, as I stand here before you, I say that these athletes, cut down in the prime of their lives, stood for something sacred. They stood for *possibility*. They stood for the *future*. And, we, too, must stand together against these brazen acts to safeguard a *future* where all things are *possible* for all of you. With this in mind, I give you the *Future Games*," he announced, knowing how the name alone would have bundles of his pricey silver discs leaping off retail shelves by nightfall. If *World of Warcraft* players were now pushing 12 million globally, then 15 million for *Future Games* was certainly not out of the question.

"A pageantry of competition," Mills explained to the camera, "of cultural sharing, and, of course, modern technology, all in the form of a computer gaming show-down of epic proportions. It's a cyber Olympics, if you will, with vast riches going to the winner – that boy or girl, man or woman, who tracks down the killers behind the Sporting Murders."

People love puzzles.

"The culmination of this amazing competition," he continued, "will be held under one roof, with thou-sands in attendance and millions more watching in real time from your personal computers. This battle royal will let the terrorists know we *defy* them. We, the world, stand united against their tactics, even if their goals may seem worthy. And, with every copy of my new game purchased, I will donate some of the proceeds to the cash award already being offered for information leading to the capture or killing of the *real* Sporting Murderers, starting with $5 million of my own money!"

Now, he knew he had them, for what could be more enticing than solving the mystery behind a real-world crime, even if it was only in a game? For not only was he offering his customers a new, cutting-edge form of enter-tainment, with the juicy prospect of a global competition to showcase their skills, he was giving them something far more valuable. He was giving them a sense of per-sonal worth, a belief that with each dollar, euro, or yen plunked down on his product, they were making a difference in the world.

Three dozen hands shot into the air.

"To learn more," Mills said, anticipating the reporters' questions while ignoring their requests, "you must purchase my newly released Portal 3000 software, *Future Games – Defy or Die*. Here you will find the rules to the game and all the information needed to join this battle of the century. And here you will learn the date and site of the Future Games Championship."

A collective groan emanated from the reporters, who couldn't believe they had traveled all this distance, to these bleak surroundings, only to be told they now must shell out additional cash for some crappy computer program before they could report on this most astounding news.

"Give us a clue!" one of them shouted.

"Give us *something!*" another begged.

Always the showman, Mills Greenblatt leaned forward on his crutches, staring straight into the camera's lone red eye, his asymmetrical head tilted slightly to one side, as if listening to millions of hearts pounding back in expectation of his next words.

People love riddles, too.

"The Future Games," he said at last, "will take place in just over a week's time, in a land of historical significance, where cultures have clashed, religions have wrestled, and East and West stare upon one another across an illustrious body of water."

25

"**I**srael?"

"No, *Istanbul*," Rory answered Rani, as they cut through the concourse at Romitsae Inter-Island Airport, outdated and largely devoid of people, save for a few cinnamon-skinned staff workers in loose-fitting tropical garb and the obligatory uniformed gun-toting guards.

"So it's not the Red Sea, that illustrious body of water separating Jordan from its Jewish neighbor?"

"No, it's the Bosphorus," said a third voice, belonging to a man who might best be described as a grizzly bear. He stood taller than Rory and nearly twice as wide, with big inflated feet, a barrel for a belly, and a round head covered with frizzy red hair and matching beard. "It's the one that puts half of half of Istanbul in Europe and leaves the rest of Turkey hanging out in Asia."

"But nice try," said Rory, handing Rani the newspaper given to him moments earlier by the other man, who met them upon landing and introduced himself to her as Sebastian Crowley.

"My friends call me Seb," he said with a faint Irish brogue. "And, for fook's sake, if you're a friend of Rory's, then Seb it is!"

"Then Seb it is," Rani replied, handing him back his newspaper with an impish grin that left both men exchanging looks with each other.

"You have to hand it to Mills Greenblatt," Rory said, before Seb had a chance to inquire about their personal status. "He knows how to play the game."

"And how to sweeten the pot," Seb said, confident his old friend would tell him all about it later. "Look, here, in the paper, it says 'the $5 million contributed by Greenblatt brings the total reward to $20 million now being offered for information leading to the capture or killing of the Sporting Murderers.' No wonder you dragged me to this island swamp."

Rory caught Rani's questioning look and deflected Seb's comment by directing them toward the baggage carousel. He started for their luggage, but Seb beat him to it, easily plucking their bags off the conveyor belt and throwing one under each arm.

"So, are all of Rory's friends giants?" Rani asked.

"Better to protect him that way, given all the crazy shite he seems to get himself into," Seb answered.

"And better to make us targets," said Rory, as they moved away from the sparsely populated baggage claim. "This place makes me nervous. Where are all the passengers?"

"It's been like this since I landed yesterday," Seb said. "Very few people seem to be coming in and even fewer are getting out. It's as if the island were on lockdown."

They soon reached passport control, where they were greeted with no lines, no bribes, and no hassles whatsoever.

"Toto, we're not in Lagos anymore," Rory said to Rani with a wink, before retrieving their passports and starting toward the airport exit.

"You might wish you were," said Seb. "Get ready."

As they reached the exit and the door slid open, Rory understood what his friend meant. His senses were bombarded by a pair of nasty intrusions. First, the heat outside was remarkable – *almost as hot as that oil platform back in the Delta* – while the stench was unforgivable.

"What the hell happened here?" Rory asked, covering his nose while fishing for his sunglasses in the pocket of a linen shirt already moist with sweat.

"Don't worry," Seb laughed. "As far as I can tell, it only affects half the island."

He led them toward the parking lot, which also stood nearly empty. In the distance, a cropping of coconut palms swayed under a stale breeze that did little to relieve the heat and only made the smell of charred refuse even worse. Further on, past the palm trees, a wall of smoke rose up from a densely wooded mountainside, like black curtains draped over the base of the sky.

"Government's handiwork, I'm guessing," said Rory.

"You're guessing right," said Seb. "From what I could gather at the hotel bar last night, the government sent its militiamen into the hills to root out the rebels, slashing and burning everything that got in their way – land, animals, a few humans, too, plus a fair number of the priceless coffee plants that fuel the local economy here."

"Which would explain that foul stench," said Rani, wrinkling her nose.

"And a new flavor Starbucks won't be serving soon," Rory added, as they stopped before a battered Land Rover with no top covering. "So, does this mean Daemon is actually out of prison, as we were told in Nigeria, getting his men ready to go to war?"

"Don't know," Seb answered Rory, while placing their luggage in the back of the Land Rover, next to his own. "That bit of information no one at the bar either knew or was willing to tell a stranger, and I thought it better not trying too hard to find out. By the way, if you don't mind, what is your plan?"

Rory hesitated. "Visit the prison."

"And?"

"Try to find out."

"For fook's sake, that's right up there with stealing the Hope Diamond or breaking into Fort Knox."

"Do you have a better idea?"

"Yeah, not answering my phone the next time you call." Seb shook his head before placing two fingers to his lips and sending a shrieking whistle across the parking lot.

From beneath one of the coconut palms in what seemed to be the only shade for miles, a figure slowly rose to its feet and started toward them. From a distance, the man coming their way looked as thin as a blade of grass, and that impression didn't change much upon closer inspection. Even more striking than his narrow body was his long ponytail and what appeared to be blood dripping from his mouth.

"This is Paupua," said Seb, making introductions. "He'll be our driver. He doesn't speak a word of English, but comes highly recommended, at least by the bartender I heavily tipped last night."

"Nice to meet you," Rory said, shaking the man's hand, which was then offered shyly to Rani, before the four of them climbed into the Land Rover.

"From what I understand," Seb said, tucking his bulky frame into the passenger seat, while Rory and Rani got situated in the back, "Paupua has it pretty rough here. The barman said he lives like a slave. His master is some powerful bloke from another tribe, who bought Paupua out of hard labor, for charges real or contrived. It's not clear. Superstition runs rampant on the island, and his master convinced Paupua he has mystical powers, an 'evil eye.' He placed him under a spell and told him no matter where he is he can see what Paupua is doing. If he tries to hide, his master will appear out of nowhere and slit his throat with a knife. Paupua turns over his proceeds from driving and doing other odd jobs for a small room above the bar, owned by his master. The barman says he can hear Paupua praying at night for release from this curse."

"Why doesn't he just run away?" Rani asked. "And what's wrong with his mouth?"

"Nowhere to run on this island," Seb said, as Paupua started the Land Rover angling across the empty lot. "And there's nothing wrong with his mouth. He's been chewing on a root they call *daeng* here. It functions as a light narcotic, like the *khat* they chew in Yemen. Some say it provided the original zing to what later became known as Red Bull. *Daeng* makes your lips red but gives you super energy and a wicked buzz, the barman told me."

"While turning your brain to mush, I'm sure," Rory added. "You seem to have become quite well acquainted with this bartender."

"Spent a lot of time in the bar," Seb laughed, before pointing to his right. Paupua turned the vehicle in that direction and onto an unpaved road leading away from the burning hills behind them.

"Well, as long as it keeps him awake," Rory said, settling in for the journey, "I suppose it can't be all that bad."

Rory would soon be eating his words. The only frame of reference for what came next was a carnival ride he once took as a kid at the Maryland State Fairgrounds. That ride had been called the "Coaster of Doom," but at least it only lasted ten minutes. During the next two hours, Paupua hauled a reluctant Land Rover up and down twisting hills, over sharp rocks, and along narrow cliff ledges at near suicidal speeds. The road, which rose ever higher into verdant hills capped with abundant coffee plants, was so rough in most places it made talking futile. To pass the time, Rory gazed out his side of the vehicle at the magnificent landscape flying past them. The island was called Romitsae after some ancient warrior princess of the same name. It meant "dangerous beauty" in the local language, and their surroundings certainly fit the bill. He was struck by the lush valleys full of exotic trees – including the distinctive spiny tualags – that fell off far below them as they continued winding up a series of increasingly steep hills, often with jaw-dropping views to either side.

Rory's reverie was shattered, though, when Paupua banked the vehicle off a giant tree root. Their tires came within inches of spilling them into a deep ravine, causing Rani to cry out.

"Slow down!" Rory shouted.

"Wouldn't recommend it," Seb said from the front seat, seemingly unfazed by Paupua's stoned, daredevil driving. "Not if we're going to make it to the prison by nightfall."

"What happens after nightfall?" Rani asked, and Rory noticed how her knuckles had turned an unnatural shade of white from gripping the metal roll bar for too long.

"Not sure," Seb shouted back, "but I for one would rather not find out."

Just then, the Land Rover rounded a corner and started up the first paved road they had seen since leaving the airport.

"How are you doing?" Rory asked Rani, now that they were able to talk.

"Fine," she lied, but at least she had relaxed her grip. "I don't know how you do it."

"Do what?"

"Stay this calm."

"Lots of practice," Rory said, drawn to this vulnerable side of Rani. He wanted to take her in his arms, to comfort her and more, yet he knew this wouldn't be appropriate, or possibly even reciprocated. Instead, he decided to help steady her nerves at his friend's expense. "Seb lives for high adventure. He spikes his Bloody Mary each morning with a double shot of adrenaline."

"More like valium to make it through a day with this crazy nutter," Seb said to Rani, as the Land Rover topped a hill and found flat ground. "So, has Rory told you about the Chivalrous Cheetah, or whatever it is he calls himself?"

"The *what*?"

"It's the Jag," Rory corrected Seb with a frown, before turning to Rani. "But I'm sure there are much more interesting things to talk about."

"Okay," said Rani, curious but sensing Rory's discomfort. "How about this: how do you two know each other?"

Now, Rory looked at Seb and started to laugh. "He locked me up."

"In prison?"

"Yeah, and a maximum security one at that."

"*Bloody bollocks*," Seb scoffed. "It was an overnight jail, wasn't it, you big girl, and you deserved far worse than you got."

"What did you do?"

"I threw myself into a heated land dispute, at great personal risk, and would have sorted the whole thing out, until *he* showed up." Rory gestured at Seb, who turned around in his seat to face them.

"If I remember correctly, and it has been a few years now, by the time I arrived, you had several large guns pointed in your face," Seb said, "from both sides."

"Fair enough, I was just getting started back then."

"As a conflict resolution expert?" Rani asked Rory, who nodded.

"And you were a cop?"

"One of Stroke City's finest," Seb said, thumping his chest.

"Where's that?"

"Derry – or *London*derry – Northern Ireland, depending on who you choose to ask."

"Did you ever shoot anyone?"

Here, Rory laughed even louder. "Only himself, right in the ass!"

"Aw, c'mon, why did you have to tell her that?"

"Because it's true, and pretty damn funny."

"What happened?"

"He was chasing after some violent criminal, so he says, when—"

"No, no, let me tell it," Seb interrupted, with a sigh. "You always get it wrong. Here's what happened. I was having me morning tea on a rare fine Irish day, when this bloke comes running out of a chips shop right across the street, waving a pistol. Highly illegal in the UK, but as luck would have it, I had a weapon of my own. Not my standard issue, but a sweet little six-shooter I won playing cards. I started giving chase, running after the bloke with my revolver out in front of me" – Seb held up a finger and thumb in the shape of a gun – "not at all sure what I'm going to do next, because, well, I'd never actually fired at a person before, see, when I round this corner and – *bam!* – I crash right into a kid holding a football. My gun goes off, the bullet strikes lord-knows-what, ricochets around, and down I go like I've been hit by a train."

"My God," Rani said. "What did you do then?"

"Started crying like a baby."

Seb ignored Rory.

"I hobbled home, called the station, and quit my job. Same day, I did. For fook's sake, I could have killed a kid."

"And what happened to the gun?"

"I kept it, but never fired it again. It still has five bullets."

"Where did the sixth one hit you?"

"Right here," Seb said, patting his sizable rump. "Still in there to this day. Want to see?"

"*No!*" cried Rory and Rani in unison.

"Funny that," Seb said, turning back in his seat. "No one ever does."

Ahead, toward the top of another steep hill, a village was just coming into view. Paupua shifted gears while the other three continued their conversation.

"So, what did you do after leaving the police force?" Rani asked.

"If I remember correctly," Rory said, "you became a reporter, right?"

"A war correspondent," Seb clarified, turning around to face them again. "Then an aid worker...a conscientious objector...a paramedic...a socialist...a scuba instructor...a high-priced gigolo, although that last one never really panned out."

"Don't forget, a world-class photographer," Rory said. "His series of anti-hunting photos for *National Geographic* won several awards."

"Right. 'Save a life, shoot a camera.' That was many moons ago."

"But still good advice," said Rory, as they crested the hill and entered the village. "There's a lot you can learn from this man, Rani. He's an excellent teacher."

"You're a *teacher*, too?"

Seb laughed. "Could you imagine *me* in a classroom? Probably kill half the students."

"And sleep with the other half," Rory said.

"So, what do you do now?"

Seb thought a moment. "Not sure what you'd call it. I guess I'm a professional problem-solver. I go to places others don't want to go and get involved in things others don't want to do."

"Both of which we might be doing again soon," Rory said, as the Land Rover approached a series of thatched huts on either side of the road, yet no residents visible anywhere.

Seb turned back in his seat, motioning for Paupua to slow down. They continued rolling through the village, scanning the huts for signs of life.

"Something isn't right here," Rory said.

"Where are all the people?" Rani asked.

"That's part of it," he answered, "but there's something else."

"The flags," Seb said.

"Right, the flags."

"What flags?" Rani asked. "I don't see any."

"Exactly," Rory said, pointing. "Look, over there, on the ground, they've all been knocked down."

Rani followed Rory's finger and spotted the swaths of orange-and-yellow fabric tied to crude sticks. She counted several of them, flat in the dirt, in front of the vacant homes, with many of their flagpoles snapped in half.

"Why are they like that?"

"Not sure," Seb said from up front. "But I've got a hunch and it isn't good."

"Agreed," said Rory. "I've seen this kind of thing before. Those flags represent the government in power and, if I had to venture a guess, I'd say the people who live here put them up as a symbol of their professed allegiance to the state."

"Then who knocked them down?" Rani asked.

"I'm guessing again, but I would bet one of the militias did."

Rani thought a second, more confused than ever. "But didn't you say the militias work *for* the government?"

"They do," Rory said, "which is why this situation is so bad. The guys who knocked down these flags did so to make it look like the people are *opposed* to the government."

"Exactly," Seb said, as they passed by more of the modest dwellings. "Later, they will come back, under orders, and kill anyone without a flag up."

Rani stared out across the sea of colored fabric. "That's everyone."

"Unfortunately, I think you're right," Seb replied. "It's a crude yet effective scare tactic employed by the governing junta to demonstrate its power. See how this entire village has fled."

"And the next one, too, I'm willing to wager," Rory said, as the Land Rover reached the end of this sad ghost town, with all its fallen flags, and started climbing up another steep hill.

By now, the evening sky had begun to darken. The setting sun offered a pleasant respite from the day's heat, but added to the gloominess of their surroundings. Rory glanced out his side of the vehicle and imagined the fear these people must be feeling, scattered somewhere in the forest on this mountaintop, living like wild animals waiting to be hunted down.

This situation could get a lot worse, he thought, looking over at Rani and wondering if he had made a mistake suggesting she come along. *Or hadn't that been her idea?*

"Let's stop here," Seb said, breaking the silence while signaling to Paupua to pull over. "I need to stretch my legs, and we could all use a bite to eat."

Paupua steered the Land Rover off the paved road toward the lip of a gaping valley before bringing it to a stop. He left the engine idling as they all climbed out. Seb went around back to dig up sandwiches he had packed for the trip, while Rory walked to the edge and looked down. Staring into the valley, a troubling thought crossed his mind. *We've hardly seen another vehicle since leaving the airport.*

"So, where do you think the militias are now?" Rani asked, joining him.

"Down there," Rory said, pointing into the valley, which plunged far below them. From this vantage, under a darkening sky, they could see pockets of smoke rising up from the jungle floor. They could also hear the distinct if distant crackle of gunfire.

"What's down there?" Rani asked, looking anxiously over at Rory.

"I don't know," he said, meeting her eyes before taking her hand, which she allowed him to do. "And I'm afraid there's only one way to find out."

26

From the glass-encased comfort of his air-conditioned skybox, Mills Greenblatt stood alone. Training his eyes over the sprawling mesh of modern technology and romantic antiquity that spread out before him, he wondered if there could be any better place on Earth to stage the world's preeminent computer gaming showdown.

Vodafone Arena, having recently replaced BJK Inönü Stadyumu as home to the renowned sporting club Beşiktaş J.K., occupied a sizeable space in the Beşiktaş district of Istanbul, a short distance from the city's famed attractions. To the south, not far from the Grand Bazaar, stood the regal Topkapi Palace, commissioned in 1453 by Mehmet the Conqueror and presided over by a series of sultans and imperial princes, who caged their concubines like songbirds in the palace harem. Just beyond Topkapi rose Hagia Sophia, or the Church of Divine Wisdom, holding sway as the supreme cathedral in all of Christendom for nearly a thousand years before falling under the Ottoman sword. And still further on, the seven minarets of the fabled Blue Mosque soared high above the Old Town and Sultanahmet, pointing forever heavenward, like sharpened spears protecting the faithful. It was all here, Mills marveled, the bloody battles and intel-lectual advances spawned by the inevitable coming to-gether of great Eastern and Western civilizations.

Redirecting his gaze straight downward, toward the stadium floor a few stories below, he watched as an army of architects, engineers, electricians, and construction workers toiled under a punishing midday sun. Soon they would be joined by stadium officials, media consultants, ticket takers, concessionaires, and so many other cogs in an amalgamated wheel all spinning out the details of Mills' enlightened design.

Propped up on metal braces, wearing a baggy polo shirt with the Future Games logo – "Defy or Die" – stamped on his cadaverous chest, the planet's leading cyber gaming tycoon stared at his reflection in the glass before answering his own question.

"Yes," he said to himself, as a warped smile slithered across his pinched weasel face, "this is brilliant."

* * *

"This is *bullshit*," said Zulu, standing at the front of a long line of workers that snaked around Vodafone Arena, while towering over the check-in official seated before her. "Can you check your list again?"

"I did, and you are not on it," the official said in flu-ent English.

"Then we have a problem."

"No, *you* have a problem." A veteran of several large-scale events, the official wasn't about to be bullied by this black woman, no matter how tall and attractive she might be.

"Why isn't this line moving?" said a new voice, belonging to a Turkish security officer. Like his many comrades manning the stadium entrance, he wore a crisp black uniform and carried an automatic weapon.

The check-in official looked up. "This woman insists she's on the list, but I can't find her name anywhere," he said, staring at his computer screen again.

Zulu felt slick perspiration pooling on the back of her neck and heard a buzz of interest growing behind her.

"Maybe it's under a different name," the security guard suggested, while eying Zulu with mounting suspicion. In light of the Sporting Murders, he had been instructed by his superiors to bring in for questioning anyone who acted even the slightest out of order.

Then it dawned on her. *Bettina switched envelopes! I'm supposed to be somewhere else.*

"Passport," the guard demanded, stepping forward, into her personal space. "*Now.*"

"Sure," she replied, as casually as she could, adding a helpful smile in stark contrast to the anxiety fizzing up inside her. "Just give me a second."

As Zulu dug in her purse, the guard signaled for two of his fellow officers to join him.

"Here you go," she said, handing over the booklet, while silently cursing Bettina. *As much as I love you, bitch, you're going down for this one.*

* * *

Many miles away, going down, down through the clouds, Bettina sat alone near the back of a private jet, a plush Cessna Citation Mustang rented at premium rate for the flight from Bangkok to Romitsae.

Peering out her window, she couldn't stop smiling.

* * *

Alone at the conference table in the Sanctuary, Tito sat frowning.

"Keep it down in there!" he shouted at some of the others in the next room, who had been at it for hours, glued to their PCs while chattering away about how "Defy or Die" was the greatest computer game ever invented.

Normally, he would have joined in on the fun, even if he had his misgivings that any of them would ever be permitted to accept one of the "D-or-D" Mega Prizes – an all-expenses-paid trip to Istanbul to take part in the Future Games Championship for posting a top score. Listening to them praise the game's enhanced 3-D graphics, which dropped an almost perfect electronic replica of each player into the role of a detective armed with an arsenal of high-tech weaponry to wield against history's most notorious villains, was frustrating enough. While hearing how the ingenious programming, which enabled one's avatar to move across time and space in a quest to discover who was behind a growing number of murders that held a chilling resemblance to those being committed in real life, had made him consider leaving his post more than once.

But he had a job to do.

"Ring, dammit," Tito said to the disposable phone, positioned on the glossy tabletop next to his opened envelope. He thought about taking a quick break and showing those gamers how it was done, but his instructions were clear. He also knew his concentration would be crap, for he couldn't stop thinking about Bettina and how she had left in the middle of the night, without so much as a text.

Why do I even waste my—

Tito's phone suddenly buzzed to life, causing him to jump before answering it.

"*Da.*"

"I did it."

It was a woman's voice, but not Bettina's. It belonged to that silly Paki girl, the one they had been instructed to call Ramona.

"That's not in the script," Tito hissed, while pulling an index card from the envelope and reading the words written on it. "Did you find the store?"

"Yes," said Ramona, "I did."

"Did you return the package?"

"Yes, I did."

"And no one saw you?"

"No, they did not."

"Are you certain?"

"Positive," she said with a giggle. "When you look like me in this part of London, it's not hard blending in, mate."

"Good," said Tito, returning the card to the envelope before ringing off. "Then just don't fuck it up...*mate*."

*   *   *

Ramona shrugged, clicked off her phone, and turned up a long street running parallel to the Grand Union Canal.

"Cheers," she said, passing by a shawarma stand and continuing to put distance between herself and the "store" – a small flat in the immigrant-heavy west London suburb of Southall. In one hand she swung a rainbow array of department store bags, made much lighter by the "package" she had just "returned" – several clay-like bricks of C4 plastic explosive. The recipient was a cousin, newly arrived from Azad Kashmir, and the only one who had seen her entering his grungy, rented space. She made sure of that. She wasn't worried, either, about his talking since he was so pitifully poor and desperately in need of the funds they had promised him – half now, half upon completion.

A pretty good deal, Ramona thought, smiling to herself as she rounded a corner and headed for the Underground. Far more than her cousin could ever hope to make at his day job as one of the hundreds of unskilled laborers toiling inside Wembley Stadium.

* * *

Several Tube stops away, in a no less squalid quarter of London, another woman waited for a rendezvous with a relative. Her name was Fatima, and she sat alone at the only window in a sparse flat on the third floor of a rundown building anticipating her husband's return. She knew he would come home soon, for he always did. But that never made the waiting easier.

Fatima comforted herself in the knowledge that Fahad was a good man. He was a caring husband and an excellent father to their children. She knew his absences were part of a routine, an obligatory religious and social ritual. They were also part of who he was, of why she loved him so much. She also understood how he really had no choice in the matter. He must frequent the mosque every night when the sun fell. She even saw the necessity of his meeting up with the other men for tea after the sermon. He wanted to be accepted, to fit into their neighborhood and these strange new surroundings.

Admitting all of this to herself still didn't make the waiting any easier. It had been one thing when they were back home in Damascus. There, she had friends and sisters to talk with. There, she had others to share in the cooking, the cleaning, the laughing. There, they didn't even want Fahad or the other men around, she thought with a smile.

But here in London, everything was different. Here, she had no friends or sisters or anyone else her own age to talk with. Here, she didn't even know the language. Here, there was no laughter, and it was always cold outside, she thought, her smile fading.

Then she remembered what Fahad had told her. "I will get a good job, *warditi*. Our children will be happy. We are the lucky ones, Fatima, the ones who got out."

Fahad was right. He usually was, and his words gave her strength. They gave her peace and hope as she sat alone by the window, staring through her beautifully innocent eyes, rolling her prayer beads through delicate fingers, waiting for her husband to return.

*   *   *

"It's not a *quota*," the darkly clad member of the Strategic Engagement for Counterterrorism Operations with Results explained, settling into place and assembling his weapon.

"I don't see the difference," his SECTOR associate replied, attaching a silencer to his own high-powered rifle.

They were speaking in Mandarin, one of several languages they discovered they held in common and assumed anyone who might overhear them would have difficulty understanding. Given their hidden position on the rooftop of an abandoned warehouse, just after dusk, it was unlikely they would receive many visitors.

"A quota signifies *quantity*," the first man said, checking his ammunition. "Our paymasters don't care about numbers. Just that one of us starts showing results."

"Okay, that I understand," the other said, raising his assault rifle to his shoulder. "But how do we know this guy is the *right* guy?"

"We don't," answered the first, training his own weapon on a window across the street, a few stories below them. "But that doesn't really concern us. He fits the profile. He's been to the right places, or the *wrong* ones, depending on your point of view. Anyway, someone else will pass by soon to sort out the details. They always do."

"I suppose you're correct," the second agreed, taking aim at nearly the same spot. Through his computer-enabled rifle scope, the woman by the window, a few hundred feet away, might as well have been sitting on the rooftop in front of him. Using some of the best equipment government money could buy, he was able to count the beads moving through her delicate fingers and easily discern the color of her beautifully innocent eyes as he burrowed a bullet right between them.

His partner's shot was equally accurate, driving a searing lance through the trachea of the fallen woman's husband as he entered their apartment and attempted to mouth the name "Fatima."

27

Dusk turned dark as Paupua guided the Land Rover into the valley, along twisting roads that zigzagged down toward the jungle floor and the island's main detention facility.

"Abduh Naggi Penitentiary grabbed international attention a few years ago," Rory explained to Rani, still holding her hand in the back seat, as they made their descent. "When Romitsae's monarchy fell, it came to light that an absence of prison records made it impossible to determine why most of the men detained there were behind bars."

"What happened?" she asked.

"The military junta that assumed power devised a simple solution to the problem," Rory said, as the tualag trees fell off to either side, becoming increasingly faint in silhouette. "They randomly released half the prison body – white collar criminals and rapist-murderers alike – back into the general population to make room for the hundreds of opposition figures, Daemon included, they were preparing to hunt down, lock up, torture, and in many cases put to death."

The road finally flattened out as they reached the base of the valley. The air here was heavy with smoke and the odor of burning wood.

"So, do you think Daemon is out of prison again?"

"I don't see how he could be," Rory answered her. "I'm sure I would have heard about another jailbreak. The last information I had, from a trusted source, claimed that Daemon remained incarcerated for life in Abduh Naggi."

"Damn shame," Seb said, turning to join the conversation from the front seat. "He might be the only person who could sort out this bloody mess."

"Or make it a whole lot worse," Rory replied. "Unless, that is, we get to him first."

"And what makes you think these prison officials are going to let us waltz in there and hold a conversation with public enemy number one, for fook's sake?"

"A whole lot of bullshit," Rory said, with a smile, "and a little bit of cash. Put yourself in their shoes, which I'm guessing are pretty threadbare at this point."

"I'm not sure I follow."

"I plan to tell them I'm prepared to give each of them a nice slice of that $20 million reward being offered for the Sporting Murderers if they give me ten minutes with Daemon."

"And do you have said reward money with you?"

"Enough to make them think I'm not completely full of it," Rory said. "Mrs. Markham is fronting me, and with annual income on this island even in the best of times being around a thousand dollars, I'm hoping it won't take much."

"And, if you *do* get to see Daemon, what then?" Seb asked.

"I'm going to find out what, if anything, he knows about these Sporting Murders," Rory said, "and then I'm going to play to his humanity. It's a long-shot, I realize. But before the tragic events that shattered his life, he was essentially a man of peace. Just look at his early writings. Daemon, or Dr. Jekriél, as he was still called back then, dedicated his research to finding ways to bring democratic change to this island without resorting to armed combat. His groundbreaking dissertation centered on the notion that long-simmering tensions between Romitsae's disparate ethnic groups were resolvable through traditional, non-violent dispute resolution mechanisms, such as forgiving past transgressions. Success to him resided in one party taking the first step."

"And you think if we remind him of all this, he'll just turn the other cheek, call off the war he has been dying to wage against those who gunned down his men and massacred his family?"

Seb looked doubtful as they rounded a corner and left the forest fires simmering behind them. Paupua slowed the Land Rover, finding it difficult to maneuver on the unpaved, unlit roadway, while all around them they heard the metallic *whirr* of cicadas high in the trees, like alien voices from a science fiction movie.

"I know it's a stretch," Rory said, "but if you put yourself in Daemon's shoes, you would have to see that there can be no positive result from waging an all-out civil war. The more mercenaries he rounds up, the more militia forces the government recruits. Such escalation can only lead to a bloodbath, leaving this tiny nation vulnerable to attack and even takeover from neighboring states. Then they're all screwed. Daemon's a wise man who should be able to see the bigger picture. We just need to convince him that there are other ways to act and that there are people out here, especially now, with this Second Message, who are willing to help, provided he calls for a path to peace."

"And what if you can't convince him?" Rani asked.

"Then we move directly to Plan B," Rory said.

"What's *Plan B*?"

"We improvise."

Paupua suddenly slammed on the brakes, throwing them all forward.

"What the hell!" Rory cursed, checking to make sure Rani was okay.

"Yes, fine," she said. "Thanks."

"Quiet," Seb cautioned, pointing straight ahead. "We have company."

Paupua cut the engine, and Rory strained to see out his side of the Land Rover. Through a tangle of trees, on a slightly elevated ridge not more than a hundred yards away, he spotted high beams from several trucks. There must have been a dozen or more of them idling there, pointing in the direction away from the Land Rover. Each flatbed carried a pack of men, and even from this distance he could see they were armed.

"Militia," Rory said in a hushed voice to Rani.

"Are you sure?" she whispered back.

"Fairly, these islanders don't own a lot of trucks."

"Where are they're going?"

"I don't know, but according to the map, the only rebel stronghold on this side of the island is a small village not far from here called Anailam. My guess is that's their destination."

Distant shouts could be heard, followed by a rumble of engines, as the convoy started to move.

"And where are we going?" Rani asked.

"Fortunately," Rory answered, "somewhere else."

A few minutes later, the Land Rover found hard pavement again yet still no street lights. The forest receded here, the cicadas stopped screaming, and a nervy silence ensued, which Seb felt compelled to break.

"I don't like this."

"Afraid of the dark?" Rory teased.

"Hardly. It's just by my calculations we should be able to see the prison by now. It should be all lit up with floodlights."

"So, what are you thinking?"

"Either we're lost, or something is really wrong here."

"We're not lost," said Rani.

"How do you know?" Seb asked.

"Look over there."

She pointed out her side of the vehicle to where a series of large, squat buildings stood faintly visible through the dark. As they drew nearer, a mesh of razor wire could be seen atop a fence running the length of the compound. A sign in both English and the local script told them they had arrived at Romitsae's Abduh Naggi Penitentiary.

"I told you I didn't like this," Seb repeated, motioning to Paupua to bring the Land Rover to a stop just beyond the gated entrance.

"Where's the security?" Rory asked, catching sight of the empty guard house.

"And why is this gate open?" Seb signaled to Paupua to turn them around, but Rory intervened.

"Maybe we should go in."

"And maybe we should get the hell out of here," Seb said. "Daemon can't be in there. And even if he is, he's sure to be dead. Just look at this place, it's completely deserted."

Rory thought a moment. "I suppose you're right. And if Daemon is not in there but still alive, then this whole island could go up in flames any minute now."

Seb motioned again, but this time Rani interjected, grabbing hold of Paupua's arm, and startling the three men.

"We've come this far," she said. "Let's at least verify if he's in there or not. I think we should go into the prison tonight, not wait."

"And I think we should fooking flee."

"And I think I agree," Rory said. "The longer we sit here, the more dangerous things could get. I've got to side with Seb on this one. If anyone is in there, it's unlikely they're still alive and—"

That's when the first shriek cut through the night.

28

On the shores of the Bosphorus, not far from the Atmeydani, or Byzantine Hippodrome, where legend holds the fate of an emperor rested on the cracking whip of his champion charioteer, stands the imperial Çirağan Palace Hotel. Appraised at more than $1 billion, this sprawling property, which once served as the grand residence and final resting spot of Sultan Abdülaziz, is decidedly not for sale. The Çirağan Palace remains the most luxurious resort on Istanbul's fabled river and, for the time being, its proprietors are making too much profit renting out the regal estates and executive chalets to an elite clientele who number among them princes, prizefighters, and other privileged playboys.

Withered and old, Mills Greenblatt hardly measured up physically, although in some circles he was considered royalty. Standing naked and alone in the master bathroom of one of Çirağan's penthouse suites, he cast an indifferent eye on the body of water surging below him, cleaving its formidable path through the continents of Europe and Asia. The billionaire cyber king was too preoccupied to appreciate the view. Spread across the Carrara marble countertop like a

pharmacist's bounty lay all the paraphernalia necessary to accomplish the job at hand: migraine strength
ibuprofen, anti-inflammatory salve, mentholated rubbing oil, medicated mouth wash, hydrogen peroxide,
denture crème, fine French cologne, and lastly, but far
most importantly, a tall glass of water and a blue tablet
of Viagra.

The latter item he reached for first. A compulsory
inconvenience, it did require a certain amount of lead
time (though, if truth be told, the ramp up of anticipation
often rivaled the end result.) Chasing the wonder drug
with a gulp of water, Mills took stock of his liver-spotted
face and saggy physique. Unlike many of his business
associates, the mirror never lied.

"You're one ugly little fucker," he told his reflection.

It really didn't matter. For far less than he made in an
hour, he could have just about anything he wanted: one
girl, two, a bed full of women, grown men, teenage boys,
or any combination of the above. They were all there
for the taking. And, at one time or another in his fabu-
lously successful and fundamentally perverted life, Mills
had sampled them all. Prostitutes, princesses, party girls,
schoolgirls, secretaries, shrinks, masseuses, masseurs,
maids, professional colleagues, their wives, daughters,
even a few of their sons. He had made them perform
filthy acts in his honor, degrading them for his personal
pleasure, and never giving a moment's consideration to
the moral consequences of his actions. *Why should I?* No

one put a gun to their heads. No one made them do any-thing they weren't ultimately willing to do.

"We all have a price," Mills said to his reflection, "our own special needs."

Trite as it sounded, there did remain one desire his endless stream of cash could not procure. *Love?* Screw that. Roses and kittens he had no time for; he was too busy making money. *Affection?* What was the point when it always melted away or wound up being nothing more than pity in his case?

No, what he was talking about was something else al-together. Something he had long dreamed for yet rarely achieved – actually, never achieved, if he and the mir-ror were being completely honest. But it was something waiting for him now, waiting for him on the other side of the bathroom door.

A partner who was willing.

Well, at least as far as their verbal contract stipulated she must be. Although, there did seem to be a look in those dark eyes that suggested this one might want him for reasons non-fiduciary. No talk of money had left those perfectly sumptuous lips over dinner, no discussion of currency proffered in that singsong voice during cof-fee and cognac.

Grimacing as he massaged fire oil into his nearly useless spine, Mills took another accounting of himself in the mirror. Contrary to most of his game-playing customers, he harbored no illusions. Vast fortune aside, his place in the copulating food chain didn't rank much higher than a minnow or a gnat. He knew he was sexual plankton. And, again, he really didn't care.

With greasy fingers he shut off the lights and opened the door. Hobbling forward, he felt that glorious rise beneath his belly and smiled a smile of utter contentment. For there she was, on the bed, waiting for him, completely naked.

Seeing her there, a lifetime of physical humiliation faded into oblivion as he realized just seconds from now he, Mills Greenblatt, would be fucking the hell out of Zulu.

In the end, they both had their own special needs.

*   *   *

Bettina exited Romitsae Inter-Island Airport and stood waiting for the car and driver she had just hired inside. A few minutes later, a drab gray minivan rolled up to the curb beside her.

"Do you speak English?" Bettina asked the man behind the wheel. He was a gaunt creature with unnaturally red lips and a nest of dark, tangled dreadlocks.

As a rule, the driver, who called himself Bagdana, shook his head "no" to this question, eager to hold whatever advantage he could over his foreign passengers. But this girl was alone, she was beautiful, and, as far as he could tell, she posed no danger to him whatsoever.

"Just a little," he lied.

"Good," she said, before walking around the front of his minivan and climbing into the seat next to him. "Then take me to the action."

Beautiful and easy, thought Bagdana, with a lick of his *daeng*-stained lips, as he pulled away from the curb. "I take you downtown, lady, show you good time."

"Not that action," Bettina said, handing him a scrap of paper and a wad of banknotes. "Military action."

29

"What the *hell* was that?" Rory asked, as the shriek faded into the night.

"I have no idea, but it can't be good," Seb answered.

"Look at Paupua," Rani said. "He's frozen with fear."

"There may be some truth to those island superstitions, after all," Seb said.

Rory turned to Rani. "Do you still think we should go in there?"

She nodded. "I do."

"And will you be joining us?"

"If my only option is waiting out here with him," she said, looking at Paupua, who sat stone-faced and rigid behind the wheel of the Land Rover, "then yes, I'm joining you."

The three of them climbed from the vehicle, leaving their driver behind, and started across the parking lot toward Abduh Naggi Penitentiary, cast in gloaming darkness. Fortunately, the Land Rover came with a pair of flashlights, which Rory and Seb trained on the open gate as they approached, Rani sandwiched in between them.

"Do you think we'll see him again?" she asked, as they passed by the empty guardhouse.

"Paupua? I hope so," Rory said. "Although, he did look pretty wigged out."

"I *know* so," said Seb. "He seems a loyal chap, plus I haven't paid him a quid yet for his services."

Rory had chuckled then, but fell silent now as they neared the prison entrance. He focused his beam of light across the stone walls and fortified bunkers leading to the front door. Again, this barrier, like the main gate, stood open. If not for the scream they heard, he might have figured the place to be abandoned.

As they passed through the doorway, Rory was starting to consider that possibility again, when they were greeted by a second cry. Low and haunting, it sounded more like a wail than a scream, but no less unsettling.

"I don't like this," Seb said to Rory. "Maybe Rani *should* stay back in the car."

"We already had that discussion and did you not see the look on our driver's face? That guy, Paupua, was paralyzed with fear, practically catatonic. If something happens, I don't trust him to defend himself, let alone Rani. I think it's better not to get separated. She's safer with us."

"I'm right here and I'm not leaving," Rani said, moving closer to Rory. Without thinking, he placed his arm around her shoulder and she leaned in next to his body.

"All right then," Seb said, stepping past them and handing Rani his flashlight. "I'm going in first and I'm going in with *this*."

Rory watched as his friend drew a handgun from the pocket of his jacket. Nickel plated, with a pearl grip, the six-shooter looked like a prop off the set of an old Western. "How the hell did you get *that* onto the island?"

"You've got your ways, I've got mine," Seb said, cocking the pistol. "It still has five bullets."

"Nice," Rory said. "Just don't trip this time. I value my ass."

"Funny," Seb scoffed. "Now stay behind me and let's get this bloody thing over with."

At first the going was slow, for there were no lights in the prison and no way to determine which direction to take. Rory and Rani kept the flashlight beams aimed at the stone floor to illuminate their path without attracting too much attention, while Seb shuffled forward, his loaded weapon out in front of him. As their eyes began to adjust, Rory noticed how they were moving along a corridor flanked on either side by low walls made of rough brick. Punctuating these walls every four or five paces were steels doors, the majority of which were closed. Occasionally, a door stood open and Rory was able to glimpse inside, shining his light quickly as they passed. The cells looked cramped and dingy, with slabs of concrete for beds and simple holes bored in the ground for toilets. Nothing more: no desks, no chairs, no windows.

"What's that smell?" Rani whispered.

"Better not to ask," Rory answered.

"*Shh*," Seb said, pulling up suddenly and turning his head to one side. Another wail could be heard, soft at first but growing louder and coming from somewhere up ahead, off to their left. Seb pointed his gun in that direction before advancing again, with Rory and Rani trailing close behind.

Along the corridor they walked in silence. Rory placed his arm around Rani's shoulder again and this time he felt her trembling, perhaps from the cold air permeating this place but more likely out of fear.

I'm not thrilled about this either, he thought, still wondering if he had made a mistake bringing her into all of this, when another cry echoed off the walls. This time it sounded like it came from the other side, to their right. The three of them exchanged puzzled looks before continuing up the corridor.

Soon they reached the end of the hallway and stopped in front of an open area, which looked to be some sort of atrium. The space here was circular, with a high, domed ceiling, yet still sparsely lit. A set of passageways, similar to the one they had just taken, branched off in several directions.

"Helps explain the mystery," Seb said.

"Right, but which way do we go?" Rory asked.

"I have no fooking idea. I still think we get the hell out of here and come back tomorrow with a better plan."

Just then another scream lashed the air, from somewhere up ahead, off to their left.

"I guess we go left," Rory said, as another wail greeted them from the opposite side.

"Or right," Seb suggested.

"We go straight," Rani said with a certainty that surprised the two men. "Not to the left or right, we go straight."

"How do you know that?" Seb asked.

"I guess you would call it *women's intuition*," she answered, before pushing past them into the center of the circle.

"Can't argue with that," Rory said with a shrug, following after her.

Seb remained in place a moment longer, muttering to himself. "Made for each other, they are…both fooking crazy."

Across the circle, the atrium opened onto another passageway, long and dark and much like the one they had just traversed. Seb caught up and moved back into the lead, his pistol out in front of him. Moving slowly, with his other arm held back, he kept Rory and Rani a pace or so behind. Again, Rory noted the prison cells to either side, but here all the doors were firmly shut. He also noticed how there were no more screams coming down this hall. *Maybe Rani's intuition is off*, he thought, and was about to say as much, when Seb suddenly stopped and Rory nearly crashed into him.

"What is it?"

The big man held a finger to his lips and pointed his gun straight ahead.

"Thought I heard something," he whispered to Rory.

"Another scream?"

"No, softer. More like a moan."

"Where? At the end of the hall?"

"I think so. I don't know. Listen."

They did but couldn't hear anything.

"Are you sure?" Rani asked.

"No," Seb replied. "At this point, I'm not sure of anything."

Rory peered down the hall. "I think we should go investigate."

"Are you serious?" Seb said.

"There's a $20 million reward."

"Not down there, there isn't."

"Information *leading* to the capture or killing of the Sporting Murderers…"

"Who, again, are not down there," Seb said, looking at Rory. "If the money means so much to you, why don't *you* go investigate?"

"You've got the gun."

Seb stared at his friend and sighed. "All right, sixty-forty split. Not a penny less."

"Done," Rory said with a smile. "And I would have given you fifty."

Seb shook his head before starting off again toward the door at that end of the hall. Rory and Rani followed, dimming their flashlights and nearly throwing the corridor into total blackness. The air here stunk of sweat and urine.

Seb kept moving, slowly, with one hand on the wall to steady himself in the dark. Rory remained a step or so back. Rani pressed in tightly behind him. At last they reached the door, which turned out to be larger than those fronting the cells behind them. It also had a handle. Again, Seb put a finger to his lips, and Rory stepped beside him to listen. From within, strange sounds could be heard: a muffled grunt, a muted cry, the scraping of metal against metal.

Seb stared at Rory, who looked back quizzically. They both turned to Rani, who bit her lip and shooed them on.

So Rory grabbed hold of the handle, while Seb raised his pistol, and Rani held her breath.

Seb nodded once.

Rory threw open the door.

And another howl ripped through the air.

As Rory stumbled into the room, he was met by several surprises all at once: the size of the space, far larger than he had expected; the number of people in it, more than two dozen men and young women, even some teenage girls; and, most disturbingly, the activities taking place.

Immediately in front of him stood six men in loose-fitting shirts, simple tunics, naked from the waist down, with large, muscular legs shaded brown and bare feet planted on the stone floor. In front of each man stood a young woman, darker of skin, and completely naked. The women weren't standing so much as hunkering, their arms stretched out in front of them, grasping at metal rails, like ballerinas in a warm-up exercise. Only, these dancers were chained, bound together by heavy bracelets, pegged to the wall, just as they were being pegged from behind. They couldn't get away, even if they had wanted to, and judging from the looks of raw fear and misery on their faces, that was exactly what they wanted to do.

Further on, Rory saw a row of cages, like one might use to hold small dogs. Only, these occupants weren't canine. They were more of the naked, dark-skinned young women and girls, crammed into little boxes, like too many pups in a kennel. Several of them had been beaten, their faces, arms, and legs speckled with bruises and lacerations. One girl, who looked to be no more than 12 or 13, covered her tiny breasts with bloody hands as she stared straight at Rory through eyes swollen nearly closed. Behind her, another woman lay slumped in a corner. She may have been dead.

Next to the cages, Rory saw a man with a gun in one hand and a long stick in the other. He peered past Rory toward Seb, who had his own weapon raised but wasn't sure where he should point it. On the opposite side of the room, another man, dressed in a filthy white jacket, cradled a clipboard, upon which he seemed to be taking notes, perhaps recording the tenor and tone of each grunt, groan, and scream pouring from the women in the room.

And then that was that. A few seconds of utter bewilderment before Rory's mind snapped into place, comprehension hitting him like cold water.

Rape camp!

Rory had heard of this horror before, read about it in journals. It had been going on for centuries, since man first began conquering man. Some of the modern cases were well known: the Nanking Massacre of the 1930s, called the Rape of Nanking, in which hordes of Japanese soldiers may have raped and sodomized hundreds if not thousands of Chinese women and girls; Hitler's "experiments" in the death camps; the savage impregnation of scores of Bosniak women and girls by Arkan's Tigers and others during the Yugoslav War; and, more recently, ISIL's sexual enslavement, gang rapes, and other abuses meted out on those captured in Syria and Iraq.

But never did Rory imagine he would see such depravity up close and personal.

And then several things happened at once.

A blur of motion.

A thump on his shoulder.

Seb's voice loud in his ear.

"*She's gone!*"

"Who?"

"*Rani!*"

And now Rory was running, running out the door, running down the hall, flying over hard stone as fast as his legs would carry him.

Rory burst through the front door of the prison and into chill night air. His chest heaved, his heart pounded, and it felt like someone had plunged a knife deep into his hamstring. He had no idea how he found his way out and didn't care. He only had one thought on his mind.

"*Rani!*"

He frantically scanned the courtyard and was about to shout again, when he spotted her several feet away, standing in the dark, doubled over, hands on her thighs, rocking back and forth. He hurried over, reaching out, but she jerked away.

"Don't."

"Okay." He wanted so badly to touch her, to hold her, to gather her up in his arms and let her know she was safe now. But he respected her wishes. *Put yourself in her shoes.*

"I'm sorry," Rani said, still turned away from him.

"Don't apologize." *She must be in shock.*

"I didn't know."

"How could you?" he said, not understanding what she meant but trying to comfort her with his words. "None of us knew what to expect in there."

She shook her head, wanting to say something else, but she was crying too hard, her voice lost in heavy sobs. At last, she looked up at him, and her face was a mess. Strands of hair had fallen out of place, while tears ran down her cheeks, smearing her mascara. At that moment, he thought, she never looked more beautiful, more in need of loving.

Then, just like that, Rani was in his arms, saying, "I didn't know…I didn't know…"

"Of course you didn't," Rory said, holding her against his chest, stroking her hair, wishing they could stay this way forever.

"Better…move…"

It was Seb. He had caught up and was visibly out of breath.

"You…were…right," he said, running by them.

"About what?" Rory asked, still holding onto Rani.

"Paupua…gone."

Rory looked to where Seb was pointing, past the guard shack, toward the main gate of the prison. The door stood open, but the parking lot was empty.

"What do we do now?" Rory called after Seb.

"Keep moving…unless you want…to see them… again."

"I don't," Rani said, tugging at Rory's hand.

"Me neither," he agreed, hurrying after both of them.

30

At the conference table in the Sanctuary, Tito sat alone. The younger members in the next room had finally taken a break from their relentless pursuit of "Defy or Die" top scores, today being the last day to qualify for the Future Games showdown in Istanbul, even if he still doubted any of them would ever be allowed to go. He hadn't seen Confucius now for several hours and wondered where the man disappeared to all the time. Still no call or text from Bettina, either, which really sucked.

Tito buried his face in a paperback, hoping the fantasy novel would help him forget about her. *Do I even have a chance? She's so freaking beautiful, but she doesn't see me anymore. Not like before, when we used to talk or listen to music or...and then she went and shaved her head...and then she killed Lazarius...and now she's become such a...*

He closed the book and stared at his phone, wrongly assuming Bettina to be somewhere in Istanbul. He didn't know she had switched envelopes with Zulu, who, to his mind, also had changed since the murders. *She's too happy all the time, while Confucius is angry or absent, and Bettina, well, she just might be losing her—*

Tito's phone suddenly buzzed to life, and he grabbed it.

"*Da?*"

"We may have a problem." Again, the Paki girl, Ramona.

"What problem?"

"Well, he can do it, but maybe not during the play."

"What are you talking about? You know this is an open line."

"Of course I do," Ramona said. "But these phones are *disposable*."

"So are you."

A pause followed before Ramona continued, much less cheerily. "I said he, my, you know, he can do it, he says, but probably not during the actual play."

"What does that matter?" Tito snapped, although privately he thought it would be pretty cool if it did happen while the game was going on. "Just don't fuck it up."

And with that sage advice, Tito terminated the call before Ramona could say another word. He then constructed a short text, which he sent to Confucius, wherever he was:

Game time

Task completed, Tito put down his phone and returned to the novel. But it was no use. He just couldn't get Bettina out of his head.

"I ought to take the next plane to Turkey," he said out loud. "Give her one hell of a shock."

But he knew he wouldn't. And not pursuing this course of action had less to do with how Confucius would react, should he disobey orders and leave his post, than with his own fear of what he might find waiting for him there in Istanbul. Probably catch her in bed, ankles to her ears, enjoying the screw of her life from some fat, sleazy Turk.

He couldn't have been much further from the truth.

*   *   *

Bettina squatted by the side of the road. Normally, she would have preferred more concealment for the operation at hand. But there was no time for that now, plus it was fairly dark outside, and there was really nothing normal about what she was trying to do.

They had been driving for hours, away from the airport, high into the hills on the far side of the island. Her driver had introduced himself as Bagdana and then promptly shut up, per her instruction. He soon grew tired and irritable as the buzz from the *daeng* he had been chewing wore off.

To keep awake, Bagdana let his mind wander, eventually coming around to a devilish plan. *This bitch is beautiful*, he thought, giving Bettina a long look. *I could pull over and hump her white ass. Who's going to know? Hump her and dump her right here in the forest.*

Bagdana watched as Bettina stared straight ahead, her face set in place, striking and emotionless, like some rare stone. *I'm going to enjoy you*, he thought, while steering the minivan along a narrow cliff ledge. No fear from the girl. Like most Western women, she was foolishly optimistic. *I'm going to enjoy you, and then I'm going to dump you.*

Bringing his eyes back to the road, Bagdana remembered those human rights activists from America. They had been optimistic, too, he was told, right up until they were dragged from their car, beaten, raped – even the men – and left for dead in the woods, not far from here.

Bagdana swerved to avoid a fallen tree, yet still nothing from the girl. Not a peep. The silence was beginning to gnaw at him. They hadn't exchanged words for over an hour, and these crazy ideas dancing in his head were starting to crystallize.

"Pull over." Her command startled him.

"What?"

"I said pull over. *Now*. I won't be long."

The tree she chose provided scant cover and, out of respect, Bagdana shut his eyes. Even he had limits. They weren't closed long before he began nodding off, weary from the drugs and all that silent driving. The last thing he remembered was a pinprick sensation on his neck.

Straightening up, Bettina admired her work. On the ground by her feet sat her driver in the dirt. His arms hung by his sides, shoulders slung back and slim body supported by the trunk of a tree. His eyes were closed, as was his mouth, stained red at the corners. The look on his face seemed natural, almost serene.

"*Wunderbar*," she said with a smile, positive anyone passing by would think he was just resting there. Unless, that is, they actually took the time to stop, move in a little closer, and notice how the top of the man's head had been completely shorn off.

Dropping his bloody dreadlocks into her leather satchel, Bettina wiped her blade clean on the front of the dead man's shirt. She then climbed back into the mini-van and continued on her journey across Romitsae.

31

It took over two hours, hiking through the hills, changing course more than once to be safe, before they found a suitable spot to rest for the night.

"We should really push on," said Seb, looking over his shoulder, as he had done several times since leaving the prison behind. "We can't be sure we're not being followed."

"We haven't seen anyone since we left the prison," Rory replied. "Honestly, my hamstring is killing me, we're all exhausted, and there's no way to know how far it is to the next village."

"I agree," said Rani, stifling a yawn. "Let's stop here. Please."

"All right," said Seb, out-voted. "At least this place looks deserted and backs onto water, giving us some protection. But we leave first thing in the morning, no debate."

None was given.

The site they chose was some sort of vacation spot, this part of the island having served as a refuge for backpacking eco-tourists before the situation on Romitsae deteriorated. A series of thatched bungalows lined a promontory overlooking the sea. To reach these lodgings, they came first upon a reception building constructed of stone and topped with Spanish tile. Entering, they found an abandoned lobby decorated with worn teak furniture grouped around a small television set. "Electricity," Rory observed, while Rani flopped onto one of the couches and almost immediately dozed off to sleep.

Seb called out, but no one answered. He then stepped behind the counter and picked up the phone. "Reception is good, too. Should we try calling Paupua?"

Rory laughed. "I think we've seen the last of that guy."

"And our luggage, too," Seb said, hunting around until he found a stash of bottled water, two of which he handed Rory. "You take the bungalows. I'll stay here and keep a lookout, in case anyone shows up."

"I think we should all stick together."

"Nonsense," said Seb, motioning toward Rani. "She needs sleep and I'll be fine on my own." He placed his revolver on the countertop before spotting a small refrigerator. Much to his surprise, there were two cans of beer inside. "Better than fine," he said, holding up the liquid trophies. "Want one?"

"All yours," Rory said, shaking his head. "Although, if you happen to find a steak and some garlic mashed potatoes in there, let me know."

"Will do," Seb laughed. "Now, go take care of Sleeping Beauty."

"Thanks, my friend," Rory said with a nod. "And good night."

Back outside, he walked a bleary-eyed Rani toward the nearest set of bungalows. She was half asleep and wobbling down the path, so he placed an arm around her shoulder. This time, unlike outside the prison, she did not object to being touched. The grass ran high here, overhanging much of the trail, and Rory needed his flashlight to guide their way. Neither of them spoke, listening instead to the night sounds – a stir of insects, a croaking bullfrog, the splash of water against the shoreline further on.

They soon reached the first bungalow, which turned out to be larger and more modern than Rory had expected.

"You take this one," he said, pointing with his light. "Unless—"

She looked up at him. "I don't think—"

"—that is you want—"

"—given what happened—"

"—some company—"

"—tonight."

They said the last word together and laughed.

"Stupid idea," Rory said, releasing his arm from her shoulder.

"No, it wasn't," Rani replied. "It was sweet, just not tonight."

Rory thought a second. "Then are you saying perhaps *another* night?"

"Perhaps," she said with a smile.

"Is it because I lied to you?" Rory asked. "You know, about my reason for coming here, the twenty million dollars."

"No, Rory, that's who you are," she said, smiling again to let him know she wasn't upset. "It's just, well, I'm still a little shaken by what we saw back there and I'd rather be alone. You know, get some sleep."

"Sure," he said. "Sleep is good. Here, take this." He handed Rani his flashlight, she having lost hers during the mad run through the prison.

"Thanks," she said, squeezing his hand before accepting the light.

"Try not using it too much," he added, while opening the door for her with a numbered key from the reception desk. "We don't want to attract attention, but should you need it, you've got it. And, should you need me, for anything, I'll be in the next bungalow over."

"Got it," Rani said, holding up the flashlight. In her other hand, she held her cell phone. "I need to make a call, if I can, and then it's straight to bed."

"Your family?"

"Huh?" A strange look came over her face, as if she had said more than she intended.

"The call, is it to your family?"

"My family," she said, still looking somewhat distressed.

Rory guessed at the meaning. "Man, I'd hate to meet your father."

"Why?" she asked. "He's a nice man."

"I'm sure he is, and he'd probably put a fist right through my face, given everything I've put you through on this trip."

"No, he wouldn't," Rani laughed, easing the tension before stepping through the doorway, only to turn back briefly. "I think he'd like you."

It was a relatively short distance to the next bungalow, yet with no flashlight it took Rory some effort getting there. He tripped once, sending a shriek of pain up his wounded hamstring, causing him to hobble the rest of the way. Upon entering the bungalow, he tried the overhead light but it was out. He felt his way to the bed and found a lamp, which actually worked, casting the room in a soft red hue.

"Romantic," he said, taking a look around and wondering if he had chosen the honeymoon suite. "Too bad I've got no bride."

The room was spacious enough to hold a queen-size bed encased in mosquito netting, a small desk and chair, a mini-fridge, and a flat-screen TV. There was even a separate bathroom, which he limped over to now, hoping beyond hope to find a shower there. No luck, but the water in the sink ran, so he splashed some of it on his face, only to discover there were no towels.

"Some honeymoon."

Returning to the main room, Rory opened the fridge. No steak or mashed potatoes, but he did find a packet of cheese and crackers, which he devoured, sitting on the bed and washing them down with one of the bottles of water Seb had given him. He realized then that he had forgotten to give Rani her bottle. He considered returning to her bungalow, before remembering what she had said: *Just not tonight.* Not wanting to look desperate, he gave up on the idea, hoping she had a mini-fridge in her room, stocked with refreshments.

Still sitting on the bed, Rory kicked off his shoes and stripped down to his boxers before unzipping the mosquito net and climbing in. He had kept up the antimalarial regimen started in Nigeria, so wasn't overly concerned. The mesh cocoon provided additional protection, enabling him to lie above the covers without fear of infection. He contemplated watching TV, seeing if there were any new developments in the Sporting Murders, but noticed the remote on the desk outside the netting. He was suddenly struck by a wave of fatigue, which made the effort to retrieve it seem difficult and unnecessary. He could always catch up on the news in the morning.

Sinking into his pillow, Rory closed his eyes and listened to the water slap against the shore below, his mind replaying some of the day's events as he drifted off to sleep.

What a night...the prison screams...the rape camp...no sign of Daemon...no closer to stopping a war...Paupua gone... walking through the hills...finding this place...Rani in his arms...she didn't know...just not tonight...what didn't she know?

The next thing Rory knew, there was warm breath on his face. *I must be dreaming.*

But everything was real – the pain in his leg, the cool night air, the firm pressure on his midsection as Rani lowered her naked body there.

"*Changed my mind,*" she whispered.

Still on his back, he reached for her now and felt smooth skin, bare shoulders and arms, perfect breasts, as she leaned in to kiss him, her wet tongue finding his in the dark.

Eyes closed, Rory heard the waves pound the shore and felt himself coming engulfed in a sea of warmth he never knew existed.

32

This is your home now…

A tall boy, older, translated. He was from another tribe.
You will live here for some time…

Up on the platform a man spoke in a strange language.
Soviet, someone said. He spoke through a long metal hat,
which made his voice loud and clear across the field.

You will eat here, sleep here, learn to fight here…

There was a hundred of them, maybe more. They stood in
tight packs on the dusty stretch of earth. Some had dark skin.
Others light. Most were around his age. Young.

You will report to your group leader, no one else…

They arrived in the middle of the night, huddled together
in an airplane, his first flight. No one spoke during the trip.
The plane was loud. They were scared.

Your group leader will speak to you. You do not speak to
him…

Bright lights hung from trees with no leaves. The boy
next to him was from his village. The others were strangers.

You will rise at dawn, do your training…

A man like the one up on stage stopped by to hand out
bundles. He did not speak. Each bundle contained a shirt, a
pair of pants, some sturdy leather boots.

Now you will go to the barracks…

They walked together, a dozen boys. He counted. They followed their group leader toward a row of wooden buildings. The lights on the trees went out, leaving them in darkness.

Behind him, he felt a boy take his arm, lightly, no threat. He did the same, reaching forward, grasping the arm of the boy in front of him.

Connected this way, they walked through the dirt in the dark to a wooden building that would serve for the next three months as his home, his refuge, his only sanctuary.

* * *

Rory woke and knew something was wrong. *What time is it?*

There was light in the room, yet Seb had wanted to leave before dawn. It must be well after sunrise.

Rani was gone, too. Her side of the bed was empty, but the television was on. It hadn't been that way, he knew, while she was still there – *while they were making love* – and he couldn't imagine why she would have turned it on before leaving the bungalow.

Sitting up, he rubbed sleep from his eyes and stared through the mosquito net at the TV. The volume was low, but it didn't take words to tell him what had happened. The image on the screen was jarring: a wide shot of London's famous skyline, with Big Ben, St. Paul's Cathedral, and Westminster Palace all in their postcard positions on what would have been an otherwise lovely spring evening if not for the fist of black smoke punching through the sky.

Someone had bombed Wembley!

The camera caught a scene of chaos outside the stadium. There were people running and policemen shouting and ambulances with lights whirling through ash and debris, as funnels of smoke billowed from a tangled wreckage of glass and concrete on one side of the vast structure. Through the haze, a platoon of firefighters in maroon-and-yellow uniforms could be seen launching sheets of water through bulging hoses at the violent flames.

"*Damn...*"

Rory searched for the remote but it was no longer on the desk. It was inside the mosquito net, on the bed beside him.

What the hell is going on? Why would Rani put it here? Where is she now? And where is Seb? Does he know this happened?

Rory grabbed the remote and increased the volume, just as the camera cut to a makeshift medical station, not far from the carnage. An attractive reporter stood to one side of the screen, beyond a flurry of paramedics, who were doing their best to patch up the wounded. As they tended to the patients, several of whom sat or lay bloody on the ground, the reporter held up a microphone to the face of a giant. The man was huge, with dark skin and hair, powerful thighs sprouting from taut black shorts, and bulging arms bound in a dark polo shirt. A bandage wrapped around his head was stained bright red.

Rory was just putting the pieces together when the words scrolling across the bottom of the screen filled in any missing blanks:

Wembley bombed, several Black Boas dead

So that was it, he realized with a shudder. The stakes had been raised again. The Sporting Murderers had struck once more, this time their target being an entire team. And not any team, but one of the world's top rugby sides, the Black Boas of Samoa, along with many of their supporters.

Rory focused on the interview and what one of the surviving Samoan players was saying.

"—as we were coming down the tunnel to warm up. Then we heard that first explosion. *Boom!* And before we could move there came another and another. *Boom-boom!*"

"And what do you make of the message?" the reporter asked, holding her microphone up again.

"What message?"

"On the big screen, after the explosion…"

"I don't know. I was flat on my back, and then I got out of there, fast. What did it say?"

As the reporter answered, the camera cut back inside Wembley, where a shot of the jumbo screen in the stadium revealed the following:

**STOP ALL WARS
YOU'VE BEEN WARNED!**

And then it hit Rory. It him with such power his head hurt and he dropped the remote. Several years earlier, he had agreed to submit himself to a psychological assessment conducted by a renowned behavioral scientist at Georgetown University Hospital trying to better understand Rory's abilities. The session came about after one of his more celebrated cases, in which Rory returned an abducted child to her mother, a cosmetics heiress, while identifying the kidnapper as the woman's ex-husband and the child's own father. It was the first time Rory had used his talent of putting himself in another's shoes for large financial gain, and others took notice. "It was literally his shoes," Rory told an appreciative district attorney during the trial. "When I first met the man to discuss hostage negotiation tactics, I couldn't help noticing his brand of footwear, extremely expensive and in complete contrast to his drab surroundings, his cheap car and rented apartment. It got me wondering how a man accustomed to such a lavish lifestyle could maintain it after his rich wife cut him off in the divorce. Kidnapping their child for ransom made my shortlist."

When the trial ended, the prosecutor thanked Rory and mentioned the psychiatrist, who then led him through a battery of tests – IQ, Woodcock-Johnson, Stanford-Binet, Myers-Briggs, Rorschach inkblot – before striking upon a line of questioning found particularly interesting to both men. "Have you ever experienced an *epiphany*," the doctor asked, "you know, one of those sudden, intuitive leaps, when the stars of perception align – one finds religion, loses it, accepts his own mortality – so rare yet so potentially life-changing?"

Rory thought a moment, taking so long to answer that the psychiatrist was about to repeat the question, when, at last, he nodded and smiled. "Yes, doctor, all the time."

And he was having one again now.

I didn't know.
I was clearly ahead of you.
To Romitsae, to stop a war, partner.
I think we should go into the prison tonight, not wait.
We go straight, not to the left or right, we go straight.
There's no gain without risk…you must keep fighting.
I guess you might call it women's intuition.
Stop all wars, you've been warned!
You're in big trouble now!!

"No!" Rory screamed. "It's not possible."

But he knew it was, as he tore back the mosquito netting. Rani's words were there in his head, all the pieces falling into place, as he threw on his clothes. She had been guiding him from the start, showing him where to go, telling him what to do, always one step ahead, he realized, as he stepped over his shoes and charged out of the bungalow.

Rory knew exactly what was happening, he just wasn't sure why.

Racing barefoot through the grass, he took no notice of his hamstring, a spike of adrenaline negating the pain. He thought briefly of Seb, wondering where his friend was and what Rani might be capable of. *But that isn't who she is, is it? Plus, Seb is armed.*

Reaching her bungalow, Rory shoved on the door without hesitation. It flew open and he called out as he entered.

"Rani!"

But the place was empty. *Did she flee?*

Rory dashed back outside and started for the reception desk, when something caught his eye. The next bungalow over, the door stood open. He couldn't remember if it was like that last night, the sky quite dark when they arrived, but he and Rani had needed keys to enter their rooms. He looked back to the reception building before deciding to check out the bungalow first.

This time, he approached with some trepidation, pulling up short of the door and craning his neck to peer inside. The light was dim and the curtains were drawn making it difficult to see, so he stepped forward, pushing the door further open before entering.

There, in a chair by the desk, sat Rani. Her back was to him and her hair down, falling over her shoulders.

"You're still here," he said, stepping all the way into the room.

But she didn't respond. She just sat there, showing him her back.

"Rani," he said, taking another step forward and sensing something out of place. Her hair was too long and braided in crazy dreadlocks. And, if that was Rani, then whose body lay in the corner by the bed, slumped in a pool of blood?

Suddenly, the chair swiveled around.

"Hello, Mr. Crandall," said the woman sitting there. "I've been waiting for you."

"Who the hell are you?"

The woman smiled back, and Rory saw she was holding Seb's revolver.

"You can call me Bettina."

Endgame

33

*W*as he dreaming?

Or was he awake now and this whole experience one long dream?

A nightmare.

Maybe all of this, the scorching hot days, the bitter cold nights, the loud angry voices, inedible food, backbreaking work, constant mind games and, worst of all, the endless hours and days and nights of sheer loneliness.

Maybe all of this was the dream.

Maybe reality was what he saw before him now, his father and mother, sister and brother, all his friends gathered around him at the big table in his father's house, talking and laughing and eating together, drinking sweet drinks and waiting for him to do something.

But what did they want him to DO?

Say something? Tell a joke? One of his stories?

Maybe something else, something important, vital, essential, mandatory, obligatory. Yes, they were cheering him on, goading him on, smiling and laughing and waiting for him to make the first move. But what did they want from him?

And then, he remembered, for he saw it there in front of him, the answer to the riddle.

He knew what they wanted him to DO.

Play the game.

So, he laughed back. He smiled and laughed with them over the object before him, the object of their desire, the round and fat and fantastically enormous frosty white cake.

Cut the cake!

Cut the CAKE!!

CUT THE CAKE!!!

But it was a dream. For they were all dead now, burned to the ground with this table, these chairs, this whole bloody house.

Blood and ashes, all gone.

Only he was alive, alive in this place, alive and alone in this miserable place, with these horrible men and sad wicked boys.

And now, as he climbed out of the dream, up the prickly trestle of his tattered mind, through the ghostly black fog that filled his days and haunted his nights and tormented his every waking hour, he remembered exactly where he was and precisely why he was there and perfectly well what they wanted him to DO.

For there in front of him, there on the ground, lay the true answer to the riddle, the unmistakable object of their desire, staring back at him through their hellish chants with those soft pleading eyes, that round and fat and fantastically innocent human face.

Kill the fake!

Kill the FAKE!!

KILL THE FAKE!!!

Oh, leave me alone, let me be, give me peace, take me away...

KILL THE FAKE!!!

What do I do? Grant their wishes? Meet their demands? I won't...

KILL THE FAKE!!!

But I do, of course I do, I start kicking, like always, the soft little ball...

KILL THE FAKE!!!

The round rubber ball, the beautifully smooth and innocent round rubber ball...

KILL THE FAKE!!!

That isn't a ball at all. Oh, why did you tell me? At night all alone...

KILL THE FAKE!!!

Thought I would listen, not go to the others, but I was trained...

KILL THE FAKE!!!

We were all trained, trained to kick the rubber ball...

KILL THE FAKE!!!

The rubber skull...

KILL THE FAKE!!!

The live human skull...

KILL THE FAKE!!!

Of my only true friend...

GO AWAY!!!

KNOCK...KNOCK...KNOCK...

"Sir?"

Dead silence.

"Sir?"

Confucius stood in the hallway on the top floor of the Sanctuary. He waited outside the door before knocking again. Three crisp raps with his knuckle, as he had been instructed by the man on the other side of the door.

KNOCK...KNOCK...KNOCK...

Still nothing.

So Confucius reached into his pocket and extracted a single key. He turned to the man standing next to him, whose head was hidden beneath a black hood.

"Not a word from you, unless spoken to, or I'll kill you with my bare hands."

The other man nodded through the head covering. Confucius watched him and then inserted the key into the keyhole before cracking open the door.

"Sir, I've brought him to you."

More silence. Then, at last, there came a cough, followed by a command.

"Good, let him in."

Confucius obeyed, pushing the other man forward. As he entered the room, the hood was pulled from his head, and he was greeted with a question.

"My God, is that you?"

"Yes it is."

"Rory."

"Dr. Amwaj."

34

"Surprised?"

"Well..."

Rory left his answer hanging there in the air, which held a stale, musty feel, like inside a hospital ward or retirement home. "Yes, you could say I'm surprised, confused, dismayed, disgusted, shocked, bewildered, appalled, revolted. What else do you want me to say?"

"Nothing. Not yet. Just tell me what you *think*."

Seated, with a quilted blanket draped over his legs, Dr. Amwaj swept a hand to indicate his surroundings. It was no less than Rory would have expected. Maps covered one wall, photographs another, with books stacked on the floor and papers tilting this way and that on an antique roll top desk. A tremendous globe held sway in one corner, while nearby a voluminous tome lay open on a filigree stand. Above it, Rory couldn't help noticing a collection of exotic-looking weapons mounted on silky red mats within glass-encased frames, including the curved blade of an ancient *sica*. From hidden speakers, jazz music filled the room, blending pleasantly with the soft crackle of fire in the hearth. Further on, past a four-poster bed, stood a vast picture window, like a matinee movie screen or a portal to the world, a magnificent canvas upon which to craft one's final masterpiece to humanity, or, in this case, one's sinister abomination.

How fitting to situate this clandestine studio of terror, Rory thought, recognizing the landscape below him, high in the hills over Sarajevo, a living graveyard and silent witness to some of the most horrific scenes of carnage committed during the past century. And while you're at it, why not choose an abandoned dungeon, Rory remembered, spotting the infamous turrets he had seen several times in history books. A fortress of rock and mortar constructed by the Partisans during World War II and later captured by the fascist Ustaše, who obligingly installed underground torture chambers from which to carry out the Fuhrer's diabolical schemes against their Slavic brethren. Converted lock, rack, and baking ovens two generations later, the Chetniks under Arkan used the cells to inflict a new round of agony on their Croat and Muslim victims. Rory recalled the old professor's lecture well. Legend held the prison walls seeped human blood, and the voices of the damned could be heard wailing at night. Villagers mockingly referred to this place as *Sklonište*, or Sanctuary, and avoided it like an incurable virus. Dr. Amwaj told this story to his students to illustrate the power of myth. To Rory he privately conveyed a different tale, a personal aspiration of one day turning this hellish landmark into a peace center. Transforming *Sklonište* into a genuine sanctuary had been a quest of his for years, part of a quixotic crusade by Dr. Amwaj to right past injustices, to even historical balance sheets. And now look what it had become.

"I've done it," the professor said, gazing with pride across the city far below.

And look what *he* had become. "Yes, you've done it, all right," Rory said, still standing, staring down at the old man slumped there before him, this false prophet he had once blindly worshipped. "You've gone on a killing spree. You've taken innocent lives. You've become a terrorist wanted the world over. What the *hell* happened to you?"

Rory took a step forward and felt sharp talons dig into his flesh. He had completely forgotten the other man standing there.

"Easy now," Dr. Amwaj said to Confucius.

"Are you certain, Sir?"

"Yes, yes, of course, let him go. Rory is our guest here and should be treated as such."

Confucius did as ordered, yet only after adding an extra twist of pain to Rory's arm.

"In fact," Dr. Amwaj continued, "why don't you leave the two of us alone?"

"But Sir, don't you think—"

"I'll be fine," Dr. Amwaj said, shooing him away.

Confucius nodded but did not look pleased by his dismissal. Dr. Amwaj waited for the door to close before turning back to Rory.

"Now, where were we? Ah, yes, Rory, please take a seat. I fear this may prove a little more difficult than I had hoped."

Rory kept standing, rubbing at his wounded arm. "What are you talking about?"

"Winning you over."

"Winning me over for *what*?"

"For the reason you came here. What else?"

* * *

Confucius remained on the opposite side of the door, listening in. Once convinced this conversation did, indeed, seem harmless, he pulled himself away and started walking up the hall, his mind reeling out questions as he went. *Who is this guy, Crandall? What does he mean to Dr. Amwaj? Why wasn't I told he was coming here? And why am I being tossed aside, swept from the room?*

He hadn't gone far when he reached a second door, more questions piling up in his head. *Why is Bettina here at the Sanctuary and not in Istanbul? Where is Zulu? And what the hell does Tito know about any of this?*

In a ragged anger now, he threw open the door and stormed inside. The room he entered was slightly smaller and far less cluttered than the one he had just left down the hall. It was arranged how he liked it, with a certain minimalist charm: simple black leather couch, matching table and chairs, a bed in one corner, with a well-worn copy of "On the Theory of Evolutionary Peace" book-marked on the nightstand, beside a molded-iron weight set, stacked neatly on the floor. Best of all, no one at the Sanctuary – save for Dr. Amwaj – knew about this room. None of the others had ever been permitted above the fifth floor.

"Screw them all," Confucius said aloud, as he stood there, considering what to do next. "I'm in charge here, so why am I being left out in the cold?"

Slamming the door behind him, he snatched up the lone object on the tabletop. A remote control device, he aimed it at a closed-circuit TV anchored just below the ceiling, which no one at the Sanctuary – *including* Dr. Amwaj – knew existed, determined to find out why.

35

Rory remained standing, halfway between the closed door and his old mentor, still seated before him. "I don't know what you're talking about. I came here because you dragged me here, after you kidnapped me and drugged me and killed my—"

"Yes, yes," Dr. Amwaj said with a wave of his hand. "We shall get to all that in good time, I promise. Right now, I fear we've stepped off on the wrong foot. I would like to start over again, more civilized this time, if you will allow me." He motioned once more for Rory to take the seat in front of him, by the fire, and again Rory refused the offer.

So Dr. Amwaj pushed on. "How was the flight?"

Now Rory laughed. "Are you serious? The flight was wonderful, Emile. I slept like a baby. What was the onboard meal again? Right, temazepam, or was it sodium pentothal?"

"I don't know, Rory. I'm not a dictator. I leave it to my associates to decide how they carry out their business. We are all free thinkers here."

"Your *associates*. Free *fucking* thinkers. That bald psychopath is a real beauty."

"Indeed, she is," said Dr. Amwaj, ignoring Rory's hostile sarcasm. "Bettina *is* beautiful. She's brilliant, too, plus ambitious and loyal as they come. A German Jew with a tragic family history, she would do anything for the success of this mission."

"Like killing one of my best friends and—"

"As I said," Dr. Amwaj cut him off again, "Bettina is committed body and soul to our cause, and what she did, while unfortunate, was entirely necessary."

"Necessary for *what*?"

"To prove a point."

"What the hell are you talking about? What *point*?"

"The one I needed you to see," said Dr. Amwaj, pausing long enough to pour himself a glass of Scotch from the old crystal decanter Rory recognized from the past. He measured a second glass for Rory, without asking. "I needed you to see that you care."

"Care about *what*?" Rory demanded, still standing, ignoring the drink.

Dr. Amwaj raised his own glass. "About something larger than yourself. Yes, Rory, that was vital, the reason we sent you on your journey. I had to be certain."

Rory couldn't believe what he was hearing. It was too much information at once. *Maybe a stiff drink is exactly what I do need*, he thought, watching Dr. Amwaj bring the glass to his lips. But he held his ground. "What do you mean, *certain*?"

"Certain you were ready to fulfill your purpose," Dr. Amwaj answered, returning the glass to a coaster on the table next to him. "You know, you could have come straight here. Once you saw the news and heard our third message, once you figured it all out. You could have gone to the authorities and collected your precious reward money. You could have had me and the others locked up forever. But you didn't. You went to see about the girl, as I hoped you would – as I *knew* you would. By doing so, you proved a point. You proved that you cared more about her than you care about yourself."

"So you killed her."

Again, Dr. Amwaj brushed off the accusation. "This mission is larger than you, Rory. It is larger than me. It is larger than all of us."

"*Us?* Who, that bald whack job that brought me here? That Oriental hit man on the other side of the door?"

Now Dr. Amwaj laughed. "Please, Rory, you must give me more credit than that. These are just two of my many colleagues."

"There are *more* of you? How many?"

"I don't know, Rory, not precisely. There are plenty of us. You would be surprised how many young people these days want to join a good cause."

"So you've corrupted a band of adolescent assassins?"

"Hardly," Dr. Amwaj said, reaching for his glass again. "Yes, many of them are students – my *star* students, in fact, as you once were."

"What are you talking about?"

"They are the elite, Rory, my 'rare finds.' They speak several languages, hold various degrees. They have lived all over the world, growing up in warring societies, with horrible grievances. There is a clever Bosnian Serb I want you to meet, and a resilient Kashmiri woman, and so many other good souls. They have all lost family and friends, seen loved ones killed right in front of them, just like you and me. They are brilliant, Rory, open-minded, inquisitive, wanting so desperately to fit in, to please, to serve a higher purpose. Need I say more?"

"No, you've said quite enough. If I understand you correctly, you've recruited a bunch of sick, troubled, young geniuses from war-torn countries to do your killing for you. Can we give this man another Nobel Prize?"

Dr. Amwaj did not laugh. He looked at Rory with disappointment in his eyes. "Have you such a limited view of who I am, of what we are trying to accomplish here? Yes, some of them are young, fresh out of school. It is such a wonderful time, wanting to change the world and being idealistic enough to think you still can. Remember yourself at that age? But not only students, Rory, there are so many more of us – doctors and lawyers, teachers and diplomats, scientists, engineers, other

Nobel laureates like myself. Where do you think the money comes from? Oh, yes, and businessmen, executives, innovators. Razinski, Kaan-Mueller, the cyber king Mills Greenblatt, Eleanor Markham, and—"

"Mrs. Markham?" Rory blurted in disbelief. "My employer is part of this madness?"

"Yes," Dr. Amwaj answered patiently. "Elle is a visionary, like the rest of us. And yes, they are all very much a part of what we are doing here. Each of us in our own way contributes what we can. That is how it works. We all have roles to play. Some of us are actively involved. Others give money to the cause."

"They give you money knowing what you are doing? Killing innocent people?"

"Yes, Rory, they donate money," Dr. Amwaj said, disregarding the second comment.

"You mean to your foundation? Your *peace* foundation. They think they're giving you money to help bring peace to the world, for Christ's sake."

"Exactly," Dr. Amwaj said. "That is exactly what we *are* doing. But not one war at a time, the old-fashioned way. That way doesn't work. It never did. Don't you see? There are always more wars." His voice began to rise with emotion. "You have now seen first-hand what people are capable of. Brothers killing brothers. Men burnt alive. Children sent into battle. Women and girls raped like dogs. No, Rory, it must be wholesale. I'm talking about massive change – *revolutionary* change – a paradigm shift, a whole new way of looking at the world!"

Here, Dr. Amwaj paused to catch his breath and take another sip of whisky before carrying on, his tone level again. "But I am getting ahead of myself, Rory. Please, I beg you, take a seat. Have a drink with me, like old times, and I will explain it all to you, so you will fully understand and—"

"*Old times*," Rory spat. "You brought me here for a drink and a nice game of chess? You're crazy, you know that."

Dr. Amwaj looked up at him with wounded pride. "You must have questions for me. Won't you *please* join me?"

But Rory remained standing, taking a step closer. "I only have *one* question for you. The rest will be carried out by a panel of judges at your trial." He pointed at Dr. Amwaj. "How did you know I would go to the places you needed me to go and see what you wanted me to see?"

Now Dr. Amwaj smiled. "What we wanted you to see is *everywhere*. That is the point. We could have sent you to most any place on the planet. It really did not matter."

"But why send me at all?" Rory asked, keeping on the offensive. "Why not just ask me to turn on the TV? Or watch a YouTube video? It would have saved us all a lot of trouble."

"No, no, *no*, Rory," Dr. Amwaj said, perturbed. "That won't do. That is exactly the problem. The way we have all become so conditioned to seeing violence, so de-sensitized through too many TV shows and movies and video games. No, I needed you to really *experience* it for yourself – to feel the fear in the eyes of those child soldiers, to smell the odor of burning human flesh, to hear the screams of helpless young girls. I needed you to be reminded of the true barbarism of it all. The choice of where to go was left up to you. The girl, Rani, she was only there to make sure you kept going."

"But my feelings for her, *those* were real. You couldn't have predicted that."

"Yes, she was carefully selected, Rory. I made the final choice myself. Do you know why she called herself Rani?"

"What? What are you talking about?"

"Rani Bai," Dr. Amwaj said. "You haven't forgotten your history lessons, have you?"

Rory waited.

"Rani Lakshmi Bai was a heroine of the Indian Rebellion of the 1850s," Dr. Amwaj said. "British officers marveled at her cunning and determination, her lust for life. Before, that is, she shred them to pieces with her sword."

Rory kept staring, not sure what to say.

"Of course, Rani was not the girl's real name," Dr. Amwaj continued. "I ask each of them to choose codenames after historical figures who mean something to them, something personal. Funny how the boys keep picking great thinkers and political figures – Che, Caesar, Confucius – while the girls tend toward rebels and warriors. I'm not sure what that says…ah, but I am getting off course."

Now Rory shook his head.

"Please, do not look so surprised, my friend. You must remember, Rory, I know you well. I know your tastes and desires, your strengths and weaknesses. Yes, Rani was a kindred spirit. Although, let's be honest, she did betray you. So, no, I am not surprised you fell for her. Nor should you be, for that was all part of it."

"Part of *what?*" Rory demanded, losing his temper. "*She was part of what?*"

"What I had to show you," Dr. Amwaj said, carefully watching his former protégé, who had taken another step forward and was now leaning over him. "Or, perhaps, what I had to see for myself. I had to see if you were capable of feeling something larger than yourself, larger than your passion for fortune and fame and seemingly little else these days."

"Yes, and in case you didn't notice, I am capable."

"I know."

"And you killed her," Rory said, pointing again.

"*So what?*" Dr. Amwaj suddenly fired back, pointing up at Rory. "So, you lost someone. We've all lost someone. Me, my entire family. Some of them out there" – he swept his arm toward the picture window – "everything they ever had. But what I have gone to great lengths to show you, even if you still refuse to see it, is the notion that there exists a cause much larger than you or me or any one of us. The total is so much greater than the sum of the *fucking* parts."

Rory couldn't remember ever hearing Dr. Amwaj swear before.

"Sometimes the ends *do* justify the means," he continued, pointing again. "They *fucking* have to, don't you see? It's a simple game, Rory. This isn't chess. It isn't even checkers. It's law of the jungle. It's survival of the fittest. It's survival of the whole *goddamned* human race. And someone had to put evolution back on track."

"And that someone is you?"

"No, Rory, *damn it*, it's not me. It's *us*. It's always been *us*."

"There is no *us*," Rory insisted. "There hasn't been for some time, and there certainly isn't now."

At last, Dr. Amwaj dropped his hand, although he kept looking up at Rory, holding him in his gaze. "There once was an *us*, you know that, and there can be again. That is why I brought you here. That is why you are still alive. I could have had you killed at any point, you know. I still can."

"Then why don't you?" Rory said, glaring down at Dr. Amwaj.

"Because I need you, that's why."

"You need me for *what*?"

"I need you to listen to my offer."

*   *   *

Down the hall, Confucius stood scowling. *What offer?*

He wasn't getting the answers he needed and was growing increasingly impatient. Lowering the volume on the closed-circuit TV, he opened his cell phone and punched up a number.

"I need to see you," he snapped, keeping an eye on the screen overhead. He didn't much like the way this guy, Crandall, kept pointing at Dr. Amwaj.

Bettina's voice could be heard on the other end of the line. "Why?"

"Because I do, that's why." His anger was mounting, although he was pleased to see Crandall back away from Dr. Amwaj and finally take the seat offered him. "Sixth floor, as fast as you can get here."

A pause followed before Bettina spoke again.

"I've never been up there before. Did *he* ask for me?"

"No, *I'm* asking for you," Confucius shot back. "So get your ass up here – *now* – and bring Tito with you!"

36

In a bustling café off Beyazıt Square and the main campus of Istanbul University, Zulu was doing her best to fit in. A pair of textbooks on architectural photography, which peeked out from a book bag purchased at the student store, served as a basic prop, while a table in the corner by the window provided an open view of the busy coffee bar and the world outside. Being dark-skinned, standing nearly six feet tall, and looking model gorgeous didn't make the task any easier. *But that's half the fun, right?* It didn't hurt, either, that the student body at Turkey's oldest establishment of higher learning featured an array of nationalities, many of which were represented here washing down sticky sweet baklava with thick Turkish coffee.

Plus, she didn't plan on staying long.

Paying her bill and collecting her belongings, Zulu exited the café and started across the campus grounds. She passed by an impressive heap of Byzantine ruins and a landmark gate used centuries ago by the Ottoman Ministry of War, according to a brochure she had found at the student store. This literature also informed her that Istanbul University, established during the 15th

century by Mehmet the Conqueror as a *madrassa*, or religious school, was modernized in the 1920s by Atatürk
and now housed nearly 70,000 students on five separate
campuses. This information was interesting, but the real
reason she picked up the flyer was for the map on the
back, which guided her now toward her intended destination, the ancient Beyazıt Tower.

A moment later she came upon the 250-foot edifice,
once used as a fire-watch tower for the city – then called
Constantinople – but now serving mainly as a place to
bring visiting parents or hold clandestine make-out ses-
sions after dark. This being neither family day nor late
enough for such extracurricular activities, the tower
stood practically empty.

Climbing to the top, Zulu lingered on the observa-
tion deck, pretending to read an informative plaque there
while waiting for a pair of elderly tourists to descend.
Once alone, she dug into her bag and retrieved a camera
with a long-range lens, as any good architecture student
might do. Scanning over the city, she trained her lens
first on Beyazıt Square and then past the late afternoon
traffic clogging Karaköy. It didn't take long from this
elevated perch to locate her target: Vodafone Arena and
the site of the Future Games Championship scheduled
to begin just a few hours from now.

Focusing on the stadium, Zulu briefly thought about
how she had been earlier denied access there, after Bettina
switched envelopes on her, and the awkward backroom

interrogation that followed, until she was compelled to bring up Mills Greenblatt's name. She fully intended to settle that score the next time she saw the bald bitch, but right now she had a job to do.

Through the zoom lens, the stadium was swarming with activity. Cars and buses and motorized scooters streamed onto a field adjacent to the sprawling complex, while thousands of people marched toward the entrance, corralled by more security guards than one could imagine possible. A virtual sea of policemen – on foot, on motorbikes, on horseback, even in helicopters swooping over the stadium – patrolled the area in matching black uniforms and heavy riot gear, making their presence oppressively felt. And not only cops, but what appeared to be at least a couple units of Turkish Land Forces. Several hundred armed soldiers in combat fatigues stood in formation around a pair of battle tanks in a dramatic display intended to dissuade anyone foolish enough from trying something in the days following the fatal bombing at London's Wembley Stadium. That the Futures Games were proceeding at all spoke to the persuasive influence of its main backer, Greenblatt, who had publicly refused to back down to terrorist demands while personally footing much of the bill for this immense outlay of security.

Finished with her viewing, Zulu returned the camera to its bag, placing it next to a jangle of keys, a slim penlight, and a set of credentials on a plastic string featuring an image of her face and other pertinent biometrics, all courtesy of the same Mr. Greenblatt. "It's all been taken care of," he promised, while handing over the items after they had finished their business together. *And whatever the old boy lacked in size,* Zulu thought, remembering, *plus, well, most other ideal masculine traits, he more than made up for in desire and an ardent willingness to please.*

Zulu smiled to herself as she slung the bag over her shoulder and started down the tower steps, marveling at the sheer magnitude of forces required these days to protect a bunch of computer geeks and their friends, families, and other supporters from harm's way.

She was still smiling when she reached ground level and set off on foot in a direction away from the stadium, toward the much smaller, calmer, and far less secure overflow arena.

37

Dr. Amwaj smiled at his former protégé, who had finally taken the seat across from him. "Good, this is progress."

But Rory was not swayed. He sat toward the front edge of his chair and left the shot of whisky still untouched on the table beside him.

"So, what's your *offer*?"

He sneered at the old man seated before him, surrounded by his maps and papers and books. With the fire in the hearth and the jazz music filling the space between them, it might have been 15 years ago, back in Brussels, Rory thought. Only, the creature sitting across from him now was no longer a friend of mankind. He was more like a henchman to the Devil.

"I killed a man once," Dr. Amwaj said, as if confirming Rory's silent assessment.

"Yes, I know. It's all over the news – several of them, in fact, including a young girl who might have become the world's next tennis champion. I still don't see what any of this has to do with me."

"I killed this one myself. I kicked his head in."

"What?"

"Twenty, thirty times, maybe more. His brains leaked out of his skull, all over my leather boots."

Rory stared back in disbelief. "You must have had a good reason."

"The best, and worst, reason of all," Dr. Amwaj said. "It was not self-defense, or hatred, or even revenge, as you might think. I loved the man. He was like a brother to me, my only friend at that time. I killed him for *acceptance*."

"For *what*?"

"Acceptance holds an amazing power," Dr. Amwaj said, picking up his drink. "It is seductive, primordial. The reason we came down from the trees, abandoned our safe little caves. Acceptance is the true opiate of the masses."

"I thought that was *religion*."

"What's the difference? Throughout history, more people have died in the name of acceptance than all other reasons combined. Jesus was crucified over acceptance. We fought the Crusades in the name of acceptance. Hitler gassed the Jews over, well, you see where I am going. We all want to fit in, be connected, part of the winning team. Yes, to avoid being cast out of our comfy little communities, we kill our next-door neighbors" – here he pointed to the picture window again – "purge our political opponents to frozen tundra, maim innocent women and children in—"

"What are Sarajevo, Siberia, and Sierra Leone for one hundred?" Rory said, feigning a game show contestant.

"Please, spare me another history lesson and get to your damn point."

"That is precisely what I am doing, Rory, getting to my point." Dr. Amwaj took a sip of Scotch before returning the glass to its coaster. "It is utter madness, yet we accept it. We accept it all. Suicide bombing *martyrs*, pedophilic *priests*, ethnic *cleansing*, and my all-time favorite, *holy* wars. It is so preposterous it makes your head hurt. But we accept it, Rory, because that is what we've been programmed to do. Since the day we were born, in our schools and mosques, in our temples and churches, we preach peace as we learn to accept war. We glamorize killing. We trivialize pain. We romanticize violence. We not only accept it, we *revel* in it. We hold up brutality as something intrinsic, beautiful, *fucking* artistic."

Rory started to object, but Dr. Amwaj waved him off.

"This is not why I am telling you the story."

"Why are you telling me any of this?"

"Because I keep having these dreams, nightmares really."

"Given what you've done, I'm hardly surprised."

Dr. Amwaj ignored the comment. "The dreams usually end the same way. With me standing over my best friend, while all those around us shout: 'Kill the fake! Kill the fake! Kill the fake!' And I do – in the dream, as I did in reality – I mash his head like an insect. I kick his skull into a bloody pulp, for the very reason I just mentioned.

I longed so badly to be accepted then. I was young and stupid, desperately lonely and very afraid. I had been taken away after my village was burned down, my entire family, well, you know. But this does not excuse what I did. Not in the slightest. I am responsible for every one of my actions. We all are. You always have a choice."

There it was, Rory thought, remembering Rani's same words, spoken to the Nigerians back on the boat, as Dr. Amwaj continued.

"And I have been paying for this choice my entire adult life, trying in vain to wipe this lurid vision from my mind. But it is no use. In the end, I am the fake."

Here, Dr. Amwaj trailed off, turning to stare out the picture window. Across the valley, Mount Igman cast a dark shadow over Sarajevo. An ember popped in the hearth, as Coltrane's sax slid through a timeless refrain, and Rory found himself reaching instinctively for his whisky glass.

"That's a bit hard, don't you think?" He regarded the silky liquor at the base of the tumbler without trying it yet, as he remembered the roll call of amazing feats this once great man had accomplished. Selfless acts of peace and compassion, many of which they had worked on together: Cypress, Northern Ireland, Colombia, the Congo...

"Please, Rory, let me finish," Dr. Amwaj said, returning to him. "I *am* a fake. My entire life's work has been a sham. I call myself a peacemaker. They write books about me, produce documentaries, bestow important awards – the Nobel Prize, for God's sake – all intended to prove it. Yet, what have I done? Really? Stage countless negotiations in Israel and Palestine, where human bombs eviscerate busloads of innocent people. Convene endless talks in Jammu and Kashmir, where Indians and Pakistanis swim in each other's blood. Hold tireless conflict resolution exercises in America's inner cities, where crack babies are slaughtered in drive-by shootings. Don't even get me started on the cesspool we call Africa. Do you know, Rory, on average, somewhere in the world at least two people become casualties of war every minute of every day? Of course you do. We all know the figures, the truth about rape camps and child soldiers and human trafficking and indentured slaves and extrajudicial killings, human shields, torture chambers, beheadings, crucifixions, genocide. The list goes on and on and on..."

Dr. Amwaj shook his head and fought back strong emotion. "I saw on the news today where a twelve-year-old girl in Darfur was raped so many times by a gang of men that her legs were torn apart and now she's a cripple. An eight-year-old boy in Syria was forced to eat his own tongue when he refused to reveal the location of his mother. With so much evil in the world, it's a wonder we get out of bed each day. Have we learned nothing? Is it our fate to keep killing each other, as we have been doing for centuries, devising ever more effective means of inflicting pain and suffering on our fellow man and woman?"

All of a sudden, Dr. Amwaj broke into a fit of coughing, like he had done back Brussels, Rory remembered. It was so strong it caused the professor's entire body to shake, as Rory sat by watching, making no effort to help. *I'll listen to his tale, that's all.*

Dr. Amwaj eventually brought the spasm under control, before reaching for his glass again, continuing.

"Then came that date."

"What date?"

"The date that changed everything."

"I don't understand."

"September Eleventh."

"You mean 2001?"

"Yes, of course, Rory. I mean Nine-One-One. The emergency cry for help. I sat there watching it unfold on television like everyone else. Watching that first airplane careen into the Twin Towers, praying it was some horrible mistake, a piloting error, or air traffic control. I had nearly convinced myself, when that second craft came veering onto the screen, confirming all of our worst fears. This was no fluke, no steering malfunction. This was a deadly purposeful act engineered by a rare cast of villains. A truly abysmal day in the course of human history, I remember thinking, as I fell back in my chair, wondering how this could have happened. Who could have done this? Toward what end? And before I could answer my own questions, another thought entered my mind. Not a thought, so much, as, I don't know a… *premonition*. Yes, it was a powerful sensation, a convergence of myriad ideas difficult to accurately describe. I have tried many times to attach the proper word to what I felt at that moment, that moment of truth and clarity, as I sat there alone in my study, in reverent silence, watching those serpents of black smoke twisting into the sky. The nearest I can come to is—"

Another harsh cough and again Rory waited, finally taking his first sip of Scotch. *Smooth.* He watched as Dr. Amwaj cleared his throat and then uttered a single word.

"Hope."

Now Rory's mouth dropped open. "*Hope?* September Eleventh gave you *hope?*"

"Yes, *hope*," Dr. Amwaj repeated, nodding. "Not at first. No, at first, I felt the same as most everyone else. Horror. Shock. Sympathy. Remorse." He watched Rory's questioning eyes. "Right, *remorse*, for the way I figure, we all had a hand to play in letting things come to this. But the more I thought about it, the more I realized that within this terrible tragedy lay the seed of a brand new beginning, a second chance, an historical rebirth, if you will. For surely, I surmised, this must be it. This must be the moment when the world finally sits up and takes notice, the moment when we decide, as people, that enough is truly enough, the moment when we all become conscious that our present system is failing, that our rules of engagement are ineffective, outdated, in need of drastic reform. The moment when we finally grasp that war only begets more war, and we decide, once and for all, that we can no longer *accept* it."

"The moment when peace evolves," Rory said, taking a second sip of whisky.

"Yes, my words exactly," Dr. Amwaj said. "My dreams would be realized, my life's work justified, my demons vanquished. And, at first, in the immediate aftermath of those terrorist strikes, I was encouraged. Truly, I was. America, the world's self-anointed policeman and single remaining superpower, whatever that means, acted with reason rather than revenge, compassion in the face of controversy. And not only the United States. Remember, more than five hundred of the nearly three thousand people who perished in the World Trade Center came from ninety-one different countries. In response, a multinational coalition was formed, bringing together good souls from every corner of the world. Old enemies put aside their differences in a true act of humanity, bound as we all were by this new challenge, this common goal, this collective desire to root out evil wherever it dwelled. Saddened as I was by the tragic events in New York, Washington, and Pennsylvania, I was also elated, Rory, I must admit. For these were the days I had been dreaming of for such a long time. These were the days I had been laboring over for more than two generations. And these were the days when I lost all hope."

"What? I don't understand."

"Nor did I, Rory," Dr. Amwaj admitted, as a log shifted in the fireplace, stirring up cinders, spitting out a sharp hiss. "Not at first, Rory. In my infinite optimistic ignorance, I had fooled myself into believing that the world would finally change. At last, we would realize that we could no longer remain on our present course if we intended to survive, Rory. But what happened next?"

Why is he looking at me that way? "I don't know," Rory said.

"Yes you do, Rory."

And why does he keep using my name? "I don't know what you want me to say."

"The truth, Rory. I want you to say the truth."

All of a sudden, his head felt funny. *I've hardly had anything to drink*, Rory thought, as he experienced a flashback of their times together, sitting in a room much like this one, listening to familiar music, sharing whisky, the all-knowing professor and the eager schoolboy. It was always this way, always had been. Rory stumbling around in the dark, trying to match wits with this superior mind, the answers being coaxed out of him then, just as they were being coaxed out of him now.

"All right," he said at last, "*nothing* happened."

"Correct, Rory," Dr. Amwaj agreed. *Good boy, have a biscuit.* "Absolutely nothing happened. We went right back to where we had left off, didn't we? Our government officials telling us this time it would be different, as tanks rolled down the streets of Beirut. Our so-called leaders promising to put an end to the violence, as killings flared up in Kabul. Our guardian angels flapping their useless wings as innocent people were blown to shreds in Bali, Madrid, Istanbul, Casablanca, London, you name it. Serbs went right back to killing Albanians, and vice versa. Monrovia became the next African blood bath, or was it Mali, Madagascar, Mogadishu? What difference does it make? North Korea kept threatening us with nuclear warheads, while body bags ran scarce in Baghdad. And what did we do? What did we all do on this occasion? Oh, I won't waste either of our limited time together waiting for your response."

But Rory answered anyway. "Nothing, we did nothing, right?"

"No, Rory, that answer is *in*correct. We did *more* than nothing. We *accepted* it. We willfully, collectively, impotently accepted it all over again. Just like before. Just like always. Yes, I am afraid, the wakeup call came on September Eleventh and the world decided to hit the snooze button."

Now the elderly professor moved forward in his chair, and Rory realized he was leaning back in his own. *When did that happen?*

"Well, not *all* of us," Dr. Amwaj resumed, his voice rising. "Not anymore. Some of us decided *not* to accept it this time, *not* to conform. A small group of us decided that enough truly was enough and that we could no longer sit idly by while the world committed mass suicide. We decided to take action. We saw no other choice. We had to obliterate the status quo."

The words seemed to be coming at Rory from all sides. "So let me get this straight," he said, trying to gain control over the proceedings. "You decided to shake us all out of some great global slumber by killing off our favorite athletes?"

"They could have been actors, pop stars, politicians. It didn't really matter."

"It did to *them*."

Dr. Amwaj pushed aside this feeble rejoinder. "We had to find a way to wake the world up. It was that simple. When we took over that hotel in Dubrovnik a few years ago we—"

"That was *you*?"

"Not me in the lobby, Rory. I'm a little old for that, but I did come up with the plan, which was then carried out by others who—"

"Those fiends I met?" Rory interrupted again, feeling he'd just won a point.

"Our network is large, Rory, I already told you." Dr. Amwaj was now speaking as if to a difficult child. "When we struck in Dubrovnik, we came in peace. No one was injured. Our weapons weren't even loaded. You know how I abhor guns. Our intentions were modest. We had only one demand then. We wanted people to take a good look at what was taking place in the Sudan. Two *million* people dead, even more wounded and displaced, curable diseases running rampant, widespread starvation. We wanted others to stop and ask themselves a simple question: Is this the way people should be living in the twenty-first century?"

"Of course not," Rory said, or at least he thought he did, for his head was starting to swim now. The fire in the hearth was too hot. *What's happening to me?*

"Of course not," Dr. Amwaj repeated. "But the world didn't listen, nothing changed, the violence kept coming, just like before, just like always. Aceh, Bogota, Cairo, Damascus. *A-B-C-D.* The names change but the results remain the same. It's an alphabet soup served up in a bloody red broth. Yesterday's Kashmir becomes today's Kosovo, tomorrow's Kampala next week's Kyrgyzstan…"

Rory was trying to keep up while fighting against something inside him he couldn't quite name. "What about Libya? Qaddafi is gone?"

"And chaos looms," Dr. Amwaj shot back, as if anticipating the question. "This is nothing, Rory, just baby steps going round and round in circles, always ending up in the same place. What I am talking about is a *revolution*. You know, we used to accept slavery and public torture and witches burned at the stake. But world views change. History is not static. We can move forward. Why is it so hard to believe, then, in a world entirely free of war? People just need to be shown what is possible – *forced* to see it, if that what it takes."

Rory suddenly felt constricted. "But our leaders are trying, they are."

"*Bullshit*," Dr. Amwaj cursed again. "Who do you think makes all the weapons? Sells them? Gets filthy rich off of them? Stays in power because of them? Benefits most from people killing other people? And we all let them do it. We, the people, are ultimately responsible for it all. Our laws are bent and carefully crafted to ensure we keep protecting the very people we should be protected against. And, again, we accept it. Yes, it has been this way for ages and will continue this way indefinitely, I fear – I *know* – unless someone does something to change it."

Now Rory wanted to stand up, move about, get some fresh air, but the lecture wasn't over yet, the words kept coming.

"People get busy," he heard Dr. Amwaj say, "busy making money, busy going to films and sporting events, busy getting fat on restaurant food. Too busy with their own personal affairs to stop and think about the suffering of some unseen other on the opposite side of the planet. Too busy with their own precious little lives to consider objecting, taking a stand, refusing to accept the unacceptable. So that's where we came in."

"You came in," Rory mouthed the words, as if in a dream. He felt lost in a fog, finding it increasingly difficult to fight back. He stared at his drink. *Have I been drugged?*

"Yes, we came in," Dr. Amwaj said, moving even further forward, toward the front of his chair. "We came together. Like-minded people committed to change, determined to leave an imprint on history. But what could we do? I used to think I had the answers. Christ, I've earned two PhDs. I know all the theories. I've written half of them. 'Be patient,' I used to say. 'Build bridges, foster trust, find win-win solutions.' But it was all rubbish, wasted breath. What we needed was *real* change, a fresh approach, a brand new way of looking at the world, of seeing what was possible. So we took small steps at first and—"

"You call the death of innocent sports stars *small*?" Rory interrupted.

"Yes, in the grand scheme of things, I do," Dr. Amwaj said, unfazed. "This is not how I wanted it, Rory. I am a man of peace, you know that. But when the world would not listen to our simple request, we realized then that there was no other way. We had to speak to people in the language they understood. We were forced to use violence to prevent much greater violence. In the end, Rory, we are all expendable, and the death of a few pampered playboys seems a small price to pay for a chance at world peace, don't you think?"

Rory no longer knew what to think. "But she was only sixteen," he said, trying to focus on the slain tennis star, hoping her image would help him climb out of the fog.

"Yes, and the girl on CNN this morning was twelve. The boy killed in Sana'a yesterday nine…my sister four-teen…my brother five. So what's your point?"

"My point," Rory struggled, "is that peace must evolve. You said so yourself."

"Yes, Rory, peace must evolve. I believe that now, just as I always have. But sometimes peace needs a little help."

And then Rory began to understand what was happening.

"Sometimes evolution needs a little nudge, my friend."

He knew what was going on, as he listened to the other's powerful words.

"And this is where great men become involved."

Rory wasn't drunk.

"Men of vision, men of wisdom, men of courage…"

He hadn't been drugged.

"Men who step up when called upon…"

No, he was finally letting go.

"Men who step beyond the bounds of convention…"

He was fully giving in.

"Men who step outside the law in the name of the greater good…"

He was giving in to *reason*.

"Men who take it upon themselves to change the world…"

"I want to change the world," Rory heard himself saying.

"Of course you do," Dr. Amwaj replied, staring deep into his eyes. "But I had to be certain you could be trusted."

"I can be trusted."

"Of course you can." Dr. Amwaj kept staring. "I know that now, and that is why I brought you here. That is why I am prepared to make you an offer."

"What offer?" Rory asked, wanting desperately to please. Like a rush of morphine, it felt so soothing to surrender.

"I want to offer you a job, Rory."

"*What job?*" He was ready to acquiesce to anything.

"The job you were born to assume."

And now Rory waited, waited eagerly for Dr. Amwaj to reveal his fate.

"I want you to be our leader."

38

"**O**ur *leader!*" Confucius seethed, as he muted the volume on the closed-circuit TV. "I've killed for that man. How can he offer this *fucking* outsider my job?"

He glowered at the remote in his hand, ready to hurl it at the screen, when a knock came at the door. He had nearly forgotten.

"Come in," he barked, pulling himself together.

Bettina entered first, and Confucius was struck by what she had chosen to wear. No longer in one of her dark Euro-chic ensembles – *did she actually change since I called her?* – she now wore a pleated, knee-length skirt made of plaid fabric, with a short-sleeved schoolgirl blouse in baby blue, unbuttoned low enough to reveal a good slice of her ample chest. Her bald head was covered in short, frizzy red hair – *where does she get all these wigs?* – giving her the appearance of a slightly slutty, very desirable Little Orphan Annie.

He was instantly put on guard.

Tito followed next, looking young and nervous in his black hoodie, with a blink of that crazy, blood-stained eye. Confucius wondered if the kid's deformity ever hurt him.

"Nice place," Tito muttered, hiding his true feelings.

"Great view," added Bettina, as she crossed the room and peered out the window at the distant Sarajevo skyline before shifting her gaze downward, into the stark rock gully that plunged a couple hundred feet below them.

"Thanks," said Confucius, watching their expressions and weighing the level of displeasure, in spite of their kind words. *Good, we're all rattled now.* "Please," he said, gesturing toward the table, "have a seat."

Bettina chose first. Tito then sat down next to her, pulling his chair a little too close, before looking up at the television overhead. "Who's that man?" he asked, pointing.

On the screen, Dr. Amwaj was speaking with hand gestures but no sound, like an aging mime. Rory watched him from his seat next to the fire.

"Well, Dr. Amwaj you know," Confucius said, taking up a position on the opposite side of the table. "And the other man – funny you should ask, for he is the very reason I called you up here. Who, indeed, is that man?" he said, turning to Bettina. "Why don't you enlighten us?"

Tito shot her a look. There were so many things he had wanted to say on their way up here. He was ready to tell her off, to tell her how sick he was of being ignored, of being insulted. He was ready to tell her how their relationship was going to change. But she had been distracted, like she often was lately, and then they had reached the sixth floor…and he had not said a word…

and now she looked so damn good…*and my God I want to fuck her.*

Bettina's mind was also in a whirl. *What does Confucius know? Why is he so upset? Did he really call me up here, or was it Dr. Amwaj? How long has Amwaj been at the Sanctuary? What is Tito doing here, and can he be of any use to me? How is Crandall involved? Am I being punished or praised for going to Romitsae and bringing him back?* She decided it best to slow play this situation and see if she could gain more than she gave away.

"Well," she started, "we only just met, as you know, and—"

"Don't tell me what I know!" Confucius slammed his fist on the table, causing Bettina to jump and Tito to look from one to the other.

"I'm going to tell you what I know and then I'm going to tell you what we're going to do," Confucius said, leaving his fist there and spreading his fingers open like an angry tarantula.

It crossed Bettina's mind, not for the first time, that Confucius had killed the Jin Dragon all by himself, and she wondered again now exactly how he had pulled that one off. Staring at the hand placed in front of her, she did her best to collect her thoughts. She still had no idea why she was here, but she had come prepared. While Confucius launched into a tirade against her, she slowly reached up, beneath the table and under her skirt, to where she had concealed Seb's revolver, strapped to a belt against her thigh. She had no intention of revealing the firearm – strictly forbidden at the Sanctuary – but it gave her comfort knowing it was there, should she need it, and she suddenly had to stifle a peculiar urge to laugh.

"—so that's what we are going to do now," Confucius was saying, looking at neither of them but rather at a point in space somewhere in between, as he continued in a tight, controlled voice. "We are all going to sit here until Bettina tells us exactly what she knows about this guy Crandall and why she felt it her prerogative to change orders, orders handed down by me and directed from none other than Dr. Amwaj. Then she's going to—"

"I want to see him."

Bettina's interruption and the gravity of her request caught Confucius by surprise.

"That's not going to happen," he said, sweeping his eyes around to meet hers, as Tito joined the party.

"I want to see him too."

"Neither of you are going to see him," Confucius said, still in his deliberate manner, although he was finding it increasingly difficult to contain a brewing rage.

"Why not?" Bettina asked, to which Tito repeated like a parrot.

"*Da*, why not?"

"Let me tell you why not," Confucius said, watching them both. "There's a simple concept you may have heard of. It's called *chain of command*. Every good organization has one, from the—"

"What's the point of all this?" Bettina cut in again, as she secretly edged the palm of her hand around the pistol's grip. "I said I need to see him."

"The point of all this," Confucius continued, still restraining himself, "is that whether you like it or not, I'm in charge here. He speaks to me and to me alone. I am Number Two on this mission and both of you are Numbers Two-Plus-Something-Else. I give the orders and you follow them. I report to him and you report to me. I hand out the assignments and you, well…you seem to fuck them up."

Now he turned on Bettina, shoving his index finger up toward her pretty little face. She let out a gasp and Tito wondered if the rumors about Confucius blinding a boarding school teacher for giving him bad marks were really true. As much as he enjoyed watching Bettina squirm, for he was still angry at her, Confucius had no right treating her this way.

"What you did was inexcusable," Confucius kept going. "You not only breached protocol, you jeopardized our entire mission and—"

"Which is why I need to see him," she interrupted him once more, her voice surprisingly calm given the finger and its razor-sharp nail sashaying less than an inch from her eyeball. Underneath the table, Bettina had worked the handgun free from her belt. "I need to explain to him how what I did was necessary for our mission and—"

"How the *hell* do you know what's necessary?" The finger circled her eye like a shark. "I wouldn't be surprised if this little stunt spells the end for you, Bettina. You've gone too far this time." The finger kept dancing. "You've been a major disappointment." *One-two.* "You've disobeyed orders." *Three-four.* "You've put Zulu's life in danger, this entire mission at risk." The finger finally came to a stop, grazing the edge of her lower lashes. "If you want any chance of saving yourself, then you better start telling me everything you know about Crandall. *Now!*"

Bettina swallowed as she calculated just how quickly she could swing the loaded weapon up over the tabletop and blow this Asian maggot's brains across the walls of his spiffy bachelor pad. She opened her mouth to answer, while curling a finger around the trigger, ready to act, when Confucius suddenly dropped his hand from her face and flew out of his chair.

39

ory had known it was coming, known it all along. *You wouldn't be here if you didn't have a clue. You could have gone to the authorities, like he said, but you didn't. You've wanted this, wished for it, longed for it your entire life – a place in history, beside men of great power and influence, fighting a vital cause in a role beyond your wildest dreams...*

"To be your leader," he said aloud.

"Yes, Rory, that's right, to be our leader."

"Why *me*?"

"Because we need you, Rory," Dr. Amwaj said. "*I* need you. At first, you had no place in my plans. You were never part of my original equation. I must admit, I had not thought much of you in years, the way you were going about your business, making money, chasing fame. Until, one day, just like that, you called me, and then you showed up on my doorstep."

"I needed your help," Rory said, remembering.

"And I needed yours," Dr. Amwaj replied, not missing a beat. "Your arrival at the Peace Institute gave me an idea, the inspiration for a wonderful new plan. At that point, if you recall, we had yet to make our first announcement to the world. In fact, your arrival helped launch our first message. It also gave us the perfect—"

"*Alibi*," Rory finished the sentence.

"Not only an alibi, Rory. Hearing from you again, seeing you there in the flesh, after all of these years, I knew you were the best man for the job, the *only* man for the job. You may have lost your way, but you came back, back to the Sanctuary. Don't you see, Rory? You are like a son to me. You always have been, even if we have had our differences. You are the one in six thousand."

"What are you talking about?"

"It's simple, Rory," Dr. Amwaj continued, leaning forward, taking him by the hand. "I need you. I need you here by my side. I need you to run this operation."

"But what about *you?*"

Now Dr. Amwaj hesitated. "Well, yes, I will be here, too, for as long as I can be. You can think of me as an advisor, a technical consultant, someone to help guide you on your way."

"And these talks, they will continue?" Rory asked. "Just like before?"

"Of course they will," Dr. Amwaj smiled, squeezing Rory's hand. "But the day-to-day activities, those will be yours. You will make the decisions required to fulfill our vision."

"And what about those others?" he said, with a nod toward the door.

"Don't worry, Rory. I will let them know and they will listen to me. They are extraordinary young people, but they are not ready to lead a mission like this, not on their own, not yet. No, that job is yours. I am offering you the opportunity of a lifetime here, but you keep playing me coy. Please, Rory, we haven't much time. I need your answer."

It was true. Rory was stalling. He had given himself over to Dr. Amwaj, and it felt so good, so liberating, yet there was still something he was trying to work out.

"Aren't you holding the world hostage?" he said at last, as much to himself as to his mentor.

"If that is how you want to see it," Dr. Amwaj said, releasing Rory's hand. "I prefer to think we are offering the world a chance to save itself, possibly its last chance."

"But what if you are *wrong*?" Rory asked. "What if peace must evolve at its own natural pace, as you once believed? What if you've done all this killing for nothing?"

"Well, then, Rory, I would have to pay the consequences," Dr. Amwaj responded, like back in the old days, back in the old house in Brussels, patiently explaining it all. "I would become the next Jim Jones. David Koresh. Charles Manson. Just another crazed psychopath, a false messiah who manipulated others and murdered at will to feed his bloodthirsty delusions, a real killer for the ages. I would go down in history with a permanent black stain by my name. 'The peacemaker who went postal,' they would write about me. But this is a gamble I am willing to take. For what if am *right*? What if my instincts are spot on? What if everything I have ever done in my life has been a prelude to this? Then Jim Jones becomes Christopher Columbus. Koresh, Copernicus. Manson, Einstein. A paradigm shift occurs. We all move a step forward. We begin to live our lives in an entirely different way. The long-held dream of global peace finally becomes a reality. You know as well as I do, Rory, sometimes the ends do justify the means."

Of course they do, Rory thought, rolling it around in his head. A chance to play God was being offered here and who better to share it with than the man sitting in front of him? This brilliant man who had taken Rory under his wing, into his world and his eminent trust, given him a home, a purpose, a direction in life, this great man who had served as mentor and friend when he had no other, who had truly acted like a father to him after his own passed away. Dr. Amwaj was right. Their mission had always been the same – to see a world free of war, free of waste, free of so much needless suffering, where people could pursue their hopes and dreams without constant fear and anxiety. Yes, looking into those ageless, all-knowing eyes, Rory realized everything Dr. Amwaj was saying was true. It all made perfect sense. Of course there were times in history when men of vision were compelled to take action, to do the right thing, to march against conventional wisdom. Lincoln. Gandhi. Martin Luther King. Of course there were times when those who knew best needed to step up, to offer a guiding hand, to steer mankind back on track. Of course there were times when the ends justified the means, no matter what the cost.

Only, Rory knew in his heart, this was not one of those times.

"She was only *sixteen*," he said, for he had been having dreams of his own.

"What?"

"She had her whole life in front of her." The same dream, really, and in it Rory stood alone in a room, a brilliant white room, with shimmering white walls, white ceiling and floor, all whitewashed clean save for a single speck of red, no larger than a teardrop, until that red speck began to grow…take on a new shape…a dot…a line…a letter…a word…a phrase.

"You are not making sense," Dr. Amwaj said.

"*Help me*," Rory said in response, for that is what the phrase said, the words on the white wall, scrawled in a young girl's blood. That is what the girl said to him in his dream, time after time, night after night. *Help me, Rory!* That is what she cried through gray and grotesque lips, through a razor-slashed face, through pulpy flesh shredded and hanging from a mutilated skull. But he was too late. Too late to reach her. Too late to protect her. Too late to save her from the monster staring back at him now.

"How more can I help you, Rory? I am offering you the world."

"No, you are offering me a job."

"Yes, I am offering you a job, a priceless opportunity."

"To work for you."

"No, Rory, to work *with* me – as partners, collaborators, comrades. It is all yours for the taking, my son," Dr. Amwaj smiled back at him. "What do you say?"

"I say this," Rory started, moving forward in his seat.

"Yes?"

"I would rather serve Hitler in Hell!"

Dr. Amwaj reeled back. "*What?*"

"You heard me, old man."

Now Rory was out of his chair. "I would rather pimp for ISIL than spend one miserable hour working for you."

"You are making a terrible—"

"No, Emile, the mistake is all *yours!*"

And now Rory was coming straight at Dr. Amwaj.

40

Bettina saw a flash of silver and realized what had happened.

"Oh, Tito."

But it was too late. The knife was out. Confucius was on his feet. Tito, too.

"Shut up!" the kid shouted. He had also come prepared. Something in Bettina's voice, when she told him he was needed upstairs, convinced him to bring his knife. Carefully concealed in the front pocket of his hoodie, it was the same knife Tito had learned to use butchering wild rabbit on his uncle's farm, outside of Banja Luka, after the war took the rest of his family. "You think I'm such a pussy I can't protect you from this asshole?"

Bettina didn't answer. She watched, instead, as Confucius started circling the table, his right hand extended, ready to ward off a strike from Tito's blade.

"You better know how to use that, boy," said Confucius, as he kept advancing.

"Shut up," Tito repeated. "Both of you, shut the *fuck* up!"

Bettina remained seated, still holding onto her hidden weapon, watching Confucius edge closer, while contemplating a critical question: *Which one of these pricks do I shoot first?*

"Because if you don't," Confucius said, "you just might find you're the one—"

"Shove it up your ass, Chink!"

"—who's *fucked!*"

And with that, his left hand shot out like a python, clamping onto Tito's wrist.

"*Ahh!*" the kid screamed, as fingers tore like fangs into his flesh.

Confucius laughed, squeezing harder. "Shove it up *my* ass. Now, there's a fitting image. Why? Because both of you have made all of us look like a bunch of *asses*."

Bettina kept sitting perfectly still, eyes riveted to Tito's hand, which was rapidly turning an unnatural shade of blue.

"A bunch of amateur *asses*," Confucius said, blue becoming violet as Tito's knife fell from his fingers, clattering on the tabletop.

"And I'm sick of it," he continued, Tito's arm trembling now.

"I'm sick of being questioned."

The boy began to moan.

"Sick of being challenged."

His body convulsed.

"Sick of listening to both of you."

Confucius kept increasing the pressure, while Tito started to whimper, and Bettina went for her gun.

*   *   *

Rory towered over Dr. Amwaj, jabbing a finger into his chest.

"You've lost your mind, Emile. You've recruited a gang of juvenile delinquents and gone on a mad killing spree."

He pressed down with his hand.

"Please, don't," the old man implored, words coming out in spurts. "I…beg…you…"

"No," Rory fired back. "I'm through listening to you."

He shoved down even harder, as Dr. Amwaj shook beneath him.

"This game is over," Rory hissed, "and you lose!"

*   *   *

"What do you say now?" Confucius demanded, as Bettina watched Tito gasp for air, his eyes rolling back in his head.

"*Help me!*" he pleaded.

"*Fuck you!*" Confucius roared.

"*Look!*" Bettina screamed, pointing at the TV.

*   *   *

Rory had his hands around the neck of Dr. Amwaj.

"I must admit," he said, clamping down, "I have been curious about one thing."

"*What?*" the other managed, clawing feebly at Rory's arms.

"All of this, why now?"

The old man croaked in a voice barely audible. "*Because…*"

"Why do you need me *now?*"

Rory kept applying pressure, strangling the life out of his former mentor.

"*Because…*" he started again in a horrible rasp, and Rory loosened his grip just enough to hear the man's final words.

"I'm not crazy," Dr. Amwaj said. "I'm *dying.*"

Rory heard the answer.

Then everything went black.

41

Everything was black, but she dare not turn on a light. Not yet.

Moving along an unlit corridor, Zulu considered how easy it had been getting in here. The credentials given to her by Mills Greenblatt had worked like a charm. No one questioned her, either, when she bypassed the main staffing area and went directly to the stairs, leading downward, below ground level. The color of her badge gave her full access.

Even so, there were security cameras everywhere, and the hall Zulu was passing through now made no sense without a degree in engineering or a set of specialized tools, neither of which she possessed. In fact, all she had with her was a jangle of keys, a disposable phone, and the penlight she was still hesitant to use.

Reaching the end of the corridor, Zulu felt her way around the corner, turning to the left, as Mr. Greenblatt had instructed her to do. Only then did she engage the light.

Now she blinked, before following the beam toward the room at the end of the next hall, the room housing the ventilation system circulating the oxygen keeping alive the 5,000 people streaming into the overflow arena directly overhead.

42

"**Z**ulu has reached the overflow arena!" a voice was saying excitedly, as Rory opened his eyes and tried to gain his bearings.

He was lying on one shoulder across a wooden bench in the corner of a large room constructed of stone, with similar benches and wooden tables pushed to one side. *The prison dining hall?* Perched almost directly overhead stood a sizeable statue of an eagle, cast in bronze, with wings thrown back and a look of brute defiance on its predatory face as it scoured the space below. Toward the far end of the room, near the main entrance, a floor-to-ceiling tapestry filled much of the wall from the arched doorway to the massive, char-stained hearth, presently devoid of fire. From the size and shape of the land masses colorfully woven in silk on this tremendous map of the world, Rory figured the tapestry was several centuries old and quite valuable. Further along the wall, positioned at roughly head-level, appeared to be the only modern item in the room, a digital clock keeping time, second-by-second, in brightly-lit, bold red numbers.

Rory closed his eyes again and felt his head throb, yet this sensation was nothing compared to the searing pain that tore through his neck, along his shoulders, and down much of his back. He had never been knocked out before and realized now that coming to from this type of enforced unconsciousness was less like waking up in the morning than like being jarred from a drunken stupor. He felt groggy, badly hung over, and it didn't help that his hands were tied off tightly behind him.

Nevertheless, with some effort and an extra helping of pain, he was able to pull himself upright, into a sitting position. The first thing he noticed was the bustle of activity going on around him. There must have been a dozen people, maybe more, all in their late teens or early twenties – *Dr. Amwaj's star students* – moving about with a buzz of purpose, as if preparing for a festive event. Rory watched an olive-skinned young woman – *the resilient Kashmiri?* – giving orders to a trio of college-aged boys setting up chairs, classroom style, across the stone floor. A slightly younger, doll-faced girl arranged coffee mugs on a table nearby, while a kid in a black hoodie stood watching it all, cradling his wrist with his other hand.

Is he the one who hit me?

Rory's stomach felt queasy, his hamstring burned, and he suddenly began to shiver. He felt a cool draft and followed it toward an open door off to his right, which led onto a modest-sized balcony. Through the door he could see the evening sky had begun to darken, throwing into silhouette the twin turrets he had noticed earlier. *This room is only slightly below the one where I met Dr. Amwaj*, he estimated, maybe one floor down, which meant they were still pretty high up. *And where is Amwaj now?*

Rory debated trying to stand, when he noticed he was being watched. The Asian fellow was staring straight at him with a look of such raw contempt it made Rory reconsider his earlier assessment. *It was clearly this thug who delivered the blow to the back of my head.*

Just then the noise level took a noticeable uptick before the room fell completely silent, everyone stopping what he or she was doing to gape at the entourage pushing through the main entrance. In the lead was an intense young man with brown skin and a slash of black hair, literally beaming with joy, his ruddy cheeks propped up by a wide, toothy grin.

"How did it go, Che?" one of them asked.

"Were you nervous?" another inquired.

"Nailed it!" the boy gushed, pumping his fist.

But then, just like that, he was forgotten, as their collective attention swung downward toward the next figure to emerge.

"Greetings," said Dr. Amwaj, as he was rolled forward in a wheelchair. Rory recognized the same quilted blanket draped over the legs of his former mentor, who was now wearing a foam brace around his neck. A giddy chatter filled the room, and Rory found himself wondering if this was the reaction Jesus Christ inspired when he greeted his disciples, or Charlie Manson each time he met the Family.

"Ah, Rory," Dr. Amwaj said, spotting him tucked away in the corner. The old man's voice sounded agreeable enough, given the recent attempt on his life. "Glad to see you back among the living. I pray you are not in too much discomfort. You had me worried there, and I should have warned you. Apparently, I am well watched these days." He glanced up at Confucius, who stared stone-faced straight ahead. "Anyhow, bygones, my friend, we must keep moving forward and…where is Bettina?"

The others looked around the room and then at each other.

"It doesn't matter," Confucius said at last. "We can start without her."

"Nonsense," Dr. Amwaj replied, wagging a finger. "She must be here to see this."

"Of course she must," Confucius said, before giving sharp orders of his own. "Caesar," he snapped, pointing toward the entrance, and Rory watched as a teenager with broad shoulders and tight, curly hair left the room in search of the woman who had drugged and delivered him here.

Dr. Amwaj was speaking again now. "While we wait for Bettina, I want you all to meet our new spokesman," he said proudly, tilting his wounded neck upward. "Che has just finished taping and soon we will send our next message to the world."

Rory couldn't help detecting a look of envy in the faces of some of the other young people around the room.

"Now, I have something to show you," Dr. Amwaj continued. "All of you follow me."

Before Rory could stand, he was hoisted to his feet, those memorable talons digging into his arms again, as Confucius appeared out of nowhere. Rory was shoved forward and nearly tumbled before regaining his balance. He followed after the mob trailing Dr. Amwaj toward the open doorway and onto the balcony, which could only hold about half of them. The others craned their necks to see where their leader was pointing.

"Yes, over there, by that second bridge. Can anyone tell me what happened down there?"

Rory knew the answer but also that the question wasn't for him. He took the opportunity to peer over the balcony ledge. What greeted him, even in the dying light, was a sight that dashed all hope of escape, at least by this route. The drop here plummeted straight down, at least a couple hundred feet, into a quarry of jagged rocks and boulders.

"Oh, come now, one of you must know," Dr. Amwaj chided the others with that professorial patois Rory had so often heard employed to pry loose information from hesitant minds. "We don't want our guest to—"

He suddenly stopped and looked over at Rory, who remained bound from behind. "No, no, this will not do," Dr. Amwaj said with a frown. "This is no way to treat a guest. Rory may not agree with our tactics, but he is still about to become part of history. He poses no threat to us now. Cut him free."

Rory felt the ties around his wrists fall away and he tried shaking off the pain, settling instead for a dull, throbbing numbness.

"So, anyone?" Dr. Amwaj asked once more. The younger members on the balcony looked to Confucius, certain he would answer first, but he was preoccupied, keeping a distrusting eye on Rory now that he was no longer restrained. Tito wasn't talking, either. He stood on the opposite side of Dr. Amwaj, as far from Confucius as the balcony would allow. Even those who knew the correct answer rightly sensed their leader desired the floor, which he took again now with his grand orator's voice.

"All right, then, I will tell you what happened," Dr. Amwaj said from his wheelchair. "It was twenty-eight June, nineteen-fourteen, just over a hundred years ago, and right down there, by the base of that bridge, running over the Miljacka, a young Serbian radical named Gavrilo Princip, not much older than most of you, fired a pistol from close range at the Archduke Ferdinand, heir to the Austro-Hungarian throne, and his wife Sophie, killing them both and setting in motion a series of diplomatic failures that would lead to the outbreak of conflict across Europe."

"World War One," a young man next to Rory blurted out, unable to contain himself.

"Precisely, the *Great War*," Dr. Amwaj replied, his face twisting into a sneer. "*Ha!* Can anyone tell me what was so *great* about thirty-five million people dead or wounded and the near destruction of Western civilization?"

None of them answered this obviously rhetorical question, so Dr. Amwaj forged ahead, his voice filling with emotion as he went.

"What Princip did down there was understandable, perhaps, in his own mind, and regrettable, certainly. But what came next, over the next one hundred years, the actions – or should I say *inactions* – of our so-called leaders and most of the rest of us, has been nothing short of *inexcusable!*"

Now, the elderly professor reached back, and, with a single motion, ripped the foam brace from his neck and flung it over the side of the balcony. Others gasped at this rash action, following the flight of the discarded object, which fluttered briefly before dropping out of sight below them. They then returned their attention to Dr. Amwaj, who was nearing full stride, his rich baritone driving through the Sarajevo sky, stamping key words has he went.

"A century's worth of *killing* and *maiming*…hundreds of *millions* of innocent people driven from their homes… mass *murder* on practically every continent. From bayonets to biological weapons, from trench warfare to atomic bombs…hell, the Cold War is over, yet we keep twenty *thousand* nuclear missiles pointed at each other, and some say it's still not enough. *My God!* Year after year after bloody *fucking* year we devise ever more effective means of annihilating each other."

Dr. Amwaj stopped to catch his breath and let the gravity of what he was about to say next sink in.

"A century after Princip fired his pistol down there, what has changed? What has really changed?" He did not wait for an answer. "*Nothing!*"

He shook his fist.

"And a century from now, what will change?"

This time, a few of the others responded, shouting back. "*Nothing!*"

"Right, *nothing!*" Dr. Amwaj replied. "Unless, *tonight*, we finish what we started!"

Swept up in his words, the others cheered wildly, pumping young fists with their leader.

"Tonight, we create *change!*" Dr. Amwaj bellowed, like a preacher from the pulpit.

"*Change!*" the faithful shouted back, the entire congregation joining in.

"Tonight, we *obliterate* the status quo!"

"*Obliterate!*" they hollered.

"Tonight, we rewrite *history!*"

"*History!*" they screamed.

"*Tonight, we end all war!*"

"*No more war!*" they cried.

"*No more war!*"

"*No more war!*"

"*No more war!*"

Standing by, watching this mad affair, Rory considered rushing forward, manhandling Dr. Amwaj over the side of the balcony and watching him sail through the air like his neck brace, splattering on the rocks below. But he doubted in his present condition he would ever make it through the crowd. *And what does it matter, anyway?* The old man already said he was dying. He must have a strategy in place for after his demise.

Rory decided, instead, to break up this manic revelry with his own words, shouting to be heard over the din. *"What are you planning?"*

At first, no one heard him, so Rory repeated the question, louder this time. And now, those closest to him turned dark eyes on this intruder, this heretic among them.

"Shut up!" snarled one of the boys, raising a fist.

But Dr. Amwaj intervened. "No, no, it's a fair question," he said, wheeling around to face his former protégé, as the others stopped their battle cries to listen in. "Although, Rory, I would have thought you, of all people, could have figured out the answer."

"Yeah," said one of the others, but Rory paid him no attention, waiting for Dr. Amwaj.

"Our last message could not have been stated more clearly," he said. "As you will remember, we announced to the world: 'Stop all wars, you've been warned!' While privately, we sent a different message to the most powerful actors on Earth – NATO, the G8, the UN Security Council – telling them they had exactly forty-eight hours to comply and—"

"That's *absurd*," Rory interrupted, to which Dr. Amwaj chuckled.

"I prefer *ambitious*, but yes, Rory, I agree with you. It is an unreasonable request, for these are unreasonable times. I would settle for just one tangible sign that the world is truly committed to finally bringing about real change. Is that so much to ask?" He pushed on before Rory could answer. "We are not here to destroy the world but to reshape it, to give peace a chance, as they say. Yet, as you have seen, there has been no sign at all that the world takes us seriously, and now time is running out." He paused briefly, glancing at his wristwatch. "In fact, there are less than twenty minutes until—"

"*What?*"

"Until we *make* the world take us seriously."

"How?" Rory asked, fearful of the answer.

Dr. Amwaj looked up again at Che, still standing beside him.

"With our next message, which will let the world know it has failed again."

He turned back to Rory.

"And then, we will kill several thousand people."

"*No!*" Rory cried, stepping forward, only to be restrained once more by Confucius.

"First Istanbul," Dr. Amwaj said. "Then, if we still have no response, another city – Tokyo...Sydney... Cairo....New York..."

He ticked them off on his fingers as he went. "Another day, another city, until, eventually, people *will* listen. They *will* act. And they *will* do what needs to be done. Yes, my friend, the world *will* stop fighting wars once and for all, I promise you."

An edgy buzz raced around the balcony, and it dawned on Rory that now was the first time many of them were being made aware of this madman's plan. *He doesn't trust his own disciples*, Rory realized, wondering whether this information might be used to his advantage.

"Istanbul," he said, thinking out loud. "The Future Games."

"Fitting name, eh?"

"But that place must be crawling with security?"

"More than you can imagine."

"Then how do you plan to pull it off?"

Now Dr. Amwaj laughed. "You still don't get it, do you, Rory? After all this time, after everything I have placed before you, you continue to doubt my means, to discount the extraordinary preparations that have gone into our mission. This is no fly-by-night operation. We are determined to succeed. We are not going to hit the stadium. That would be lunacy," he continued, while easing from the pocket of his vest a sleek silver cell phone. "One of my associates, Zulu, a wonderful young lady whom you have yet to meet, is at the overflow arena as we speak. She is waiting for my call from this phone. There may only be five thousand people there, watching the computer games showdown on a big screen, but that number should be more than sufficient to get our point across at last. And, if it is not, then, as I said, we will strike again and again and again, until the world finally stops accepting the unacceptable."

Rory couldn't believe what he was hearing, but he had nothing left to say. He watched as Dr. Amwaj turned his chair around and motioned to one of the others to push him forward.

"Enough with words," he said, as he was wheeled past Rory, who was then shoved forward by Confucius, across the balcony, through the open door, and back into the main room with the others.

"We will give the world another fifteen minutes," Dr. Amwaj said from somewhere up ahead, "and then I shall place a call to Zulu to release the gas. Now, where is Bettina? She must be here to see this."

"Right here, Sir," a voice rang out from the far side of the hall.

Rory looked up with the others. There, beneath the arched doorway, Bettina stood in rare form, having exchanged her Little Orphan Annie costume for full battle regalia – black combat boots, thick leather belt, camouflage fatigues. Even more striking was her skull, shaved slick bald again with lips splashed blood red and eyes framed in heavy mascara, like some vampire nymph.

And standing next to her was the teenager with the broad shoulders and tight, curly hair, Caesar, with a look of morbid fear on his face. For in her hand Bettina held Seb's revolver, pressed against the boy's head, as she made the following announcement.

"We have a traitor in our midst!"

43

Zulu turned a key to unlock the cage protecting the core ventilation system responsible for circulating fresh air throughout the overflow arena. Above her, she could hear the muted rush and swell of 5,000 spectators lending their support to an elite crop of cyber warriors battling on a big screen for glory and cash prizes.

The key struck resistance and her heart skipped a beat. *Damn.*

She tried again, anxiety rising, and this time the key engaged the lock and the door swung open. *Good.*

Now, with the aid of her penlight, Zulu connected a long, snake-like cord from the mouth of a cylindrical canister – filled with enough chlorine for several large swimming pools and located, as Mills Greenblatt promised it would be, in a storage locker in the next room – to the building's ventilation system. She repeated this action with two more of the metal tanks, careful to ensure each cord snapped firmly into place.

She next turned her attention to the time-release modules attached to each canister. These devices would guarantee she had sufficient time to exit the arena should the world's decision makers fail to heed the ultimatum, as she imagined they would. That was their choice, not hers, but she wasn't taking any chances. She planned to be far away from here when the real entertainment began.

Hell, I'm only 24.

Stepping back through the opening in the cage, she found a place to sit down. Her instructions, typed on a card in the envelope foisted on her by Bettina, which she had carefully committed to memory before destroying, could not have been more simple:

When call comes from A: release gas
No call by 9: abort mission, walk away

Zulu glanced at her watch – 8:45. Exactly 15 minutes to go.

She checked her phone – signal strong, battery charged, volume set. She would have no problem hearing his call.

Satisfied, she doused her light and sat waiting in the dark. She listened to the noises overhead and considered the implication of what was about to take place.

Soon there would be no more cheering, no more applause.

Soon there would be only the sound of screaming and gagging, as the sting of chlorine gas penetrated soft lung tissue.

Then there would be no sound at all.

Zulu smiled and then whispered in the dark. "When you're on the verge of making world history, what's a little collateral damage?"

44

Bettina entered the room, pushing Caesar in front of her with the gun.

"What are you doing?" Dr. Amwaj demanded from his chair. "You know firearms aren't allowed."

Watching her march by the grand tapestry, past the empty hearth, stopping a few paces in front of them, Rory had some thoughts of his own. *Why is she doing this? What does she want? If I don't start thinking like Bettina – put myself in her shoes – I may never get out of this room alive.*

"I told you, we have a traitor in our midst," she said, again pressing the weapon to the head of the boy, who looked like he was about to cry.

"Caesar didn't do anything," Confucius said.

"I know he didn't," Bettina responded, shoving the kid aside. "But he told me who did."

And without warning she fired away, lodging a bullet smack between the eyes of Che. The room filled with a bone-jarring *crack* and a potent whiff of gun smoke as the boy toppled to the ground. His forehead opened like a spigot, a gush of blood spewing out and pooling around the wheelchair of the man speaking now.

"My God, Bettina, what have you done?"

Others went screaming or cowering or running for the door. The girl with the gun let them go before turning her weapon on those still in the room.

"Our *spokesman*," she spat, eyes bulging wildly. "That job was *mine!*"

Rory wondered what she would do when she learned of the position he had been offered. And then it hit him, as it often did, just like that. *She craves power.*

"You're out of control," Confucius said, stepping toward her. "This is not our way."

How much power?

"It's *my* way!" Bettina shrieked, pumping her next bullet into his gut.

All of it.

Rory watched as the Asian dropped to his knees and then into a heap on the floor, clutching his stomach as his face contorted. Rory remembered reading somewhere that without medical attention this slow torture was one of the worst ways to die.

She knows what she's doing.

"Anyone else have something to say?" Bettina dared the people still remaining in the room. In addition to Rory and Dr. Amwaj, there was the wounded man, Confucius, the Bosnian Serb, Tito, the Kashmiri woman, Ramona, plus Caesar and the doll-faced coffee girl.

"I do," said Dr. Amwaj, rolling forward in his wheelchair with a look of utter defeat. "He's right. This is no way to get things done, Bettina."

"What are you talking about?"

On the ground, in a smear of his own blood, Confucius began to groan.

"We're not ready," Dr. Amwaj said, shaking his head. "Not like this."

He kept rolling toward her, the silver cell phone resting on the quilt in his lap.

"Far enough," Bettina said, pointing the gun at him.

She wouldn't possibly, Rory thought. *He poses no threat.*

Bettina cocked the weapon as Dr. Amwaj rolled closer.

"This is not the way to bring about peace, with hatred and jealousy," he said, finally stopping his chair. Nearby, Confucius was moaning in agony. "These are precisely the human shortcomings I have spent my entire life fighting against."

Bettina held the gun out in front of her, taking aim at the professor's chest, as Rory figured it out. *It's not his actions she fears, it's his words.*

"Listen to me," Dr. Amwaj was saying, "all of you. We have come too far to go out like this. We have opened eyes. We have made the world think about what it is doing. We are not there yet, not even close, but we have forced people to consider a new type of future. So now we must—"

"*Shut up!*" Bettina shouted, shaking the weapon at him.

"—rethink our plan," he continued, holding out his hand. "Bettina, give me the gun."

"Don't make me do this," she replied, ignoring his request. "You are not the man I gave my life to. You are weak and indecisive, like these others. You have served your purpose, old man. Give me that phone, or I *will* shoot you."

"You know I can't do that, Bettina." He looked toward the digital clock on the wall, which was just reaching 8:50. "There will be no call to Zulu, not like this."

"Then you leave me no choice," she said.

"You always have a choice."

And then she fired.

Oh Christ!

Rory recoiled as the bullet found its target, propelling the chair and the body of Dr. Amwaj several feet backward across the floor. The shaggy head of the man he once loved slumped forward, onto his blood-stained chest, and now Rory knew Bettina would stop at nothing to get what she wanted. And then another thought crossed his mind: *Is there anyone left in this room who poses a greater threat to her than I do?*

On the floor by his feet, Confucius was literally howling. Not far away, Tito looked on.

Maybe the Bosnian Serb?

"Put him out of his misery," he heard Bettina say to Tito.

"With pleasure."

Shit.

Rory watched as Tito crouched down and picked up a hunting knife that had fallen from the hand of the Asian when he was shot.

"Fuck you!" cried Confucius, as he saw Tito coming toward him. He clawed at the stone floor, trying to get away, but he was too weak. Tito easily caught him, taking hold of his pant leg, careful to remain beyond the reach of those deadly hands. With a look of glee on his usually dour face, Tito plunged the blade deep into his rival's sternum, gutting him like a fish.

"*Wunderbar*," Bettina said, enjoying the show. "Now, bring me that phone, Tito, so I can call Zulu. We haven't much time."

What do I do now? Rory wondered, as the Bosnian Serb started for the cell phone, still in the lap of Dr. Amwaj. *If Seb's crazy story is true, she only has two bullets left, even if she doesn't know it. One of them is certainly meant for me. If I run, she makes the call, and thousands die in Istanbul. If I stay, they die anyway, and so do I. What choice do I have?*

None.

Rory knew he must risk it to save himself, praying he reached the door before Bettina gunned him down. She was presently distracted, waiting for Tito to hand over the phone, and Rory figured now might be his only chance.

Turning toward the main entrance, he was prepared to make his move, when something suddenly flashed across the doorway.

It was a woman, with a slender frame, long dark hair, and—

It was Rani!

Rory couldn't believe it. *I saw her dead, didn't I? Is she really here to help us?*

Not wanting to draw attention to her, if that was the case, Rory turned back to the pair of fiends talking in front of him.

"*Da*, I will, Bettina, but first I need something from you."

"What?"

"A promise," said Tito.

Rory noticed how the others in the room all stood behind Bettina, either in a show of solidarity or more likely to increase their odds of not becoming her next victim. He decided to steal another peek toward the main entrance. And there she was again, craning her head around the doorway, her gorgeous face the color of summer sand and—

Rory's heart sank. Even if Rani had spent a month on the beaches of Romitsae, her fair complexion would never attain such a dark hue.

So who was this woman?

Leila, the Arabian Princess, craned her head around the doorway and froze. Some strange man was staring at her, while strewn across the floor were several dead bodies belonging to Che, Confucius, and Dr. Amwaj!

"You're in no position to make demands," Bettina was saying to Tito.

"You're wrong," he responded, holding up the cell phone. "I'm in a perfect position."

Rory kept staring at the girl. *Could she really be here to stop this charade, to rescue us?*

As farfetched as that idea seemed, like right out of the movies, he realized she might be their only hope. So, Rory did the best he could to reassure the girl, whoever she was, nodding ever so slightly to let her know the coast was clear.

Leila nodded back, tight-lipped, before stepping into the room and slipping behind the grand tapestry for cover.

"I have something you want," Tito was saying, "just like you have something I want."

"What are you talking about?" Bettina demanded. "We don't have time for this, Tito. Not now. If Zulu doesn't get our call, she walks."

"I know she does. That is why I'll give you the phone once you promise—"

"What?" Bettina said, before registering a look on his face. "My God, are you serious?"

"Very," Tito replied, with a wink of his blood-stained eye, confident he finally held the upper hand in this twisted relationship. "You and me together – *exclusively* – once this is over."

Bettina stared hard at Tito before answering him. "Okay, *ja*."

"*Da?*"

He was stunned by how easily that went, until he saw where the gun was pointed.

"I can't wait for you and your marmalade eye to slobber all over my body again," she said, pulling the trigger and sending her next shot right through the center of his deformity. Tito's head exploded like a pumpkin struck with a mallet, showering bone and brain matter all over the floor.

Rory had to force down hot vomit rising up from his stomach, before reminding himself. *She only has one bullet left.* He spotted the Arabian Princess stepping out from behind the tapestry, into the open room, and tried to buy her time.

"I have an offer for you, too," Rory said, catching Bettina by surprise. She turned toward him, as he hoped she would, enabling the girl to advance further into the room.

"You've got *nothing* for me." Bettina pointed the gun at Rory's chest.

"A lot of money," he said, as Leila reached the stone hearth.

This just might work.

"I don't want your money." Bettina took careful aim.

Or get me killed.

But she was no longer looking at Rory. Her gaze went up, over his head, toward the ceiling.

What is she doing?

Then he remembered. There, perched high on the wall behind him stood the statue of that magnificent eagle, its body of polished bronze acting like a perfect mirror. And framed within its belly was the image of the Arabian Princess charging across the room.

Bettina saw her, too, wheeling around just as Leila started to dive. A thundering blast roared from the gun, the others screaming, as a hole bore right through the face of the Arabian Princess, killing the young beauty before she hit the ground.

Rory stood shocked.

What have I done? This girl, who risked her life to save us, is dead because of me.

As the cries in the room subsided, it also dawned on Rory what this all meant. If Seb's story could be trusted, he was a free man now. Bettina had fired her last shot. He could walk out of here, away from this bloodbath. He could go to the authorities, collect his reward.

While thousands died in Istanbul.

You always have a choice.

Stooping down, next to Tito's carcass, Rory picked up the silver cell phone.

"*Stop!*" Bettina screamed, leveling the gun at him.

"You're out of bullets," he said, walking straight at the bald freak.

"You're *lying!*"

She cocked the weapon, as Rory pulled back the phone, ready to throw it out the door, over the balcony, hundreds of feet below.

And Bettina pulled the trigger.

45

Zulu turned on the penlight just long enough to stare at her phone.

Still no call. No text, either.

Nothing.

She watched as the clock at the top of the screen reached 8:59. One minute to go.

She had already heard noises, and not just from the crowd above. These sounds were closer, maybe even on this same floor.

Turning off the light, Zulu shrugged and began silently counting down from 60, fully prepared to walk away if she did not receive the call in time.

46

Rory heard the gun go off.
Click.

Seb's crazy tale was true. *Thank God.*

There were no more bullets. She had fired her last shot.

At the same time, he felt a torrent of pain shatter his body. Not a shot in the chest, for this ache plowed through his back, just above the kidneys, sending him sprawling to the ground.

Rory watched helplessly as the silver cell phone flew from his hand and clattered along the stone floor, out the open doorway, and onto the balcony, where it slid to a stop, inches from going over the edge.

As he tumbled to the hard surface, slamming his knee, Rory turned in time to see Ramona drop the chair she had used to smash into his back, before throwing herself on top of him. It took nearly all his strength to cast her off his body, shrieking as she fell away.

Now Rory struggled to his feet, catching a glimpse of the digital clock on the wall.

It had just passed 8:59.

He staggered through the doorway, onto the balcony, but he was too late.

Bettina had already retrieved the phone.

She held it out in front of her, taunting him with it, one thumb poised over the automatic dial, ready to place the call that would seal the fate of 5,000 innocent people in Istanbul.

"Don't," Rory begged, taking another step toward her.

But she only cackled in his face.

"You're too late, asshole. *I'm* in charge now!"

So Rory made the only choice he could and took them both over the edge.

Acknowledgments

While the act of writing is primarily an individual one, the creative process benefits immeasurably from collaboration, and I cannot thank enough all those who helped guide me on this journey. Namely, Alan, John, and Stacy for catching my errors, keeping me honest, and making me dig that much deeper; Sladja for turning my ideas into an unforgettable cover image; and, of course, Mom and Dad for your early edits, creative tips, and constant encouragement, but most of all for your instilling in me a free and imaginative way of looking at the world, which is priceless. And to Vonda, my wife, for without you, this book simply never would have been written; for all you do, I am grateful.

About The Author

Kirk Wolcott was born in Highland Park, Illinois, grew up in and around Seattle, and has spent much of his life roaming the world. He has worked as a sportswriter, a peace and conflict resolution advisor, and presently serves as an American diplomat. *A Simple Game* is his first novel.

Made in the USA
San Bernardino, CA
08 November 2015